THE
PRICE
OF THE
VERDICT

JOHN BAE

Print ISBN: 978-1-66786-600-0

eBook ISBN: 978-1-66786-601-7

In loving memory of
Choon Jai Rhee and Young Nahn Rhee

For Anita, Alex and Will

1.

Jack Hatchet finished his closing statement and sat down at counsel table. He watched the jurors disappear out of the door behind the jury box. Jack's partner Bob Tuckson put his arm around him.

"Great job, Jack."

"Thanks."

Sam Pritchard, the General Counsel of the Pearson Group, walked up to counsel table and tapped Jack's shoulder.

"Jack, that was brilliant. I think you're going to pull this off."

Jack turned to Pritchard. "The trial went well, but this is a challenging case. This would be a good time to call the plaintiff and settle."

"What? After that performance? You had the jury eating out of your hand."

Jack looked away and stood. "Sometimes we start to believe in our own bullshit. That's when we make bad decisions. We have a difficult case as I've told you from the beginning. The evidence is stacked against us. Even if we win here, we will lose on appeal."

"It's a $500 million claim, Jack. If we win, we both will be heroes."

Jack shook Sam's hand. "You are the client, so it's your call. A win here isn't a win. You'll get a significant reduction on the settlement demand if you call them now. They know they took a beating here, but they also know the evidence falls on their side. At least think about what I'm telling you."

Pritchard smiled. "Alright Jack. I'll raise it with senior management, but they're likely going to want to see the verdict."

"I understand. I would like to be in on the discussion when you speak with the CEO."

Pritchard nodded. "Sure thing. I'll let him know."

Jack picked up his briefcase and headed out of the courtroom. Bob caught up to him. "You really think we're going to lose?"

Jack didn't slow his pace. "Yes. Ultimately."

"Well, I have a feeling they're going to want to wait for the verdict."

"I agree, which is why I need to be involved when they make their decision."

"What're you going to do?"

Jack stopped and turned to Bob. "I'm going to save Pritchard's job."

"Well, he's not going to want to settle because he's taking the heat for this lawsuit. A victory here would help him greatly."

"But for how long?"

Bob didn't respond.

"He'll save his job for a few months, but the company will have to write a big check when the case is reversed. Pritchard would have hung onto his job a little longer, but at what cost to the company?"

Jack started walking again. "Bob, you're right. Pritchard's not going to be very happy when I convince the CEO to settle, but I'll do it in a way where Pritchard won't have to take a hit."

"How're you going to do that?"

Jack grinned. "I'll figure it out as I go."

Jack walked in his office and sat down on his couch. As the company's General Counsel, Pritchard had selected the lawyers to represent the Pearson Group in negotiating the supply agreement with the plaintiff. Pritchard relied on his lawyers' advice and signed the contract. He later realized the contract, as drafted, failed to require the plaintiff to deliver a critical component. The contract would have required the Pearson Group to procure another supplier to provide the missing part, which would have doubled the company's manufacturing costs. Later recognizing this problem, Pritchard took the position that the plaintiff misled the Pearson Group regarding what it would deliver under the contract. Of course, the plaintiff did no such thing. When Pritchard terminated the contract, the plaintiff sued for $500 million, which was what the Pearson Group would have had to pay the plaintiff for the life of the contract. Even though this lawsuit was a direct result of the malpractice committed by the Pearson Group's lawyers, Pritchard still took the heat for it, since he selected the law firm.

Jack's phone rang. He heard his assistant Margaret on the intercom. "Mr. Pritchard is on the phone."

Jack picked up the phone on the coffee table. "Good afternoon."

"Jack, this is Sam. I'm here with Mark Pintos, the company's CEO. The CFO, Steve Lombard, is also here."

"Nice to meet you both," said Jack.

"Jack, this is Mark. I heard you destroyed the other side. Congratulations."

"We shouldn't celebrate yet. Also, much credit goes to Sam for getting me the information I needed to put up a viable defense."

"So, what's our next step?" asked Lombard.

Before Jack could answer, he saw Bob standing at his door. Jack motioned for Bob to come in and take a seat.

"I suggest you let me call the other side to negotiate a settlement," said Jack into the phone.

"Why would we do that?" asked Pintos. "Why would we pay money to settle a case we're going to win?"

"For your share price."

"For my what?" asked Pintos.

"The company's share price took a hit once news broke about this lawsuit. You might see a slight uptick after today's trial, but the risk of the company taking a $500 million loss is already baked into your stock price. If we can settle this case for a significantly lower amount, your stock price will spike. If you don't settle, you'll be stuck with the depressed stock price until the appeal plays out. And, anything can happen on appeal. You are better off paying some amount now and distancing yourself from this lawsuit. The expected uptick in the stock price will more than make up for the check you'd have to write."

Jack could hear the three men discussing. After a few moments, Lombard said, "How much do you think you can settle for?"

"Give me authority to settle for $200 million, but I'll try to get it done for less."

"Let us discuss internally, and we'll come back to you," said Lombard.

Jack hung up the phone and waited.

"So, you're really pushing to settle this case, huh?" said Bob.

"It's the right path."

Jack's phone rang. "It's Mr. Pritchard again," said Margaret.

Jack answered on the speaker phone. "Hey Sam. Bob is here with me."

"Hey Bob. Jack, you have authority to settle for up to $200 million."

"Great, I'll see what I can do," said Jack as he hung up. He pressed the intercom. "Please call Jimmy Coyne."

"Mr. Coyne is on the line," said Margaret.

"Good afternoon," said Jack.

"Nice job in court today."

"You too."

"What can I do for you?"

"Now that we've beaten each other up a little, let's see if we can resolve this case."

"I'm all ears," said Coyne.

"My client will wire $75 million to your client within five business days, and we'll sign mutual releases and go our separate ways."

"Well, I don't know, Jack," said Coyne. "I know you guys had a good day in court, but we feel pretty good about our chances on appeal."

"You guys are going to want to accept this offer. Your client was in court today and saw your case get derailed. Yes, you could win on appeal, but what if you lose? Do you really want to be the lawyer who advised his client to walk away from a $75 million cash settlement? Remember, this is free money. Your client did not suffer any damages. This case is purely based on a contract that my client should never have signed."

"Alright, I'll take it to the client."

"Please understand, we are not interested in a counteroffer. It's either $75 million or we wait for the verdict. Also, keep in mind what'll happen to your client's stock price when the verdict is rendered."

"Understood," said Coyne as he ended the call.

Bob shook his head. "Don't you think we at least should have considered the client's desire to wait for the verdict?" asked Bob. "They are the client, and it's their money."

Jack's phone rang again. "Mr. Coyne's on the line."

"Hey Jimmy," said Jack into the phone.

"You have a deal."

"Good. We'll send you a draft settlement agreement this afternoon."

Jack pressed the intercom. "Please get Sam Pritchard for me." A moment later, Margaret said, "He's on."

"Sam, we settled for $75 million."

"What?"

"$75 million."

"That's amazing, Jack. How'd you get them to agree to this?"

"They recognized that nothing's ever certain in litigation. Just like you, they chose not to gamble. Certainty is always better than hope."

"Well, you did a great job, Jack. Thanks again."

Jack smiled. "My performance can only be as good as what the client allows. You took my advice. I know when a client has to fight to the end. This wasn't one of those cases."

As he ended the call, Jack turned to Bob. "Yes, there certainly is merit to letting the client decide its fate. No one would blame us for abiding by the client's wishes. But that means we are just hired guns—hired to just fight the enemy the client points to, irrespective of how the fight will impact the client. Hired guns are a dime a dozen. I refuse to be that that kind of a lawyer. Either the client lets me fix its problem, or I won't take the engagement. It's not negotiable."

2.

Being a senior associate at a major New York City law firm assured Henry Lane of only one thing—a check every two weeks to pay the bills. But for him, who had no patience to spend the rest of his life building a career, the stability of a salary wasn't enough. He stacked the twenty black chips in front of him and slid them across the green felt toward the croupier. The dealer dealt the first card, and Henry stared at the king of spades. The anticipation started to grow. The dealer dealt his card down. The dealer dealt the next card, and it was another king. Henry had twenty. His friends called this a "no-brainer" hand, because there was no decision to be made. You just sit back and wait to see what happens to the dealer's hand. The dealer was dealt a six of diamonds. Henry was going to win this hand because the dealer was going to bust.

He thought about Elaine, sleeping in their bed, like she always was. Her therapist said she'd get better, but he couldn't say when. They were just empty words to give him hope, to keep Elaine going back for more sessions at five hundred dollars a pop. The depression was eating her alive, but he didn't believe there was anything anyone could do about it, other than temporary fixes with meds. She was alone in having to figure out a way to crawl out of the darkness she was trapped in. It pained him to know that, deep inside, he was responsible for keeping her locked up in that place.

Henry tilted his head back and allowed the Scotch to flow down his throat. It used to burn him, but not anymore. He was going to win this hand and then win some more. Elaine would be happy if he could bring home the winnings. It would help to pull them out of the hole he had put them in. He wished Elaine hadn't seen the letter from the collection agency. In her state, that was the last thing she needed. Why did she pick today to go through the mail? She never before cared about what the USPS slid through the mail slot. Those assholes didn't have the patience to wait. He was angry at them for sending the letter and upsetting her. He just needed a little more time, the right card or roll of the dice. All the debt would have been repaid, and life would have gone back to normal. She cried in anger and fear when she saw the letter. "How could you?" she asked. "How could you gamble away everything we have?" Those words echoed through his mind, and his heart ached. He couldn't go back and change anything in the past, but he could change everything right now. He could start to win it back tonight.

Henry put down his glass. He had drained the last twenty thousand dollars left on his fourth Visa. In front of him was a winning hand. He'll win. It was time to win back his life. The croupier turned over the hole card. It was a ten of clubs. Sixteen. The dealer had to take a hit and most likely bust. He waited in anticipation. Henry declined to take another card. The dealer dealt himself a five of diamonds. He stared at the cards sitting in front of the croupier, who swept the chips away from him. No, he wasn't going to fix anything tonight. He would drink some more Scotch to numb the anger.

3.

Peter Cantor waited at the diner on Main Street with a half full cup of coffee. He stared at the curves of Patty Kullen as she poured coffee into the empty cups of the four men sitting two booths away. He knew she saw him staring. She always noticed, and she loved it. Was it the prospect of making a few dollars for giving him company or was it the idea that men still found her desirable? It didn't matter at the end of the day. It had been a while since he was with her. He couldn't afford her anymore. Business was crap and there was nothing in the works. All he had was the plan that was hatched a month ago. It was a short phone call. It didn't have to be a long one to make him buy in. He believed in the strategy. He checked his watch and then looked out of the large window shielding him from the heavy rain outside. He didn't hear Patty sneak up on him. "You've been waiting a long time, Peter. Who're you waiting for?"

"I'm waiting for David," he said as he turned to her. "Looking good this morning, Patty."

Patty leaned down and brought her face to within an inch of Peter's. "You look pretty good too. Have something in mind?" she asked, staring at his lips.

Normally, he would have kept it going, and maybe even would have tried to talk her into meeting him that night on credit, but he had too much on his mind. He turned away from her and looked out at the drenched street outside of the diner.

"Maybe another time, Patty."

She straightened up and smiled. "What are you two up to?"

"Nothing, Patty. Just getting together with an old friend."

"Right. Old friend. I thought he hated you. After what you did to him."

"He doesn't hate me."

Patty shook her head and smiled. "Sure."

"He doesn't," said Peter, smiling back.

Patty rolled her eyes and walked off to the next booth. Peter saw the blue Cadillac pull into the parking lot. A surge of excitement filled his head. His heart raced. A few moments later, he saw David Chen walk in the door. He shook off the raindrops from his coat and hung it on the wooden coatrack by the cash register. Peter waved and David walked over and slid into the booth. Patty came over with the pot of coffee and poured a cup for David. "You two gonna eat something, or just take up my table to discuss your master plan?"

David looked at her. "What master plan?"

Patty laughed, "You know, the one that Peter's going to tell you about."

Peter shook his head and glared into her eyes. "Patty, you need to leave us alone, so we can talk."

Patty turned and walked away. David took a sip of his coffee. "What was that about?"

"Nothing. She's just being Patty. If you would've met me at my house like I suggested, we wouldn't have to worry about her or anyone else bothering us."

"Look, I know this is going to be a waste of my time, and I wasn't about to drive cross-town to be at your house. So, this is the best you're going to get from me. I need to get back to the office for a ten o'clock appointment. Why'd you want to meet?"

Peter smiled. "I won't take that much of your time. I know you're busy. I'm going to be bringing a lawsuit and I need your help."

"You want my help? After what you did to me?"

"Stop living in the past. It's pointless. And, I didn't do anything to you that you didn't have coming. You know you misdiagnosed her, and her family was entitled to be paid. Your insurance took care of everything anyway, so stop whining about it."

David stood up and put his hands on the table and leaned in toward Peter. "I didn't misdiagnose anything," he said in a hushed voice with gritted teeth. "You fucking had that doctor lie on the witness stand. You don't think I paid? Do you know what your lawsuit did to my insurance premium? I knew this was going to be a waste of time."

Peter took a hold of David's wrist before he could pull away. "David, please. Just sit for five minutes and hear me out. I'm sorry. I didn't bring you here to rehash that case. Just five minutes, and if you don't like what I have to say, I'll stop bothering you."

David grunted and sat back down.

"Thank you," said Peter. "I asked you to come here to discuss an opportunity that'll make real money—something that'll more than make up for whatever you lost from that lawsuit."

David picked up his coffee. "I'm listening."

Peter noticed Patty hovering nearby, so he lowered his voice and leaned in toward David.

"I'm going to bring a lawsuit against Pearl-Line for its YF Cream."

"For what?"

"The cream. It makes people sick. Autoimmune disease."

David furrowed his eyebrows. "What? Autoimmune disease?"

"I know someone who got sick from using it," said Peter with a wink. "And I need you to prepare the medical diagnosis."

David laughed. "You must be joking."

Peter lowered his voice to a whisper. "We can make a lot of money. My client is willing to sue, and all I need is for you to prepare whatever it is we need to show that she's suffering from the disease. It's that simple."

David shook his head. "And what makes you think you can win? You think Pearl-Line will write a check just because you sued them?"

"Lower your voice," said Peter. "I've got that worked out. If you're on board, I'll give you the details."

David leaned in toward Peter. "And if I do this and put my medical career on the line, what do I get for helping you?"

"A lot of money."

"And, how exactly will I be able to prove that YF Cream causes auto-immune disease?"

"You won't have to worry about that piece. Like I said, I have a plan, and if everything goes the way I think it will, we'll win no matter what."

"What'll I have to do?"

"You'll have to prepare and sign the medical reports. Opine that the plaintiff is suffering from this disease, and talk about the pain and suffering she's going through."

David stared at his coffee for a few seconds, then looked at Peter. "I can get in a lot of trouble for this."

"It's foolproof. We play this right, we'll be fine."

"I need to know what I'll get out of this."

Peter leaned in closer toward David. "We'll work something out."

"If you want my help, we need to work this out up front."

"What do you have in mind?" Peter asked.

"How much do you think you can make off of this?"

Peter smiled. "That will depend on the jury, but I have a feeling we can make many, many millions."

"I want half."

"You can't have half. There are others involved. There are six of us, including you, and we have to divide the money evenly."

"Who are the others?"

"That's not important right now. The point is they're on board and we're ready to pull the trigger. But I can't tell you who they are or any more details until I know you are game."

Patty walked to the table. "You two gonna order any food?"

Peter smiled at her. "No, Patty. Can you just bring us the check please?"

Peter continued after Patty walked off. "Do we have a deal?"

"Yes, but I want a written agreement."

"Don't be stupid. Are you going to sue me if I don't pay you? You'll get your money."

"How do I know you aren't going to cheat me?"

"Because you'll always have the threat of blowing the whistle on me. Everyone involved will have that same arrow in their quiver, and that's what'll ensure everyone does their part."

"What good will that do? I can't blow the whistle on you without getting myself in trouble."

"You're a smart guy, David. I'm sure you can figure out a way to do it without incriminating yourself."

David nodded, thinking through what Peter said.

Peter reached his hand out toward David and said, "You do this with us, you are guaranteed to make millions. We are going to be rich."

David stared into his eyes for a long while, and then slowly took Peter's hand.

Peter sat back and watched David walk out of the diner. Peter had a grin on his face as he picked up his coffee. He looked forward to the day he would be able to stand in a courtroom again to present his case to the jury, and the big payday that would follow. It would be just like the Greene case—the case against David Chen. He remembered the jury, staring at him, hanging on every word. David sat on the witness stand, with sweat dripping down the sides of his face. Peter had just shown the jury the picture of Liz Greene taken two days before her death. The jury was shocked at the image of the emaciated Liz, lying in the hospice, just waiting for death to come and take her. He also showed the jurors pictures of Liz before she got sick. They saw her beautiful face and radiant smile. He remembered the questions he had asked David that doomed him long before his lawyer put on his defense.

"Dr. Chen, Ms. Greene was a patient of yours, correct?"

"Yes."

"When did you last examine her?"

"I, uh, I think it was in March."

"March. Let's see. Do you know when she was diagnosed with cancer?"

"I believe it was in June."

"When you examined her back in March, were you able to diagnose her cancer?"

"No, I mean, I, uh, I didn't examine her for that."

"Weren't you her primary physician?"

"Yes, but we just did a routine checkup, and nothing turned up. There were no indications that she had cancer."

"But you just testified that she was diagnosed with cancer in June, mere three months after you had examined her. Isn't that right?"

"Yes."

"Ms. Greene had advanced cancer, did she not?"

"Well, yes."

"But, you were not able to diagnose the cancer in March, isn't that correct?"

"Objection!" shouted David's lawyer. "No foundation. Counsel is assuming facts not in evidence."

"Sustained," said the judge. Of course, the judge's ruling was correct. He had not yet put in any evidence that Liz was suffering from cancer in March when David examined her. But, the judge's ruling was irrelevant. The jury had already heard his question and David's prior admission that he didn't diagnose the cancer in March. All he had to do was put on his star witness, Dr. Marty Schultz. And when Marty got on the stand, he testified that he examined Liz in April and detected the lump in her breast. He told her that the tumor had been growing for some time and she needed to get a biopsy. Of course, Marty never even had met Liz, much less tell her to get a biopsy. Two months later, she was diagnosed with cancer by Dr. Tina Jahar, and five months later, she was dead. Though there never was a lump in her breast back in March, all Marty had to do was fill out a false medical report saying he detected it, and that was all he needed to get to the jury. That and the picture of what was left of the once beautiful Liz Greene were all he needed for the jury to see blood. The verdict was read just an hour after the defense rested. The multi-million-dollar verdict was nice, though the money had to be shared with everyone involved, with Liz's estate receiving the bulk.

That money paid for a lot of things, but it wasn't enough to last more than a few months. It had been a while since he had a decent case. Cases like Liz Greene's didn't come around very often.

Patty went into the kitchen and began to write down everything she could make out from Peter's conversation with David. She remembered Peter saying he was going to sue Pearl-Line. David looked nervous, but she thought she heard him say he wanted money. She couldn't hear much more detail, but she heard enough to know that they were up to something. All she needed was to see David's expression and hear them talk about money. She knew anything involving Peter Cantor would be shady. He crossed the line many times before. The fact that he somehow got a law degree didn't change anything. She knew what he was like. Growing up in the same town lets you know what people are made of. If David was going to meet the one man he despised the most in town, there had to be a reason, and that they shook hands meant they were going to do something. She was going to find a way in. She had to keep an eye on them.

"What're you up to?" asked Billy as he loaded the dishwasher.

"Just jotting some things down," she said, without looking up.

"What?"

"Something that may be my ticket out of this place."

4.

Dr. Ulysses Ullman sat across from Susan LaColla, the host of the popular news show, "This Second." The bright lights shining in his face made him feel exposed, naked. He tried to calm his nerves. He reminded himself, *This is not hard. Just follow the script.*

"Are you feeling OK?" asked LaColla, obviously reacting to the perspiration forming on his forehead.

"Uh, yes."

"There's no reason to be nervous. Just be yourself and everything will be fine."

"Yes, of course. It's just that I've never been on TV before."

LaColla smiled. "You'll do just great." She turned to the director and gave him a nod.

The director of photography said, "We are rolling." Ulysses was now at a point of no return. He had to do his part.

LaColla stared into the camera and spoke calmly with her golden voice, "Good morning. I'm Susan LaColla for 'This Second.' Today, we bring you this special report on the popular YF Cream that will leave our viewers speechless and wanting answers. We start with our special guest, Dr. Ulysses Ullman. Dr. Ullman has spent the past several years researching the potential side effects users may experience from using the popular YF Cream, which as you very well know is the wonder cream that fades your wrinkles almost instantly. You will be shocked to hear Dr. Ullman's findings."

LaColla looked over at Ulysses. "Good morning, Dr. Ullman."

He took a deep breath and tried to force a smile. All of the rehearsals didn't make him feel any better. He swallowed hard. All he had to do was get the first words out, he thought. Then, he would be fine. "Good morning," he said in a calm voice. He had done it. It would be easy now. *Just follow the script and it'll be over soon.*

"Dr. Ullman, before we get into your findings, please tell us a little bit about yourself."

He cleared his throat and then looked into the camera. "I am a medical doctor by training, but now I spend most of my time conducting research. I run the Ullman Research Center in Ft. Myers, Florida, where all my research is conducted."

"What sort of research do you do at your research center?"

"We identify diseases that may afflict a certain group of people, and then try to understand the potential causes of the disease. For example, if you look at coal miners, you may see that particular group suffering from what is commonly referred to as the black lung disease. It doesn't take much to figure out that breathing in coal dust can cause the illness. But, there are other illnesses that people suffer from where the cause may not be so obvious. That's where we spend our time, trying to identify a particular disease that may afflict a certain group, and then trying to understand what may have caused the illness."

"Thank you, Doctor. Now, what made you want to focus your research on the YF Cream?"

"Because of my work, I attend a lot of conferences where I connect with other doctors and researchers, as well as with old colleagues and friends. As I met and spoke with numerous medical professionals, I started to see a trend of doctors treating more and more cases of autoimmune disease in women. This was all anecdotal at first, of course. Of significance to me was that the number of cases really spiked during the past few years, which I found to be quite interesting."

"And, why was that of interest to you?"

"Because the wonder cream, YF Cream, was introduced to the market approximately five years ago."

"Why would that be of interest to you? The YF Cream was released to the market several years before the spike in autoimmune patients that you observed."

"It's not uncommon, and in fact is expected, that unintended effects of a cream like this will take a period of time before they begin to manifest themselves. It's what we refer to as a latent injury. So, once I noticed this potential correlation, I decided to focus my research on this product to see if there's any possibility that the YF Cream had played any role in causing autoimmune disease in women."

"Tell us about your research."

"We broke down the cream to understand its chemical makeup. Most of the chemicals that go into the YF Cream are the same chemicals that go into other anti-wrinkle creams you find in the market, but the YF Cream has other chemicals that we hadn't seen before. I believe what distinguishes the YF Cream from all other anti-aging creams are these chemicals."

"Tell us, doctor, how does this cream work?"

"Well, these chemicals, combined with the other chemicals in the cream, seep in through the pores of the skin, which cause the tissue beneath the skin to swell. The slight swelling of the tissue causes the skin to stretch, which in turn masks the wrinkles."

"How long will the swelling last?"

"It lasts an entire day, meaning people who use the cream will be wrinkle free for that particular day. They then reapply the cream each morning."

"Tell us about the chemicals you found that are contained in the YF Cream."

"Well, there's very little we know at this point. We contacted Pearl-Line, Inc., the company that produces this cream, to see if they would give us information relating to these chemicals. Unfortunately, they refused to help us. They said the information is proprietary and confidential. So, we had to conduct our own research to get a better understanding of the possible relationship between the YF Cream and autoimmune disease."

"And what did you find?"

"Research focused on these two chemicals wouldn't have helped us because no one really knows what causes autoimmune disease. We therefore focused our research on identifying and studying a group of people who were suffering from this disease to see if we could find a commonality among this test group. The test group was made up of mostly women, principally because women are more susceptible to getting this disease. It was also a random sample of people from all over the United States. These women came from all walks of life. Some were wealthy, some poor. Some were stay at home women, while others were in the work force. When we interviewed each of the women, there was only one commonality that they all shared."

"What was that commonality, doctor?"

"Each person in the test group regularly applied the YF Cream, and approximately one to two years thereafter, they began suffering from symptoms of autoimmune disease."

"So, what does that show us, doctor?"

"It shows only one thing. There is a direct causal link between the YF Cream and autoimmune disease."

LaColla shook her head. "Can you tell us who these women are?"

Ulysses smiled and shook his head. "No. There are strict laws that prohibit medical professionals from releasing identifying information regarding their patients."

"Understood," said LaColla. "Please tell us what autoimmune disease is, doctor."

"To understand this disease, we need to first understand the human immune system. All healthy people have an immune system. We have what is called B lymphocytes, which produce antibodies. If a foreign substance, what we refer to as an antigen, enters the human body, antibodies will attach to the antigen and then call in what is called phagocytes, or white blood cells, which will engulf the antigen to protect the body from the antigen. We also have something called T lymphocytes, which will attack foreign substances in our body directly.

"A healthy person's immune system has a memory of antigens that enter the body. Over a person's lifetime, her immune system will remember the different antigens that enter the body, and will know to attack those antigens in the future whenever the same antigens enter the body at some later time. That's the underlying premise of giving vaccinations to people. By injecting people with a nonharmful level of a particular antigen, such as the flu virus, the body will produce antibodies to fight the antigen. Those antibodies will then remain in the body for a period of time to combat the flu virus if the person is exposed to it at a later time. Now, the antibodies in a person who's suffering from autoimmune disease do not work the same way. Their antibodies confuse good cells in the body as antigens. So, a woman's immune system thinks perfectly normal cells in her body are antigens that need to be attacked. Her immune system winds up attacking her own body.

"When this happens, the person suffers all kinds of disorders, such as chronic inflammation of the tissue around joints as well as other organs, fatigue, loss of energy, lack of appetite, low grade fever, muscle and joint pain and stiffness. These people will typically suffer from rheumatoid arthritis, lupus and scleroderma. It is an extremely painful disease that completely destroys a person's ability to lead a normal life. Imagine waking up every day with pain all over your body, not being able to sleep because of the pain and discomfort? That is what this disease can do to a person."

"Is there a cure for autoimmune disease?"

Ulysses shook his head. "Unfortunately, no. All that we can do is to try and control the pain and discomfort. We are not aware of a cure."

"What should the consumer do, if she had been using this cream?"

"Our research is ongoing, but to date, we have not seen any indication as to whether ceasing the use of this cream will cause the patient's condition to improve. From everything we have seen, women who have stopped using the cream have not recovered from their illness, which would indicate that once these chemicals seep in through the user's skin, the disease will stay with the user indefinitely."

LaColla shook her head with a concerned look. "So, once a person uses this product, she is forever doomed to suffer from this disease? Is that what you are saying, doctor?"

"Every person's body and immune system are different, so I couldn't say whether every single person who used this product will become ill. But, from what we are seeing, a large percentage of people likely will contract the disease at some point. What is truly unfortunate for people who are not yet suffering from this disease is the fear that one day they might suffer from this disease. That uncertainty and fear can be nearly as bad as actually contracting the disease. The important thing is for the people who used this product to begin medical monitoring to address the illness right away should symptoms start to develop. Proper medical care early on could help to contain the illness."

"Well doctor, that really is unfortunate—that a company would put out a cream that is so widely used that could be so dangerous to its users. Do you have any statistics on the number of people who may have used this cream?"

Ulysses stared into the camera. "We are trying to gather that information, but just based on the sheer popularity of this cream in the United States, the number has to be in the many, many millions. It would not surprise me if the number came close to or even exceeded 50 million women."

"Are you suggesting that a large percentage of those millions of people will suffer from this disease, doctor?"

Ulysses nodded. "As I said, some people may be able to fight off the disease, but from what we've seen, yes. A very large percentage of people who used this cream will suffer from autoimmune disease sooner or later. It's just a matter of time."

Susan LaColla stared into the camera. "There you have it, America. This very, very popular anti-wrinkle cream, the YF Cream, could be the cause of a very serious disease for anyone who may have used it. If you or someone you know is suffering from any of the symptoms Dr. Ullman has just described or have used this cream at any time, please, please go and see your doctor. This will end our special report on the YF Cream."

Peter turned from the television and looked over at his wife, Sara. "What do you think?" he asked.

"I think it was perfect."

"Do we have the complaint ready to file?"

"It'll be finalized by tomorrow. I just want to tweak it based on what we just saw."

Peter got up off the couch and picked up his phone off the kitchen counter. He dialed Isabella White's number and waited for her to answer as he stared down at the foreclosure notice.

"Hello?"

"Isabella, it's Peter. Did you watch 'This Second'?"

"Yes, I did. I was worried they had changed their mind when they decided not to air it the other day."

"We were all worried, but it's all good. Better late than never."

"When are we going to sue?"

"As soon as tomorrow. We have to make a few adjustments to the complaint. Just be patient."

Peter heard her sigh. "When will I see money? They're gonna shut off the electricity."

"These things take time, as I've told you, but you will get paid. I'm sure of it. You just have to hang on a little longer."

5.

The melody of the acoustic guitar flowing from the speakers soothed Jack Hatchet's mind. The smell of the coffee gave him superficial comfort—from familiarity and habit, but nothing more. He didn't want to turn on the lights. The only light he needed was the one that would soon stream in through the large window next to his desk. These few moments each morning helped him maintain his sanity. No thoughts about winning or losing in a courtroom would consume him. No questions about where she was the night before would torture his mind. No disappointment. No tears. In these few moments, Jack would just hear the music and taste his coffee, and let his mind go blank and his heart become numb. He cherished these moments of being lost, lost from the chaos in his life.

The sound of the car pulling up the driveway made him look up. He heard Angela's footsteps and wondered if she would see him sitting in the library. She walked past the door, but didn't look in. He could hear her walking up the stairs and into the guest bedroom. A few moments later, he heard the shower go on. It had been a month since she insisted on no longer sharing a bed. The guest bedroom had become her escape. From him. No, she would not speak with him this morning. He felt the pain seeping into his heart. He put down his coffee and stepped out into the garage. The soles of his running shoes were wearing thin from the countless miles he had put on them. He took in a deep breath and allowed the cold morning air to fill his lungs. The sound of the stream running along the dirt road brought back faint memories of his days as a kid, following the river to the reservoir to catch fish for his fish tank. He pushed harder and pumped his legs as fast as he could, thinking that he could sweat out the misery and run from it. The only things he heard were his breathing, his footsteps and the stream that guided his path. This was a needed distraction as much as the smell of the coffee.

He pulled off his sweat-soaked sweatshirt and stepped into the house. The guest bedroom door was closed. He walked to the master bedroom and got in the shower. The cool water running down his body soothed him, but his mind wandered back to thoughts of his wife. He knew he wanted things to go back to the way they were. But he didn't know how to get there, and there was no one to guide him. He thought he had paved a way for his life with her, thinking that life was as simple as just walking down that path. He was wrong. They had gotten lost, and now he was searching for the way back to the road they were on. But the search was pointless. She had wandered off in some other direction, and it was becoming clearer in his mind that she would not join him in the search. Where was she last night? Who was she with? Did it matter? His heart began to ache, and he was losing the battle to numb the pain with the cold water. He dried his body with the white towel and pulled on his bathrobe. He stared at the closed guestroom door. He was caught somewhere between sorrow and anger. He wondered how things could have gone so wrong so fast.

He threw his briefcase in the backseat and got in the BMW. He upped the volume of his stereo, hoping to drown out the thoughts in his head. His phone began to ring. He saw on the screen that it was Bob Tuckson. He answered.

"Hey, Bob."

"Jack, I found a new breakfast place. It's a Japanese place that serves rice balls, dumplings, soup. What do you say?"

"Well…"

"It's on 45th Street, between Lex and Third."

"I'm not very hungry, Bob."

"Come on, Jack. You have to eat. What time will you get in?"

"Around 8:30."

"Cool. I'll wait for you in the lobby. You're going to love me for this find. No more bacon and eggs."

"OK, Bob," said Jack as his thoughts started to drift toward Angela.

"Is everything OK?" Bob asked.

"I don't want to get into it now."

"Alright. I'm here if you need to talk."

"See you later."

Jack shut off the radio. He tried to focus on work. It helped him to forget about all the things that had gone wrong with his marriage. He tried to run through the things he was going to tackle. But his mind kept going back to her. Where did he go awry? How could he have let it go so far? It pained him to acknowledge that he was helpless in fixing this. Whatever love he and she once shared was a distant memory. There was nothing left. He felt the tears welling up in his eyes as he tried to grasp the fact that he had lost her.

6.

Jack parked in the garage and made his way up the elevator to the lobby of his office building. He found it easier to distract himself from thoughts of Angela when he was in New York City. He was envious of the people who ran home to escape the stress of work. For him, it was the opposite. His job was a needed distraction from his failures at home. He saw Bob leaning against a marble column in the lobby speaking to a woman. Bob was smiling, pointing toward something as the woman nodded along. Jack slowed his pace, not wanting to interrupt whatever they were discussing. He saw Bob hand the woman a business card, and she walked off. Bob turned and saw Jack and walked over to him.

"Who was that?" Jack asked.

"I think she said her name was Sheila."

"You don't remember her name?"

"No, but it's not a problem. I'll know when she calls."

"What if she doesn't say her name?"

"Jack, when she calls a complete stranger, the first thing she'll say is I'm so and so. You wouldn't know that since you don't go around meeting women like I do."

"I guess you're right," said Jack.

Bob laughed. "I have a lot of experience in this area. Did you get a look at her?" asked Bob, staring at the woman walking away.

Jack turned toward her, but didn't respond.

Bob tapped Jack's shoulder. "You ready to eat?"

Jack nodded and started toward the revolving doors. They stepped out onto Lexington Avenue and walked up to 45th Street.

"This place is exactly what we were looking for," Bob said excitedly. "How did you find it?"

"I spend hours scouring the internet, looking for something new, different. The conventional apps are good, but they're not good for finding little unknown places like this restaurant. You find these places by doing detailed research. I've had more free time lately, ever since we settled the securities class action. And on that note, I need to find a new matter to work on. I need to get my numbers up. The management committee cut my points badly last year, and with the divorce, I'm really in the hole."

"I'll get you involved with something," said Jack.

Bob put his arm around Jack. "Thanks buddy. They would've thrown me out the door years ago if it hadn't been for you keeping me busy."

"You're a partner here. They can't just fire you."

"You know what I mean. They'd cut my comp to the point where I'd have no choice but to leave."

They walked up to the red, wooden door. Off to the right was a small glass case with the restaurant's menu. "This is it," said Bob as he pulled open the door.

A young woman guided them to a small booth. The walls were covered with bamboo. Sheets of white cloth with Japanese writing hung from the ceiling. A waitress brought over a metal teapot and poured two cups of green tea. Bob flipped through the menu. "You have to order takana and cod roe for the rice balls," he said. "I'm not so crazy about the bonito flakes. Too dry. The spicy salmon is good, but a bit too rich for the morning. I just don't understand why we Americans can't get creative with breakfast. They say it's the most important meal of the day, yet we can't get beyond eggs, pancakes, bacon, ham. Now, this stuff's creative. Makes you enjoy the meal, rather than just filling your stomach."

Jack didn't open the menu. "Sounds good, Bob. Just order for the both of us."

Bob called over the waitress and gave her the order for four rice balls, steamed pork dumplings and miso soup.

Bob took a sip of his tea and then turned serious. "So, Jack. I really do need your help. I got murdered in my divorce settlement. I pretty much had to give her a big chunk of my savings and retirement just so she doesn't get a part of my partnership interest. I'm dying financially. And, with the Pearson Group case and the securities action settling, I've got nothing to do. If I don't get my numbers up, my comp's going to get crushed."

Jack nodded. "As I said, I'll get you involved with something. Don't worry."

"Also, you have a lot of influence at the firm. Could you speak with the management committee about my comp?"

Jack looked into Bob's eyes. "You know I won't do that. I'll find matters you can work on, but I won't make them pay you for something you haven't earned."

"Ouch," said Bob as he took a sip of his tea.

Jack checked his watch.

"So, Jack, what's wrong? You look like you're feeling down."

Jack sat quietly, not wanting to think about Angela. He looked at Bob and wanted to tell him nothing was wrong, but Bob had known him for too long. He'd see right through him. "Same shit," said Jack.

Bob shook his head. "Angela?"

Jack nodded.

"What's going on?"

"I don't know. I guess that's the problem."

Bob shook his head. "Shame. I'm sorry."

"I don't know where things went wrong."

"I guess things didn't improve from the last time we discussed her," said Bob. "Did you guys fight?"

Jack shook his head. "I don't think she even cares enough for us to fight. We've moved well beyond that. She just disappears at night."

"Where does she go?"

Jack looked into Bob's eyes. "I don't know, but I guess it's really not important. The point is she wants out."

"She's told you that?"

"She doesn't have to. The message is clear. She's moved out of our bedroom. She's taken over the guest bedroom."

"Maybe she just needs time."

Jack stared at his cup. "I let it fall apart."

Bob shook his head. "Come on, Jack. You can't blame yourself."

"Who else can I blame?"

"Jack, you were the perfect husband. You never strayed, unlike yours truly. You gave her a beautiful home. Always went home to her."

Jack looked down and shook his head. "Yeah, perfect husband," he said under his breath.

"What more could you have done?"

"I don't think life's that simple. Maybe that's where I went wrong; thinking that surrounding her in nice things and going home every night would be enough. Somewhere along the way, I stopped seeing what she needed. I realized that too late."

"Jack, it takes two to ruin a marriage."

The waitress returned with a tray of food and placed each dish on the table, taking way too long to position each plate, as if its placement was a work of art. She finally left.

"It's reaching the end, Bob," Jack said, not touching his food.

Bob looked up from his soup. "Have you tried counseling?"

Jack shook his head no.

Bob put down his spoon and leaned back into his chair. "Geeze. This sucks. I'm sorry. What's next?"

"Separation. Then, most likely divorce. She didn't sign up for a life sentence with someone she no longer wants to be with."

"Stop blaming yourself. She was damned lucky to have you, and if she wants to blow it, that's her problem."

Jack didn't respond.

"Jack, you are one of the few good guys I know. You have to stop blaming yourself for this. Stop beating yourself up. There actually is a good life out there that you haven't been part of. Maybe one day you'll be glad that this is finally coming to an end? You haven't been happy for a long time."

Jack looked at Bob. "None of that really matters. I need to accept what's happening in my life. I'm stuck in the present and have to deal with it."

Bob nodded. "I wish there was something I could say to make you feel better. Maybe you should take some time off? Things are quiet at the office anyway."

Jack picked up his tea. "No. Work is the only thing that's keeping me going. It's the only distraction I've got left. Besides, I need to make sure Jas is protected. I couldn't just hand her off."

"Why not? I'm sure we can find an associate who can babysit the case for a while," said Bob as he took a bite out of the rice ball.

"No. I've got to do this myself. Her ex is violating the court order. Jas called me last night. She thought she saw him following her. I need to get into court to get her better protection. He'll kill her unless I do something."

Bob shook his head. "I don't get you."

"What's not to get?"

"You spend all this time and energy working for a pro bono client. She's been a bigger headache for you than your most difficult paying clients. Why are you driving yourself crazy with her?"

"Because she needs representation and has no money. You would just let her get smacked around by this asshole?"

"No, I'm not saying that. There are other attorneys who work for you who can cover for you. That's all I'm saying."

Jack shook his head. "No. I signed on to protect her, and I'm not going to pass her on to anyone else."

Bob nodded. "Alright, alright. I was just trying to look out for you."

Jack's cell phone rang and he saw that it was Jas. He answered it.

"Hey Jas. Is everything OK?"

"I saw him again this morning. I looked out my window and saw him standing in front of my building."

"Did he try to break in?"

"No. He just stared at the door for a few minutes and then left."

"Alright. I want you to report this to the police. He's not even supposed to be on the same block as you. I'm going to see if I can run to court to get you better protection."

"Thank you, Jack. I don't know what I'd do without you."

"We'll take care of this Jas. Don't go out until I get this sorted out."

"I have to take Stevie to school."

"Can someone go with you? I don't want you out there alone."

"I'll see."

Jack put away his phone and looked at Bob. "I need to run back to the office to see if I can get into court today."

"You haven't eaten anything."

Jack stood. "See you back at the office."

7.

The paneling on the walls was beginning to warp. The cold and wet morning made her shiver. Isabella sat up in her bed and looked over at Jenny, sleeping like an angel. She took the blanket and pulled it up to her daughter's chin. Jenny opened her eyes slightly, and then smiled. Isabella felt her heart melt. She leaned down and kissed her cheek. Isabella walked out to the hallway and into the bathroom. She looked in the mirror and stared at her left eye, which was swollen shut. The bruise had turned deep blue. It was too big to hide with sunglasses. She walked to the kitchen and opened the refrigerator. She saw that she still had two eggs left. Jenny liked eggs. She started the electric stove to heat up the pan and poured a cup of coffee. Her heart ached as she knew she had no food in the house to make lunch for Jenny. She sat down on the creaky chair and felt the tears stream down her face.

Everything seemed so wonderful when they had gotten married. Everyone said she was too young to marry at eighteen. But when you think you are in love, you only see and hear yourself. Everyone else's voice is just static. They said he didn't have a good job and couldn't support a family. She didn't care. He was so handsome and smooth. Between his job as a mechanic and her waitress job, she thought they'd be just fine. But once the infatuation faded, reality set in. After Jenny was born, money became tight. They started to go into heavier debt. He began to drink more. Then the garage fired him. Russ didn't even try to look for a new job. He just kept on drinking. And when the unemployment checks stopped coming, he took his frustrations out on her. It started with light shoving. Then came the slaps. When he couldn't get his hands on the money she was saving for the grocery store, the slaps became punches.

The sound of heavy breathing made her look up. She stepped out to the living room. The large figure lying on the couch startled her at first, but she quickly recognized the familiar snoring. It wasn't a stranger. It was Russ. She had hoped he wouldn't come back. He had stormed out last night after hitting her and taking the last twenty dollars she had in her purse. She was going to use it to buy food for Jenny. That was all she had left. The restaurant scaled back two of her dinner shifts. She wouldn't get another check from Mrs. Martin for another week. They were away on vacation, and they didn't need her to assist her this week. And Russ had spent whatever money she was trying to put away at Sammy's, drinking with his friends. She could smell the alcohol reeking from his pores. A part of her wanted to take a baseball bat to his head. No, there was no point in doing that. She would wind up in jail for killing a useless man that neither she nor society would miss. Who would look out for Jenny? She wanted to pack her things and leave with her, but where would they go? Where would they sleep? It was the same conversation she had with herself a thousand times, and she always wound up staying. She had no way out. But, things were going to change. Her lawyer said to be patient, and that's what she would be. In time, after she wins, she would take Jenny and leave this sorry excuse for a man. She just had to wait a little longer. The sound of the frying eggs brought her back. She slid the eggs onto a plate and walked to the bedroom so Jenny can have her breakfast. Patience, she said under her breath.

8.

Jack made the walk down the long hallway filled with caselaw books on both walls. With the wide use of electronic legal research, these old books had become obsolete, and were largely retained by the firm to serve as decoration. The familiar smell of the aging books brought him back to when he was a summer associate at Thurman & Miller. He stopped and thought back to those days when life was both simple and filled with hope and anticipation.

"Jack, can I help you find something?"

Jack turned to see Maria, who had stepped out from the reception desk, staring at him.

"I was just admiring the books. Thanks, Maria," he said as he gave her a smile.

He walked past the open office doors with attorneys talking on phones, staring at computer screens, solving the problems of the world. Margaret wasn't at her station. He needed her to help him prepare the motion he was going to file for Jas. He picked up the stack of envelopes in his inbox and stepped into his office. The morning sun filled the room. He set down the mail on his desk and dialed the number for Judge Gomez's chambers. He heard the same voice that he always heard when he called chambers.

"Good morning, Judge Gomez's chambers. May I help you?"

"Yes. This is Jack Hatchet, attorney for Jasmine Nguyen. I need to see the judge to report that her ex-husband violated the restraining order. I need greater protection for my client."

"I'm sorry Mr. Hatchet, but the Judge hasn't arrived yet, and he will be presiding over a trial this morning. I don't know when he'll be able to see you."

Jack gripped the phone tighter. "Will you call me as soon as you know when I can come in?"

"Yes, I will."

Jack shook his head and sat down on the leather chair facing the East River. He closed his eyes to calm himself. He heard a knock on his door. "Hi Margaret," he said without looking.

"Mr. Hatchet, Margaret won't be in today," an unfamiliar voice said. "I'm filling in for her."

Jack turned to see a young woman in a business suit. She had deep dark eyes and slightly olive complexion. Her dark brown hair fell like silk on her shoulders. She was thin, but looked strong, like a dancer or a swimmer. She had a strange combination of intensity and warmth. Her beauty was striking.

Jack stood and took a step toward her. "Hi, nice to meet you," he said.

"I'm Tessa Malino. I saw Margaret's instructions on your preferences, so I'll follow them, unless you have any particular needs that are not on her list."

"I can't think of anything right now, but I'll need you to help me with a motion we need to file this morning."

"Yes, of course."

"OK. Why don't you get settled in and then we can get started in a few minutes."

Tessa smiled and went to Margaret's cubicle. Jack sat back down on his chair and stared out at the East River. He fought the thoughts of Angela trying to enter his mind. Where was she last night, he wondered, even while he knew the question was pointless. He used to feel jealousy, fueled by his love for her. He didn't know what he felt anymore. Was it the pain that comes from losing someone? Or, was it the helpless feelings of a man who knew that she was no longer his to lose? He opened his eyes when he heard the phone ring. A second later, he heard Tessa's voice through the intercom.

"Mr. Hatchet, Mark Jones from HR is on the phone."

Jack answered. "Yes, Mark."

"Jack, I just heard from Margaret's sister. She was in a car accident."

"Is she OK?"

"I think it's pretty serious. She's in intensive care. I'll let you know once I get more details."

"Which hospital?"

"She's at St. Vincent, but they are not letting her take visitors. We thought Margaret was just out for the day, but it'll probably be longer. We sent Tessa Malino to assist you for the day, but you can keep her longer until Margaret gets back. Are you OK with that?"

"I don't know. I just met her."

"Work with her today and see how things go. We can get you someone else if she can't keep up with you."

Jack stepped out of his office and saw Tessa organizing Margaret's desk. She looked up when he got to her desk.

"Yes, Mr. Hatchet."

"Please call me Jack. Margaret was in a car accident and she's in intensive care at St. Vincent."

Tessa brought her hand to her mouth, "Oh no, will she be OK?"

"I don't know. Would you contact the hospital and see what information you can get? I'd like to know when I can visit her."

"I'll take care of that."

"Thanks."

Jack returned to his office. He heard his phone ring again, and heard Tessa pick up. More bad news, he muttered to himself. The intercom buzzed. "Mr. Hatchet, I mean Jack, Susan Ines is on the phone for you."

"Who?"

"Susan Ines. She said she's with Pearl-Line."

Jack recalled the headlines in the Wall Street Journal about Pearl-Line getting hammered in tort actions throughout the country. He walked to his desk and picked up the phone. "Jack Hatchet speaking."

"Hi Jack."

It was a familiar voice, but he couldn't place it. "Hi," he said. "What can I do for you?"

"You don't remember me?"

"No, I'm sorry, but I don't."

"It's me, Susan Kelley. We were summer associates together."

Jack found himself smiling. "Wow, a voice out of the past. How are you? I assume Ines is your married name?"

"Yes."

Susan and Jack had been in the same summer associate class, along with Bob, after they had completed their second year of law school. They had become close friends during that summer. Susan wound up taking a different job after law school, and they hadn't spoken in years.

"What a great surprise to hear from you. So, what brings you to call me out of the blue?"

"Well, unfortunately, this is not a social call. My company would like to hire you."

"I didn't realize you worked at Pearl-Line."

"I just joined the company a year ago. I'm the head of litigation."

"Are you in New York?"

"No. We do have offices in New York, but our headquarters are in Naples, Florida. My husband and I moved here from San Francisco when I got this job."

"Well, welcome back to the East Coast."

"Thank you. Let me get right to the point. You may have heard that Pearl-Line has been sued all over the country for the YF Cream."

"Yes, I've heard. Unfortunate. It ramped up right after that news report, right?"

"Yes, from 'This Second.'"

"What is it that you would like to retain me for? I assume you have defense counsel in place already."

"The General Counsel Helen Tsang would like to meet you, and she'll explain the details."

"You know I don't specialize in products liability defense, right? I'm happy to meet with your GC, but I wouldn't want to waste her time."

"Jack, we know everything there is to know about you. We wouldn't be hiring you to defend the cases. We want to hire you for your ability to solve problems."

"What makes you and Helen think I can solve Pearl-Line's problem?"

"We read up on you, and we've spoken with some of your clients. We know what you've accomplished. We obviously don't know if you can help us, but we are running out of options."

"Alright. When and where should we meet?"

"She wants you and your team to be here by tomorrow morning. She would like for you to get comfortable with the facts as quickly as possible and then to prepare a strategy. You should expect to spend some time here. I know this is on really short notice, but we are in crisis mode."

"That all sounds fine, but until I know what my assignment is going to be, it's hard to pull together the right team."

"This is new territory for all of us. We are not hiring you with something specific in mind. We want you to come up with a solution to a very serious problem, and the team will be whatever it needs to be."

"OK, Susan. I'll figure something out. How many days should I expect to be in Naples?"

"I don't know, but assume at least a week. We can see where this goes and figure it out on the fly."

Jack hung up the phone and leaned back in his chair. He pressed the intercom and Tessa picked up. "Yes, Jack."

"Can you get Bob Tuckson on the phone?"

A few seconds later, the intercom buzzed. "He's on."

"Jack, you miss me already?"

"We have a new client. Pearl-Line."

Bob laughed. "That's great, Jack. How'd you land this one?"

"A call from Susan Kelley, who's the head of litigation at Pearl-Line."

"Really? I didn't know you kept in touch with her? How is she?"

"She's apparently married to a guy named Ines, but that's about all I know. She didn't have time for small talk. Do you have a few minutes to discuss?"

"Yeah."

"Please check to see if Henry Lane and Shelly Klein are available to work on this," said Jack.

"I know they recently finished a case with Larry, so I think they'll be available to help."

"Alright. I'll set up a meeting with them for later this morning."

"I'll swing by your office now," said Bob.

Jack hung up and pressed the intercom for Tessa.

"Yes, Jack."

"Please send an email to Henry Lane and Shelly Klein, and ask them to meet me at 11 a.m."

Jack heard a knock on his door and saw Bob stepping in. "Who's that at your secretary's station?" Bob asked.

"She's a floater. She's filling in for Margaret."

"Holy crap," he mouthed the words as he closed the door. "She's beautiful."

Jack didn't respond. He walked over and sat down at the round conference table on the other side of his office. Bob took a seat across from him.

"Is Margaret taking a vacation day?" asked Bob.

"No. She was in a bad car accident. I'm still trying to get information on her condition."

"Ah shit. I hope she'll be OK."

Jack nodded.

"What's the case about?" Bob asked.

"You heard about the special report on 'This Second' about the YF Cream, right?"

"Yeah, I watched the interview."

"Not surprisingly, that report triggered a number of lawsuits against Pearl-Line. The GC of Pearl-Line wants to hire us to help solve the problem. She's not hiring us to defend the individual cases, so I'm not entirely sure what she wants us to do. She wants to meet the whole team tomorrow in Naples, Florida."

Bob looked puzzled. "How do we solve the problem if we are not defending the actual cases?"

"I don't know. We'll find out tomorrow."

"Alright."

"We'll be meeting with Henry and Shelly at 11."

"Who else?"

"I'm not sure we need anyone else."

"Won't we need your assistant? You usually have your assistant travel with you on big assignments."

"Margaret obviously can't travel," said Jack as he walked over to his desk to check his emails. He shook his head when he didn't see an update from HR about Margaret's condition.

"What about the floater?" asked Bob with a smile.

Jack turned from the computer and looked at Bob. "She's never worked with me before. I don't know what value she can bring."

"I can ask my assistant to come with us," said Bob.

"He would be fine, if he wasn't completely crazy. I don't think bringing him down to meet a new client is a very good idea."

Jack turned away from Bob and stared at his computer. "I'll ask Tessa. We can get someone else, if she can't go for whatever reason. Do me a favor. Ask her to come in on your way out. I need her to work on the motion for Jas."

Bob stood with a smile. "Sure thing, boss. I'll be happy to ask her."

Jack turned to Bob. "Bob, don't embarrass yourself."

Bob held out his hands feigning confusion as he walked out of the office.

A few seconds later, he saw Tessa standing at the door of his office with a memo pad. "You wanted to see me?"

"Yes, please have a seat. Let's prepare the motion for Jas."

"Jas?"

"Sorry. The petitioner is Jasmine Nguyen. She is a pro bono client. We need to file a motion this morning because her ex-husband is violating a restraining order."

Tessa nodded.

Jack's phone rang as he was about to start. Tessa stood. "Do you want me to get that?"

Jack shook his head no and pressed the speaker phone button. "Jack Hatchet speaking."

"Mr. Hatchet, I'm Officer Schott with the NYPD. We were given your name by Jasmine Nguyen."

"What?"

"Ms. Nguyen was attacked by her ex-husband a little while ago."

"How is she? What happened?"

"He apparently was waiting for her when she was going into her building. He had a knife."

Jack closed his eyes and slammed his fist down on his desk. "What's her condition?" he asked with gritted teeth.

"She's conscious, but she's lost a lot of blood. She's headed to the ER."

"What about her son?"

"I'm sorry?"

"Her son. Was he with her?"

"I, uh, I don't know. There was no report of anyone seeing her son."

Jack checked his watch. "She must have taken him to school and was on her way back home. Which hospital?"

"She's on her way to the South Bronx Hospital right now."

"What about the attacker?"

"We have him in custody."

"Alright. I'm on my way to the hospital."

Jack hung up and stood. Tessa sat with a confused look.

Jack walked to the closet and pulled out his coat. "Can you come with me? I want to prepare papers to make sure the judge keeps this asshole locked up for as long as we can for violating his order. I can dictate it in the car."

"Yes. What should I do about the 11 a.m. meeting?"

"I'll call Bob. We'll push it back for later this afternoon. Call a car for us."

"OK," said Tessa as she ran to her cubicle.

9.

Jack leaned his head back against the headrest as Tessa put away the notepad. "We can type that up when we get back to the office."

Tessa nodded. "Do you think there's a risk the court will let him free after what he's done to her?" she asked.

Jack turned to her. "Unfortunately, yes. The prosecution will assume a high bail will keep him behind bars, thinking he won't be able to afford it. But he's tied in with a well-funded gang. He'll likely be able to meet bail. We need to make sure the judge understands that this maniac cannot be allowed to roam the streets."

"He's clearly a dangerous person. Why should the amount of money he has have any relevance to whether he should be released?" asked Tessa.

"Good question," said Jack.

"Why is he after Jas?"

Jack looked out of the window. "Her ex is with the gang that calls itself the Tide. At some point, she decided she didn't want her son growing up in a world of crime. So, she pleaded with him to leave the Tide. When he refused, she left him. He's decided if she doesn't want to be with him, she shouldn't be allowed to live."

Tessa shook her head. "That's horrible."

"Yeah."

"How'd you get involved with her?"

"Jas?"

Tessa nodded.

"My firm represents people who need assistance on a pro bono basis. She has no money, no assets. One of my associates took this case on when Jas was trying to file for divorce. After the divorce got finalized, her ex started to make threats against her and my associate. I got involved when I heard about the threats, and we got a restraining order to protect both Jas and my associate. When I met Jas with her son, my heart broke. Here she was, trying to do the right thing for her son, only to have this asshole go after her. I told her I'd protect her." Jack closed his eyes and shook his head. "I obviously failed."

"What else could you have done?" asked Tessa.

"There's always more you can do."

Tessa nodded and sat back. Jack turned to her. "I meant to ask you. Our team will have to head down to Naples, Florida for a new matter. You recall the call from Susan Ines this morning?"

Tessa nodded.

"She retained us to represent Pearl-Line, the company that's been sued everywhere for the YF Cream."

"I've read about that," said Tessa.

"For extended business trips, I like to have my assistant travel with the team. Unfortunately, well, you know Margaret's in the hospital."

"Yes."

"Would you be able to take her place and travel with us?"

"When would we have to leave?"

"First thing tomorrow morning, and we'll probably be there for a full week."

"Oh," said Tessa as she looked down.

"What's wrong?"

"It's just that I have a commitment for tomorrow evening that I couldn't reschedule."

Jack nodded. "OK, that's fine. The client didn't give us much of a chance to arrange our schedules."

"I would like to go, it's just, I've been waiting for a long time for..."

"There's no need to explain. There are others who can make the trip."

Tessa nodded. "Thank you," she said.

"You don't have to tell me if it's personal, but what's the commitment that's kept you waiting for so long?"

"I have a live preliminary audition to perform with the New York Philharmonic."

Jack smiled. "Sounds like it was worth the wait. What do you play?"

"I am a violinist."

"Well, congratulations for getting the audition. I'm sure that's a feat in of itself."

Tessa smiled with her eyes. "Yes. Thank you for understanding."

"Maybe you can fly down the following morning, if your audition doesn't keep you here beyond tomorrow?"

Tessa smiled. "Yes, I could do that."

"Good. We can discuss after your audition."

"OK. What is it exactly that we'll be doing there?" she asked.

"I don't know, but we'll know once we get there."

The car stopped at the emergency room entrance. Jack and Tessa stepped out and walked to the receptionist. They were told to wait in the waiting room. Jack paced the floor back and forth as Tessa sat and stared at him.

"Mr. Hatchet?"

Jack turned to see a young man in scrubs. "Yes."

"I'm Dr. Solomon. You are Ms. Nguyen's attorney?"

"Yes. How is she?"

"She's stable. Thankfully, the blade missed all vital organs. The wound was deep, so we had a lot of stitching to do. She'll recover."

Jack let out a sigh of relief. "Thank God. Can I see her?"

"Just briefly. She's still in a bit of shock, but she's alert."

Jack and Tessa followed Dr. Solomon to the recovery room. He saw Jas lying in an inclined bed, hooked up to an intravenous tube.

"Hey, Jas," said Jack as he walked to her bedside.

"Jack," she said in a weak voice.

"The doctor said you'll be OK."

Jas nodded. "What about Tai?"

"He won't be able to bother you. The police will hold him until the bail hearing, and I'm going to make sure he doesn't pay his way out."

Jas reached out for Jack's hand. "Thank you for coming, Jack. My son, Stevie. He's at school."

Jack patted her hand with his other hand. "Don't you worry. I'm going to pick him up from school and take him to your mother's."

Jas shook her head. "I haven't been able to reach her."

"OK. I'll stay with him until we get a hold of your mother. Don't worry."

Jas smiled as tears started to well up in her eyes. "Thank you, Jack. You are an angel."

Jack smiled. "I'll make sure Stevie's safe. Now, you need to recover. Get some rest."

Jack and Tessa climbed into the rear seat of the waiting car. He dialed the number for Bob.

"Where the hell are you? We've been waiting in the conference room," said Bob, noticeably irritated.

Jack realized he had forgotten to call Bob to push back the 11 a.m. meeting.

"I'm sorry Bob. Jas was attacked by her ex. We're leaving the hospital now. I was distracted and forgot to call."

"Is she OK?"

"As OK as one can be after being stabbed, but the doctor thinks she'll have a full recovery. Listen, apologize to Henry and Shelly for me, and see if we can meet at four o'clock. I should be back by then."

"OK."

"One other thing, can you let the daycare people know that I'll be bringing in a seven-year-old boy?"

"What?"

"Jas's son Stevie. He has nowhere to go right now. I'll take him to his grandmother's later today, but someone needs to be with him until then."

"Alright. The shit you get yourself into..." muttered Bob as he hung up.

10.

Jack held Stevie's hand as they walked to the firm's daycare center. He turned to see Tessa following closely, smiling at the little boy. Stevie didn't speak, seemingly aware that something terrible had happened to his mother. He sat down on a chair and stared at the floor with his arms crossed. Jack walked over to him after checking him in with the receptionist.

"Little man, are you OK?"

Stevie nodded, but didn't answer.

"Listen, I'm going to be upstairs." Jack pointed to the receptionist. "If you need me, you just tell her, and she'll find me right away. You just have to stay here for a couple of hours, and then I'll take you to your grandmother's. OK?"

Stevie looked up. "Yeah."

Jack smiled. "Now, your mother tells me you like cotton candy ice cream. Is that right?"

Stevie nodded.

"I'm going to bring some in, but you are not going to have any until you show me a smile."

Stevie forced a smile.

"Good man!" said Jack as he patted Stevie's shoulder. "I'll need a few minutes to get the ice cream, so you'll have to be a little patient."

"OK," said Stevie.

"Remember, you tell her if you need to see me, OK?"

"OK."

Jack walked to the receptionist. "How many kids do you have here today?"

"We have seven total today, including Stevie."

46

"I'm going to have a tub of ice cream brought in here in about half an hour for everyone. Can you help serve the kids?"

"I'm not sure we are allowed to bring in food from the outside like that…"

"Make an exception," said Jack. "I'll speak to your boss to make sure it won't be a problem."

"I understand," she said.

He and Tessa took the elevator up and headed to the conference room. Jack saw Henry Lane and Shelly Klein sitting in the room through the glass wall. Although he didn't have a lot to go on, he was confident Henry and Shelly were the right lawyers to be on the team. Henry Lane was the obvious choice. He was an exceptionally bright seventh year associate with a lot of products liability experience. Law was a second career for him. He previously worked at a laboratory, but quickly learned that working as a researcher didn't pay the bills. His background in science made him a natural fit for products liability cases. Clients liked his whole package—blond hair, all American good looks, pleasant and articulate. He was married with a young daughter. Jack knew his wife had some health issues, but Henry rarely discussed it. Jack felt badly about asking him to take the trip and be away from his family, so he'd give Henry the option to stay back.

Shelly Klein was an enigma. She had received her medical degree from Johns Hopkins, but never practiced medicine a day in her life. She immediately chose to attend law school and joined the firm three years ago. Shelly was a beautiful woman who was very well aware of how men perceived her. And she played up her physical beauty with authority. She stood at five foot six inches, and with heals on, she looked like a runway model. Her blond hair was always styled to perfection. All of her outfits were from the most exclusive high fashion designers, and she didn't go anywhere without her Hermès Berkin purse. He also knew she took care of her elderly mother. He wondered how she could fund her mother's medical needs, afford her clothes and a $30,000 purse on an associate's salary. She was a talker who wasn't particularly politic in the things she'd say, but she was a master at diffusing the situation with her charm. Jack knew he was taking a bit of a risk in bringing her to meet a new client, but he thought her medical background could be useful.

Jack poured a cup of coffee and took a seat at the head of the table. Tessa stood at the door. Jack turned to her and motioned for her to sit next to him. A few seconds later, Bob walked in.

"Hey guys," he said as he went for the coffee.

"Have you met Tessa?" Jack asked Henry and Shelly.

Shelly stood with a big smile and walked over to Tessa. "Hi Tessa, it's lovely to meet you," she said, shaking her hand. "I love your outfit. Very sexy in a professional sort of way," she whispered with a wink. Tessa gave her a half smile and sat quietly. Henry waved at Tessa and smiled.

"Tessa will be stepping in for Margaret for a while. Margaret's been in a car accident."

Shelly's eyes widened. "Oh no, how is she?"

"We don't know yet. She's at St. Vincent. I'm still waiting to hear about her condition."

Henry shook his head. "Do you know what happened?"

"No. I'll let you know once we get more information. Now, let's move on to this new matter. We were hired this morning by Pearl-Line to help it with the YF Cream litigation."

"That's wonderful, Jack. Congratulations," said Shelly. Henry sat quietly and nodded with a surprised look.

"The client asked for our team to be in Naples, Florida tomorrow for a week of meetings."

"What will we be doing for them?" asked Henry.

"That's the purpose of our trip tomorrow. The client will tell us when we get there," said Jack.

Henry nodded.

"Unfortunately, that's all I know. We are scheduled to take off in the morning out of JFK. We'll meet you at the gate. Don't forget to pack for a week," said Jack.

"What's the dress code?" Shelly asked. "As a cosmetics company, I'm sure they'd appreciate fashion. I have clothes that are out of this world…"

Jack cut her off. "We can dress business casual, but please use your judgment. It's a new client after all."

Everyone stood to leave when Jack turned to Henry. "Henry, could you hang back for a second? I need to discuss something with you."

Jack waited until everyone left the conference room. "Are you OK?" he asked.

"Yeah, sure. Why do you ask?"

"I know your wife hasn't been well. If you feel you can't travel, I understand. Just let me know."

Henry smiled. "No, I'm fine to travel. I wouldn't want to miss out on an engagement with a client like this. Thanks for asking though."

"OK, I'll see you tomorrow."

II.

The white Aston Martin Vantage convertible sat in the parking lot. Susan walked like a zombie toward it, in shock with the news she had just heard. The jury took less than an hour before returning a $35 million verdict. It was obvious they had decided the case long before Pearl-Line put up its defense. She knew this was just the beginning. There will be many more, and she didn't know if there was any way to stop them. Would Jack be able to come up with something? She thought back to when she met him sixteen years ago. He stood out from the beginning. Yes, she immediately noticed his face, the strong jawline, deep set, intense eyes, but she was more taken by the way his mind worked. The way he approached problems wasn't just a function of his ability to remember the law. More than anything, he understood how other people thought. He'd say solving problems among people required an understanding of what the other person was thinking, and to anticipate their next move. Others tried to mimic Jack's approach to solving problems. The challenge, of course, was they just couldn't predict the steps the other person would take. That was a gift that Jack had. Whether that skill would translate into a solution for Pearl-Line, she didn't know. But, she was out of options, and at this stage when the best of the best lawyers couldn't solve the problem with conventional methods, she had to look for creativity. That's why she recommended Jack to Helen. They spent weeks studying everything they could find about Jack Hatchet. What they found was a long list of courtroom victories, and an even a longer list of clients who saw Jack as their only lawyer when confronted with a serious problem.

Susan got in her car and made her way to her home in Old Naples. She saw her husband Rex getting out of his red Ferrari in the driveway—his new toy.

"How was your day?" he asked as she stepped out of her car.

"Lousy. We got hit with a $35 million verdict today in Madison County."

Rex shook his head. "Sorry, baby. Are you OK?"

"No," said Susan as she walked to the house. Rex followed.

"Why are you letting this torture you? You can just walk away. We have plenty of money."

Susan turned to him. "It's not about the money, Rex. This is my job to protect this company."

Rex looked away from her. "I'm sorry. I didn't mean to…I don't know what I was trying to say. Let's go out back and have a glass of wine. Maybe it'll make you feel better."

Susan nodded. "I'm sorry for biting your head off."

Rex smiled and kissed her forehead. He held the door open for her. "Let me go and pick out a bottle from the cellar. White?"

"OK," said Susan.

"Go get comfortable out back. I'll join you in a minute."

Susan opened the sliding glass door. The love seat with the thick, soft cushion looked welcoming. She sat down and put her feet up on the wicker coffee table. She looked out at the pool and the Gulf beyond it. The setting sun had painted the sky red. It reflected off the deep blue sea. She leaned her head back and allowed the breathtaking view to consume her.

"Here you go," said Rex as he handed her a glass of wine.

"Thank you," she said as she brought the glass to her lips. Rex sat down next to her. He swirled the wine around in the glass and then took in the aroma.

"What did you do today?" Susan asked.

"I went for a long jog on the beach. Then, I took the boat out. It was beautiful out today. I had a sandwich out in the Gulf and spent the day fishing.

I caught some snappers, which I'm going to grill a little later. I took a nap and then took the Ferrari to get some wine."

"Sounds like a nice day."

"Yes, and you could have been part of it."

Susan stared at her husband without speaking. She noticed his graying hair, and the slight wrinkles forming around his eyes. He was getting older as he was pushing 50, but he still enjoyed life like a little kid, she thought. She was amazed at his ability to simplify life. His goal was to just find a way to enjoy it, and he was doing precisely that. He had a basic formula for achieving his goal—build something a large company would want and then sell it. With all the computer giants battling for market share, he focused on building a software company they would want. After ten years, his plan paid off. He and his partner sold the company for $84 million. They split the money and he was done with work. He turned down a lucrative offer to stay on as the chief executive officer of the software division. He had all the money he needed, and he wasn't about to become a slave to work.

They were looking at houses in the Bay area when Pearl-Line offered her a job. He was ecstatic when she withdrew from the partnership at her law firm to accept the Pearl-Line job. He was happy to leave San Francisco to move to Naples, so long as he got to spend more time with her. Everything was working out exactly as planned until the YF Cream came under attack. She felt badly that she made him move to Naples, only to recreate the life in California where she spent most of her waking hours at the office. She had unintentionally misled him into thinking that this new job would be different. She watched Rex lean back and appreciate the amazing beauty of the Gulf spread out in front of them. She wondered why she couldn't join him in his happiness. It wasn't that she loved her job so much. There just had to be more to her life than just enjoying what it had to offer.

"At the rate we are going, I very well may be with you next time," she said.

Rex smiled. "You hungry?"

Susan nodded.

"Good," he said as he walked down to the dock and opened the cooler. He held up two good sized snappers.

"What do you think?"

"Looks wonderful. Want some help?"

"No baby. I'm trying a new recipe. I've got it covered."

She saw him get to work to clean the fish. He soaked the fillet in olive oil and salt. He sprinkled in a bunch of different spices and then let everything sit. He wiped his hands and came back to sit next to her.

"We've got to let them soak for a while," he said as he picked up his wineglass.

"I'm sure they'll be wonderful," said Susan as she leaned into Rex's shoulder.

"You know, if things get too bad at work, you can always come home to this. This beautiful spot where we can watch the sun set every night, and sip wine while we wait for the food. Every time you have a bad day, just think about that."

"That's sweet, Rex."

Susan sat quietly, appreciating what Rex had said. But knowing that her worst failure would land her in this world with Rex gave her no comfort. Failure was failure, and the fact that she can run from it and hide in this paradise didn't ease her mind. She closed her eyes and wondered if Jack could deliver.

12.

Peter Cantor didn't wait for the server to pour the wine. He picked up the Stags Leap Cask 23 and poured a glass for Isabella, then filled his own glass. She clumsily brought the glass to her mouth. He stared at her full lips and wondered what it might be like to kiss her. Too bad she didn't respond to his advances. He wondered if she'd give in eventually. Regardless, she was the vehicle that got him the $35 million verdict. That was enough for him to sit with her, even though she wasn't willing to fuck him. Yes, Pearl-Line will appeal, and it will be a while before they see a penny from the verdict, but things were on the right track. Pearl-Line's lawyers wanted to meet the next day. They'll probably offer a settlement, because they knew getting a reversal wasn't in the cards. He could taste the money. It's amazing what a promise of a big payday can do to people, he thought. He hadn't paid his mortgage in six months, but the bank agreed to back off from foreclosing. Even Isabella found a reason to smile, even though her life was an utter mess. Yes, just the thought of money can solve a lot of problems.

He thought back to his childhood; growing up in an orphanage, and then hitting eighteen and taking off to team up with the guys from the streets. These guys were just like him. They had nothing, but liked nice things. So, when they wanted something, they took it. They found other guys to work with for a part of the cut. The group quickly became a gang. That was many years ago. Now, he was on his own. He cleaned up his act and became a lawyer, thinking it would take him to a life of comfort. But, he was wrong. A law degree from a crap law school got him nothing, other than debt that he couldn't repay. So, he had to find a new way, and he did. The woman in front of him was what he needed. He grinned as he thought about the trial.

"That was brilliant what you did in court," said Isabella, bringing him out of his thoughts.

Peter smiled. "We all did our part. What're you going to do with all your money?"

Isabella took a sip of her wine. "Take my baby and go as far away from here as I can." She closed her eyes. "I feel like I'm in a dream…that I can just pick up and leave and be able to look forward to waking up in the mornings." She opened her eyes and looked at Peter. "How about you?"

Peter looked into Isabella's eyes. "I'm going to enjoy every waking moment of my life." He leaned in close to Isabella. "Listen, I think we both deserve to celebrate. Let's do something tonight." he said with a wink.

Isabella seemed taken aback. "Oh, well, thanks but I need to get home and send the babysitter home."

Peter nodded. "Another time," he said.

He was mildly irritated by yet another rejection, but the thought of the trial was all he needed to smile again.

It was the easiest case he had ever tried. All he had to do was show the jury that Isabella was sick and she used the cream. He didn't have to worry about tricking the judge or Pearl-Line. The jury already believed the cream causes the disease. The jury sat and stared as he put on Isabella's direct testimony.

"Ms. White, how are you feeling today?"

"Lousy."

"Describe for the jury how you are feeling right now."

"I have a constant headache. All of my joints are swollen and are in perpetual pain. I have no energy, and it's difficult for me to get out of bed."

"How long have you had this condition?"

"For two years."

"Have you had any period of time when you felt better?"

"No."

"So, you've been in this condition for two years, without ever feeling any relief, is that your testimony?"

"Yes."

"Before you developed this condition two years ago, what was your physical condition?"

"I was healthy. I never had headaches, no joint pain. Nothing."

"Now, I want you to look back to the two-year period before you started having this condition, so that would be four years ago. Did you change anything in terms of the food you ate during that two-year period?"

"No, nothing that I can remember."

"How about beauty aids? Did you change anything in terms of the products you used during that two-year period?"

"I used the same shampoo and cosmetics. The only thing I started to use about a year and a half before I started to feel the symptoms was the YF Cream."

"Have you seen a doctor about your condition?"

"Yes, Dr. Chen."

"And what is your understanding of your medical condition?"

"I'm suffering from something called 'autoimmune disorder.'"

After Isabella stepped off the witness stand, all he needed was for David to describe her medical condition and Pearl-Line was sunk. Once the Ulysses Ullman interview aired, there wasn't a juror out there who had any interest in what Pearl-Line had to say. All they cared about was how much should Pearl-Line have to pay for what it had done.

Peter held out the crimson red wine in his glass against the setting sun, and appreciated the shade. He remembered the last time he was able to sit at this table and stare out into the colorful sky. It was after the lawsuit against David Chen. It was nice to get the first verdict in the YF Cream litigation. There would be many more evenings like this. He closed his eyes and stuck his nose into the wineglass. It was so easy, he thought.

13.

Jack thanked Judge Gomez who ruled that Tai Nguyen would be held without bail, at least until the court was informed of the victim's condition. He set a hearing for the following month to decide whether Nguyen should be released on bail. That meant Jas would be protected at least until then.

Tessa had gotten in touch with Stevie's grandmother. Jack dropped Stevie off at her apartment on Wood Avenue. He drove up the Bronx River Parkway, taking glances at the running river to the left. He wondered where the river originated and where it ultimately wound up. He could easily find the answers with a simple internet search, but he found strange comfort in not answering trivial questions like these. He drove on, wondering if Angela would finally speak with him, even if it was just to come to terms on their separation. He needed the closure. He remembered the day they spent looking at houses. They were going to start a family and wanted a beautiful home they could grow into. The baby never came, and the house never became a home.

Jack drove up the winding driveway. He saw the lights were on. There was a time when she would have come to the door to greet him when she heard the garage door open. Not tonight. Not for a long time. He opened the door and saw that she was in the kitchen. An open bottle of vodka sat on the counter. Angela stared at him as she sat with a half full martini glass. She stood and walked over to him as she held onto the counter for balance.

"You came home, Jack."

Jack was surprised that Angela uttered a word at him. It had been days since she even acknowledged him.

"I came home yesterday too," said Jack, staring into Angela's blood shot eyes.

She laughed loudly for no apparent reason. "Good, I'm glad you're home."
Jack didn't respond.

She laughed some more. "Yes, I know what you're thinking. I'm drunk, and I like it. Do you want to get drunk, Jack?"

"No, I don't want to get drunk, Angela. I was hoping we could talk."

"Talk about what?"

Angela's indifference made him angry. He wanted to talk to her, but she was in no condition to participate. Jack shook his head and turned to walk away. She shouted after him. "Jack! Talk about what? Don't you walk away from me!"

Jack turned around. "I was hoping we might talk about you and me. I was hoping we could spend some time to try and understand what's happening to us."

Angela started to cry. Jack couldn't tell if she was crying for the sake of their marriage, or because of the thoughtless and uncontrollable emotions that flowed from refilling the martini glass once too many. She lifted her arms and walked toward Jack. He held her and felt her cry into his shoulder. A moment later, he could tell she was asleep. Jack carried her to the guest bedroom and laid her on the bed. He pulled the covers over her. A beep from her iPhone sitting on the nightstand caught his attention. He could see the message in the blue box on the phone screen: "A, miss u already. want 2 see you again 2nite. Meet me @ my house at 11. T."

Jack had suspected it was Tony; the way the contractor flirted with her during the remodeling of their house. The only question was whether Angela would play. She apparently had. He felt a sickening feeling in his stomach. It wasn't a surprise, but he felt every bit of the cold blade of reality cut into his heart. A small part of him always believed they could work through their troubles. They loved each other at one time. They could get it back. But tonight, he had to accept that they were too late. All his life, he believed he could fix anything. Failure was something he never accepted. Tonight, he would accept failure, because he had no other choice. Jack stared at Angela, sleeping quietly. He felt a tear on his cheek. "Goodbye," he whispered. Jack walked into his closet and packed as much of his clothes as he could. He stopped at the guestroom door and looked back at his sleeping wife. The pain he felt was undeniable, but he took in a deep breath, knowing that the torture had to end. Jack made his way down the stairs and to the garage. He heard a scream and a crashing noise. He ran back into the house and saw Angela lying on the bottom of the stairs. He ran to her and held up her head. She was unconscious but breathing. He pulled out his phone and dialed 911.

His heart was pounding and his hand trembled. He had no idea how badly she'd been injured. He closed his eyes and tried to push back the fear and emotions trying to force their way out. She didn't deserve this. That their marriage was falling apart didn't change who she was—the woman he loved.

He heard the sirens pulling up the driveway, and footsteps. He stared at Angela as he heard the EMTs rush into the house.

14.

Tessa sat behind the curtains and stared at her violin. The edges had worn and the orange varnish on the neck had faded to a dull white from the years that she held the instrument, and her father before her. She remembered the day he handed it to her. The Stradivarius was worth more than their small house in Astoria, Queens. The house was filled with brothers and sisters, aunts and uncles, little nephews and nieces, old friends and people in the neighborhood. It was raining that day as everyone cried in the living room, when he announced that he wouldn't survive the cancer. He played his final song before the inevitable trip to the hospice, hoping to bring a smile to the people he cared about one final time. Everyone applauded when he took his final bow. He asked her to play the song she wrote. She cried and shook her head to say she couldn't. She wanted to play it for him, alone. It would be their final goodbye. She didn't want to share it with anyone else. It would just be her and her father, sharing one final melody that she would cherish for the rest of her life, and one he could remember in his next. This night, she would play that song again; play it for her father's spirit. She looked up, knowing he'd be smiling down at her. The image of him in her mind brought warmth to her heart, and that made her smile. The voice said it was her turn. She stood and walked past the thick, heavy drapes and ropes that fell from the high ceiling behind the stage. Six people sat quietly in the third row of the orchestra, waiting for her to step to the center of the stage. The man in the middle with the bowtie spoke.

"Tessa Malino?" he asked.

"Yes."

"I see you studied at Julliard and graduated six years ago."

"Yes."

"What have you been doing for the past six years?"

"I've been teaching privately at a small music school in Forest Hills and have been working as a legal secretary at a law firm in Manhattan."

The man in the bowtie seemed disinterested in her response. His expression showed that her story was the same one he'd heard a thousand times—a starving artist trying to make ends meet, teaching their passion, working at a restaurant, or in this case, at a law firm.

"What song will you be performing for us?" he asked.

"The Scarlet Rain," she said.

"I've never heard of it. Don't you want to play a piece that we would know? Something from the likes of Tchaikovsky, Bach, Vivaldi, Strauss?" he asked. The others chuckled.

"The Scarlet Rain is a song I wrote for my father, and that's the song I would like to play for you."

The woman sitting to the right of the group rolled her eyes and then jotted something down on the notepad sitting in front of her.

"You get this one shot, Ms. Malino. Please go ahead," said the man with the bowtie.

Tessa brought the violin to her chin. She whispered, "For you, dad."

She closed her eyes and played the Scarlet Rain, just the way she played it that rainy day in the living room with her father after everyone had left. The strings sang loudly and delicately, with precision and beauty. The music told a story that couldn't be translated into words. With her eyes closed, she lived that moment in a secret world that she had created for herself and her father. She saw him in that world, and he looked happy. That sight brought tears of joy to her eyes. The reaction of the six judges became irrelevant. This was the moment she had waited for since the last time she played it. She was playing to her father again, and that was all that she cared about. The final note echoed through the auditorium. She opened her eyes after a long while and then placed the violin under her arm. The six judges sat speechless, staring at her with wide eyes. After a moment, the man with the bowtie gave her a smile. "Thank you very much, Ms. Malino. Thank you very, very much."

Tessa nodded and made her way off the stage. She carefully placed the violin in its case and closed it. She was startled when she heard a man's voice.

"That was beautiful."

Tessa looked up and saw Jack.

"What are you doing here? I thought you were in Naples?" she asked, looking up at him.

Jack looked down at the floor. "Some unexpected things came up and I had to push the trip back a day. We'll all travel together in the morning."

Tessa saw the distressed look in Jack's eyes. "Is everything OK?"

Jack looked away from her. "Well, not really, but I don't want to bore you with it."

Tessa finished packing up her violin and stood. "So, how did you know to come here? How did you get back stage?" she asked, perplexed that he knew where the audition would be held.

"I've decided to stay in the city tonight. I remembered your audition. I have some friends in the industry, and found out the location of the audition. I hope you don't mind I came."

"No, no. It's just that I didn't expect to see you."

Jack smiled. "Well, congratulations. I think you did great. I'll see you tomorrow."

Jack turned to leave. Tessa called out to him. "Jack."

He turned around. "Yes?"

"Would you like to have a cup of coffee?" she asked, smiling.

Jack stared at her for a few seconds. "Sure, why not? It'd be better than sitting alone at a hotel bar."

"Excuse me?"

"Oh, nothing."

They stepped out onto Broadway. "I know a little café down a couple of blocks," she said.

Jack walked next to her in silence.

"Why are you so quiet?" she asked, as they approached the door to the café.

"I have a lot on my mind," he said as he pulled open the wooden door.

"Hello there, Tessa," said Pepe with the same apron he always wore over his protruding belly. Tessa loved Pepe's kind face, and the same full beard she used to play with when she was a little girl.

"Hi Pepe. This is my new boss, Jack Hatchet."

"Anyone that Tessa brings here will always have a table," he said as he shook Jack's hand. He guided them to a booth near the back. The melody of Tchaikovsky flowing from the tiny speakers in the ceiling filled the dimly lit room. Old black and white pictures of various famous and not so famous people hung all over the walls. The fire burning in the large fireplace gave the place warmth.

"I guess you come here a lot," said Jack after Pepe walked off.

Tessa smiled. "Pepe is my adopted uncle. He was my father's best friend, and I knew him growing up."

"Where did you grow up?"

"In Astoria. I still live there," she said.

Pepe returned with two cups of coffee. "Pecan pie?" he asked Tessa.

She smiled. "Of course, Pepe."

"Two?"

Tessa looked at Jack, "It's really good."

"OK," said Jack, picking up his coffee and taking in the aroma.

"You'll want another slice after you try it," Pepe said as he marched off into the kitchen.

"So, what do you have on your mind that's troubling you?" Tessa asked, resting her chin on her right hand.

Jack let out a deep breath. "I don't want to get into it."

"Why?"

"It's personal stuff. You won't want to hear about it, and I'd prefer not to talk about it."

"I'm sorry. I didn't realize it was personal. I didn't mean to pry."

Jack smiled and sipped his coffee. "So, what are you doing, working at a law firm, with all that talent?"

Tessa let out a laugh. "Yeah, all that talent," she said as her voice trailed off. "There are a lot of talented people in this world, and they all want the same thing; to live their passion. I'd bet half of the assistants at Thurman & Miller are talented musicians, authors, actors. The talent is everywhere, Jack. The trouble is there aren't enough jobs for everyone. It really is difficult to make ends meet, trying to make a living off your passion. Do you have a passion?" she asked, looking into Jack's eyes.

Jack leaned back and let out a nervous laugh. "Passion," he muttered, then sat quietly for a few seconds, staring at his cup.

Pepe returned with two plates of pecan pie. "Enjoy," he said as he walked off to tend to other tables.

"Passion," Jack said again. "When I was in college, my life was about two things. Playing soccer and painting. Oil painting. I used to sit and close my eyes, dreaming up things to paint. It was an escape into a different world. But, I stopped doing both."

"Why?"

"I hit a dead end with soccer. I was good enough to play in college, but not good enough to do anything else with it. Painting..." Jack's voice trailed off.

Tessa waited for Jack to finish the thought.

"Not much to say about painting," he finally said. "To answer your question, I can't say if I have a passion for anything. I've been a lawyer for fifteen years and got pretty good at it, but there's something sort of wrong about saying being a lawyer is a passion. It's a job."

Tessa smiled with her eyes. "Everyone has a passion, and there are no rules on what can and cannot be a passion. I just happened to have chosen one that makes no money," she said, laughing to herself.

Jack cut off a piece of the pecan pie with his fork and bit into it. "This is very good," he said as he cut off another piece.

Tessa stared at him, without touching her pie. "Describe for me what you taste?"

"Well, it's sweet as a pecan pie should be, but not overwhelming. There's a saltiness that blends in perfectly to create a savory taste. And the texture. It's a little firm at first, but then quickly melts away in your mouth. Quite amazing."

Tessa smiled without responding. She thought about the way he was with Jas and then with her son Stevie. The way he tried to protect them, it was clear that their welfare was far more than just a job. She had never seen a man care so much for people who essentially were strangers. He had chosen to make their problem his own, and the look in his eyes was clear that he was going to do whatever he could to protect them.

"Aren't you going to eat?" Jack asked.

Tessa shook her head. "So, tell me about yourself, Jack."

Jack put down his fork. "There's not much to tell. I'm thirty-eight. Being a lawyer is the first and only job I've ever had as an adult."

Tessa cut off a piece of her pie, without eating it. "You don't want to tell me more about your painting?" she asked, playing with her fork.

Jack looked down at his plate. "There isn't much to tell. I just stopped. I'm embarrassed to say that I'm just not that interesting of a person. It shouldn't be this hard to think of something to say about myself."

Tessa laughed. "You don't think you're interesting? You don't think the way you were with Jas and Stevie makes you interesting?"

"Doing something to help people who need your help shouldn't qualify you as being interesting."

"Why did you make the decision to help them?"

"Because it was the right thing to do. I spend my days representing big companies that have serious problems. And I just do what I can to help them. It's a simple transaction. They pay me and I help them. People like Jas have problems too, and in the world I live in that's driven by money, people tend to ignore a person like Jas and what she might need. I'd say from her perspective, what she's dealing with is much more significant for her than what

Pearl-Line is dealing with. Just because she can't afford to pay me or another lawyer shouldn't deprive her of the chance to find an easier life."

Tessa nodded and stared into Jack's eyes. Jack leaned back and checked his watch. "It's getting late. We have an early flight in the morning. Let me call you a car to take you home."

"Don't be silly," said Tessa. "I'll take the train."

Jack waved at Pepe and motioned for the check. Pepe walked right over.

"Your money is no good here," he said as he patted Jack's back.

"Well, Pepe, thank you. That was the best pecan pie I've ever had in my life."

"Then you will be back for some more?"

"If you'll have me, and if you'll let me pay next time," said Jack.

Pepe smiled. "We'll discuss. Next time."

They stepped out of the restaurant to a cool, clear March night.

"Are you sure you don't need a car?" Jack asked. "It's late."

Tessa smiled. "Don't worry. I'll be fine. I'm a tough kid from Queens." She started to walk away, and then turned and walked backwards, while facing Jack.

"Thank you for coming to my audition today. I didn't think I wanted anyone to be there, but I'm glad you came."

Tessa saw Jack staring at her as she approached the subway. She waved and he waved back. As she began her walk down the stairs, she wondered if he was still standing on the street. Her heart beat a little quicker as she thought about her evening with him, and the day before. She thought about his intense but kind eyes; his dark hair that seemed a little too long for a law-yer. She thought about his kindness toward Jas and her son, and the way he made them willingly accept it, without feeling like they owed him anything. The people at Thurman & Miller told her he was the most important lawyer at the firm, but he didn't act like it. Oil painting, she said to herself and smiled. She felt like a little girl again, running through the way he looked at her, the way he smiled. The N train pulled into the Astoria Boulevard Station. Tessa walked to her home on 30th Place. The house was dark. She felt cold from the chilly March night. All she could think of was getting into her pajamas and jumping under the covers. As she placed her violin case on the table, she noticed the fireplace and the small stack of logs next to it. She smiled as she reached for the matches.

15.

Susan Ines knocked on Helen's door and stepped in. Helen looked up. Susan could see the stress on Helen's face. She had changed so much from the first time Susan had met her. When Susan first joined the company, Pearl-Line was the premier cosmetics company in the country, without a worry in the world. It was raking in the money, and the shareholders were enjoying record dividends. Helen was the General Counsel of one of the most prestigious companies in the United States. Susan liked Helen right away. She represented everything that Susan wanted to be. She was smart and confident, yet warm and caring. Helen had just turned sixty when Susan joined the company. Helen accepted her age with grace and confidence. She refused to see her age as a gauge for anything. She had more energy than an eighteen-year-old, and she didn't allow anything to serve as an excuse to change her life. She refused to dye her long graying hair. Her routine of getting up at five in the morning to run for an hour before coming to work never changed. Getting older didn't bother her at all. She welcomed it as mere proof of her wisdom. She was the ultimate professional at the office, yet wasn't shy about showing off her slim, five-foot five-inch figure that twenty-five-year-old women would envy. Helen was everything that Susan had wanted to become; to conquer life on her terms with confidence and grace.

Today, she looked different. Helen didn't hold her warm smile that Susan had seen from the first day she joined Pearl-Line. The wrinkles on her forehead and around her eyes were more visible. The YF Cream litigation was weighing on her, destroying her confidence. It killed Susan to have to share more news.

"More bad news," Susan said.

Helen stared blankly at her as Susan told her the news. She reported on another adverse verdict in Pennsylvania, two more from Mississippi.

"Have we reached settlement with Cantor?" Helen asked.

"Yes. We spoke with Peter Cantor this morning. He'll take $25 million, provided we pay by wire within twenty-four hours."

Helen shook her head. "Let's just settle it and wire the money. There's no point in dragging out the payment for a day."

"OK."

"Are Hatchet and his team definitely coming? We can't have any more delays," said Helen.

"They'll be here."

"How many more cases will go to the jury this month?" Helen asked.

"We have a bit of a reprieve. We have about three thousand cases from the initial wave where trial is wrapping up and will get to the jury in a month. After that, it's complete chaos. We have tens of thousands of cases that'll go to trial after that."

"We have a month?"

Susan nodded. "Yes. One month before the next round."

Helen closed her eyes as she shook her head. "I don't know if the company can survive that many cases. I'll need to report it to the board."

"I know. The next meeting won't be pleasant."

"You said you knew him. Is he as good as they say he is? I'm wondering if there are other avenues we should be exploring."

"You haven't even met him yet, Helen. You'll meet him and make a decision. Don't torture yourself before you've even spoken with him."

"I suppose you're right," said Helen. "What makes him so good? I know he's good based on what I've read and heard, but what is it about him that makes you think he can help us?"

"Truth is, I don't know if he can help us, but he's about the most intriguing lawyer I know. Just from the short time I spent with him when we were summer associates at Thurman, I saw his ability to see problems as a chess match. He just thinks at a level beyond the way everyone else thinks."

Helen leaned back. "Give me an example."

"I remember one case Jack and I worked on that involved a contract dispute. Remember, we were just summer associates. We had just completed our second year of law school. We were discussing a settlement where the defendant was willing to pay our client something like a hundred million dollars. Jack was reviewing discovery the defendant produced, and somehow figured out that it had limited assets, and had no ability to pay anything more than what it was offering. Our client had a very strong case and was owed a lot more than the one hundred-million-dollar settlement offer. Everyone on the team, including the partner in charge, was so confident with our case that they told the client to reject the settlement offer and not even make a counteroffer. But Jack, as a mere summer associate, realized that the strength of the case was irrelevant to the endgame. He told the partner in charge that the defendant ran a break-even business, and it would have to borrow the one hundred million dollars against its unencumbered assets to fund the settlement. There was no way the defendant could have borrowed more than that, because it had no other assets to put up as collateral. He told him that winning the case and getting a larger judgment meant nothing to what the client would be able to collect. Jack told the partner that they should accept the deal."

Helen chuckled. "A summer associate was telling the partner in charge to settle the case? I think I like him already."

Susan nodded. "I know, it's a little crazy. He told them that if we take the case to trial and win, the defendant would have no choice but to file for bankruptcy. All the lawyers on our team rolled their eyes and pretty much laughed at him, although I think they did appreciate that Jack even had the nerve to tell them what he thought. They tried to appease Jack by saying, even if he were right, they could always go back and take the settlement offer. Jack told them the money wouldn't be there at that point. He explained to them that the only reason the defendant was offering to settle now was to save its business, and an adverse judgment would make it impossible for it to borrow the money to fund the settlement. He told them that no bank would lend one hundred million dollars to a company with a six-hundred-million-dollar judgment against it. The only time the defendant would be able to pay the one hundred million dollars was before any judgment was rendered. All of that fell on deaf ears. So, they rejected the settlement and went forward with the trial. As everyone predicted, they won the case, and on the afternoon the decision was issued, the defendant filed for bankruptcy and went into liquidation. The client wound up getting pennies on the dollar of what it was owed."

Helen stared at Susan. "What happened next? What happened to the lawyers who didn't listen to Jack?"

"Nothing. No one ever discussed the points Jack raised, and Jack never said anything to anyone about it. I just happened to know what happened because I was on the team and I heard Jack tell them to take the settlement."

Helen nodded.

"I remember asking him how he felt about being ignored. He said he had no reaction, and he had no interest in discussing what happened. And that was the end of that."

Susan leaned back, thinking about Jack. "He had an intensity about him. Whatever issue we had to tackle, he just never gave up, and always came up with something. He would just dig and dig until he found an answer. He never would miss a detail."

Susan chuckled to herself. "He was just a summer associate, but his thinking was so far advanced…I don't know if he was just that much smarter than everyone else, or if he was just able to look at the situation from a different angle. I'm still amazed at what I read about the investigation he did for the Centuron Bank here in Naples a few years back"

Helen nodded. "Yes, I remember reading about it in the papers; the way he brought down the criminals behind the Ponzi scheme and the drug ring. I know he's done some amazing things, but our problem is a little different. Finding a way to stop a hundred thousand lawsuits is a little different than catching a bunch of criminals or anticipating a company's bankruptcy."

Susan nodded. "I suppose, but at this point, what other options do we have?"

Helen let out a deep breath. "You're right. We don't have any. We've hired the best products liability lawyers money can buy, and nobody's been able to make a difference. I guess we'll just have to see if Jack's as special as they say he is."

Susan saw the dejected look in Helen's eyes. She stared at her in silence for a few seconds, remembering her thoughts from the night before. "Helen, why do you take it?"

Helen turned to her. "Take what?"

"All the bullshit abuse from the board. They unfairly blame you for this mess, yet you just take it in silence."

Helen didn't respond.

"Have you ever thought about walking away?"

"No. Have you?"

"At times. Particularly last night after we heard about the White verdict. You've never thought about it?"

"No."

"Why not?"

"Why do *you* work, Susan?"

Susan thought for a moment. "Because I want to have a purpose, I suppose."

Helen nodded. "You obviously aren't working for the money."

"No, it's not for the money."

"It's because you have a need to do your job, to have a purpose and to make a difference."

Susan nodded.

"I'm embarrassed to say I started off my career with the single goal of making money. I rose through the ranks at Piedmont and Kahn and became the chair of the mergers and acquisitions group. I made more money than I had ever imagined I would make. At first, the money became the cure all for almost everything in my life. I was able to help my mother move out of Mott Street in New York City. I paid for my nephew's college tuition. And, I put a lot of money away. After all that, it dawned on me that making another dollar just wasn't that important anymore. I thought about resigning and doing something else with my life, but I just wouldn't have known how to fill my days. Then I realized I needed a purpose. Work gave me purpose. I work here because, like you, I want to make a difference. If I give up because things get difficult, I'd just be running, and I would have to live with that; knowing that I had failed. I didn't sign on to this job to run away when the company needs me the most."

Susan nodded to show she understood. She remembered her evening with Rex the night before when the thought of walking away crossed her mind. No. Helen was right. There would be no running from this. She and Helen were prisoners of this litigation, locked up by the ideals of their own creation. It did not matter that they could physically escape. Their minds were trapped and held down by a chain they had no ability to break.

16.

Isabella held the $5 million check in her hands. Peter wanted to have the money wired to her, but she insisted on a check. She wanted to be able to hold it in her hands. She jumped up and down like she used to when she was a little girl. Her heart was racing, thinking about all the things she was going to do with her new fortune. She and Jenny would escape from this miserable place and leave Madison for good. They would start over. They would move to somewhere warm, where Jenny wouldn't have to shiver in the cold anymore. *Miami would be nice.*

Holding the check made her realize she had forgotten who she was. There was a time when she believed she was pretty. But the six years with Russ were hard on her. She was only eighteen back then, but marrying Russ and getting pregnant had put her on a road to hell. The past six years had been a life of mere survival, a life where the day's worries were tied to Russ's mood swings. The mirror in the bathroom wasn't there to help her with her makeup, but to help her cover her bruises from the outside world. She stopped trying to stop him from hurting her. It was pointless. She just accepted his random temper tantrums as a part of her daily routine. It was so easy to give up when she had so few options. She had lost whatever dream she had for her life. Her existence was nothing more than a series of days strung together. Mornings didn't bring the excitement of a new day, but served only as a reminder that today would be just another where the sun would rise and set without a care about the grief that filled her life.

Today, she believed she wanted to learn to live again. She would look in the mirror and see a human being with needs and desires that were not tied to mere survival. She would create a new home for Jenny. They would learn to laugh together. Holding that check made her want to have hope, to become better, to live better. The sound of the door opening brought her back to the moment.

"Isabella?" She shoved the check in her pocket. Russ walked into the kitchen.

"I heard the great news," he said, walking over to her. "Everyone's talking about it. Let me see the check," he said as he tried to hug her.

Isabella pushed him away. "Don't touch me."

"What's the matter?" he asked. "We should go and celebrate."

"We?" she asked.

"Yeah, we. What's the matter with you?"

"There is no 'we' in this."

"What do you mean?"

"I'm through with you pissing away all our money. I'm leaving you, Russ."

Russ took a step toward her. "What?"

"I'm leaving you. It's over."

Russ shook his head. "It doesn't work like that. You don't get to keep all that money to yourself."

"What did you say?"

"I'm your husband. I'm entitled to half the winnings."

"For what? You didn't do anything."

"I'm your husband, and I'm entitled to my share. Give me my half, and then you can go wherever the hell you want."

Isabella felt the blood rising to her face. "No, Russ! You are not going to ruin this. This is my money!"

Isabella tried to step around Russ. She was going to get Jenny and walk out of that door and never return. Russ grabbed her arm as she tried to walk past him and threw her back against the kitchen counter. He held onto her arm so she couldn't leave.

"Let me go!" Isabella screamed.

"You fucking bitch!" he yelled and slapped Isabella's face. She stumbled and her head smacked against the cabinet above the counter. She felt the warm blood dripping down the side of her face. She had waited for so long for this, and this scum was going to trample all over her dreams. She swung at him with all her might, but missed him entirely. This time he punched her hard on her temple, and she fell against the stove, knocking the pots and pans onto the floor. Isabella was momentarily stunned as she fell. The room was spinning, and she had lost all control over her body. A moment later, her senses returned. Russ was on top of her trying to reach into her pockets. She struggled to push him off her, but he was too heavy and strong. She fumbled around for anything she could use as a weapon. Her right hand found the black frying pan that had fallen to the floor next to her. She grabbed it and swung it at Russ's head. The edge of the pan slammed into Russ's temple. He rolled off her as he clutched the side of his face with his left hand. He sat for a few seconds leaning against the counter as the blood gushed out between his fingers. He slowly fell to the yellow linoleum floor. His leg shook for a few seconds and then he stopped moving. At that moment, she realized what she had done. Her heart raced. She had to run. Run somewhere. The pan was in her hand. She took a dishtowel and wiped the handle, just like what they do in the movies. Was he dead? It didn't matter. She and Jenny needed to get away. She needed a plan. Patty, she said to herself. Patty's smart and can figure things out. She will do anything for her…for the right price.

17.

Jack saw the black Town Car pull up. He could see Bob waving from the back seat. The bellhop walked with Jack with the umbrella open to keep him dry as he loaded his suitcase in the trunk.

"Good morning, Jack," Bob said as he handed him a cup of coffee in a paper cup.

Jack peeled open the plastic top and took a sip.

"How're you doing?" Bob asked.

"I'm alright," Jack said, staring out of the window.

"I'm glad to get out of this weather. Naples should be pretty nice this time of the year," said Bob, trying to engage Jack in a conversation.

Jack just nodded and took another sip of his coffee.

"How's Angela?"

Jack turned to Bob. "Concussion. She'll be released today."

"And?"

"We are going to talk about next steps when I get back."

"Does she know that you saw the text?"

"I don't know, but we didn't discuss it. We didn't have to."

Bob shook his head. "I'm sorry man. It's got to be hard."

"Yeah, it's hard, but the closure will let me move on; let her move on," said Jack as he stared out into the pouring rain.

The car pulled up to the JetBlue terminal at John F. Kennedy Airport. They checked their luggage and made their way to the gate. Henry and Shelly were seated next to each other. Jack looked around for Tessa, but didn't see her.

"Hey Jack, Bob," said Henry as they approached.

"Good morning, guys. Have you seen Tessa?" Jack asked, looking around.

"Here she comes," said Shelly pointing. "What a beauty," she said. Jack and Bob turned to see Tessa, waving at them. She wore a simple khaki skirt with a white cotton blouse. She was carrying her raincoat. Her brown hair was in a ponytail, with a few strands falling down the side of her face.

"What an entrance," Bob whispered to Jack.

"Good morning," she said as she walked up.

"Hi Tessa," said Jack. He turned to the team. "We're boarding. Let's go."

They followed Jack to the boarding line. Shelly walked next to Tessa. Jack could hear them talking. "You look absolutely gorgeous," she said.

"Thank you," said Tessa.

"Don't thank me. I think you're going to steal the show."

18.

They stepped out of the Ft. Myers airport and breathed in the dry, warm air. "Welcome to Naples," said Bob as he put his arm around Jack. "Sure as heck beats a cold, rainy day in New York."

Jack smiled. "Enjoy it while you can. I doubt we'll be spending a lot of time enjoying the weather."

A white stretch limousine pulled up and the driver got out.

"Mr. Hatchet?" he said as he looked at Jack and his team.

"Yes," said Jack.

"I'm here from Pearl-Line," the man said and opened the rear door. He loaded the luggage into the trunk as everyone climbed into the car.

Bob looked over at Jack and smiled. "Not bad. I like the way they operate."

The limousine sped down Interstate 75 to Exit 105 and got onto the Golden Gate Parkway. It made its way onto Fifth Avenue South in downtown Naples.

"Such a beautiful street," said Tessa as she stared out of the tinted window.

"You haven't been here before?" asked Bob.

"I haven't. Have you?"

"A few times. There's good fishing here, out in the Gulf. I used to come here with him," said Bob, nodding toward Jack. "We had a matter down here, and once we finished our work, we stuck around for a few days to do some fishing. Ever since then, we come down here once or twice a year. Great restaurants here too."

The limousine pulled up to a small three level building with yellow stucco siding and clay shingles. It hardly looked like an office building. "We're here," said the driver.

"Are we at the right place?" asked Jack. "We are going to Pearl-Line's offices."

"Yes sir. This is it."

Bob looked at Jack and shrugged. They stepped out of the car and waited as the driver pulled out their luggage.

"Just up the stairs and through the door, and the receptionist will direct you," said the driver.

Jack opened the dark wooden door and stepped into a large room with a high domed ceiling and terracotta tiles on the floor. A round fountain in the center of the room and the sound of its flowing water made the place feel like a resort or a spa. A young woman in a white business suit stepped out from behind a glass desk on the other side of the fountain and walked toward them.

"Good morning. My name is Jessica. May I help you?"

"I'm Jack Hatchet. We're here for a meeting with Susan Ines and Helen Tsang."

"Yes, they are expecting you. Please follow me. You can leave your luggage here. We'll have them delivered to the Hotel Eva, which is where you'll be staying."

Jessica led the group up a circular stairway to a conference room with a marble table sitting on an oriental rug. A large arched window looked out onto Fifth Avenue South.

"Ms. Ines and Ms. Tsang will be with you shortly," said Jessica as she opened two sliding doors that led to a smaller room. Trays of food sat on the table in the center of the room.

"Please, help yourselves," she said as she walked out of the conference room and closed the door.

"Now, this is the way to host a meeting," said Bob as he scanned the trays of grilled vegetables, sliced beef, chicken and salmon. He picked up a plate and filled it as he walked around the table.

"You are going to eat all that?" asked Shelly. "How do you stay so thin?"

"I was blessed with good genes."

Jack rolled his eyes. He watched others take their plates to the conference table. He stepped to the window of the conference room and stared out. He thought about the summer sixteen years ago when he first met Susan. He remembered her straight blond hair, tied in a tight ponytail, her hazel eyes. She stood five-feet-eight inches; taller than him at five-foot-eleven when she wore heels. She and he were among the forty-six summer associates who had completed their second year of law school. He and Susan had become friends right away. They did everything together. Bob and the other summer associates constantly reminded them that they were perfect for each other, and wondered why they didn't date. They never felt the need to explain. Neither of them believed that a romantic relationship always had to be the endgame for a man and a woman. As friends, their interactions were simple, innocent. They had no reason to question what each other wanted; no burden of needing to explain anything to each other; no disappointments from whatever choices each made. The comfort of their friendship was just too valuable to jeopardize by running after a romantic relationship neither needed.

A knock on the door brought Jack out of his thoughts. He saw Susan standing by the door. She was just as he remembered her. He stepped toward her.

"So good to see you, Susan. It's been a long time," said Jack as they briefly hugged. Jack could feel the tension on her back.

"Yes, it really has been. You look exactly the same," Susan said as she smiled. She held her hand out toward the woman standing next to her. "Meet Helen Tsang."

Jack shook her hand. "Very nice to meet you," said Jack as he introduced his team.

"I'm pleased to meet you all. Please," said Helen, motioning for everyone to return to their lunch. She poured a cup of coffee and sat down across from Jack.

"Thank you all for making the trip on such short notice, but the circumstances required that we engage you as soon as possible."

Jack nodded. "We understand."

"We started out as a high-end cosmetics company that had a very simple operation. We started the company here, which really served as a showroom for our products. All of the actual production of our cosmetics was farmed out to various other production companies off shore. As our company grew, we built our own production facilities in the US, but kept the senior management offices here. Our company was privately held until we developed the YF Cream, which as you know was a huge success. We went public, and now the company has a $300 billion market capitalization."

Bob whistled. "All that growth from just one product?" he asked.

"Yes, in a sense that it gave credibility to all of our products. The YF Cream made our company a household name, and its success gave prestige to our other products, which is where most of our revenues are generated. It was a home run on many levels."

"It also made you a target," said Jack.

"Unfortunately, yes. Success breeds litigation—a level of litigation that we were not prepared for."

"We did some digging around before we came down, but couldn't really understand why the company's getting hit with adverse verdicts. The entire litigation appears to be built up on a researcher's observation that's not particularly scientific," said Jack.

Helen nodded. "You're absolutely right. Unfortunately, plaintiffs have been filing these actions in jurisdictions that tend to be plaintiff-friendly, and judges are letting the cases go to the jury. The judges in certain jurisdictions are elected, and the plaintiffs' bar is the biggest supporter of some of these judges' election campaigns. So, they are not doing any favors for the defense. Once they're able to get to the jury, they pretty much have a win. The Ulysses Ullman interview angered the public. Plaintiffs' strategy is not so much focused on the strength of their experts or even their evidence, but just getting past summary judgment so they can get to the jury."

"Why is the jury angry?" asked Bob.

"Because this cream became an important part of people's lives, then they learned from Ulysses Ullman that the price of the cream was much greater than the $20 they paid at the pharmacy. Rich or poor, everyone wants to hold on to their youth; to be beautiful forever. Truth and honesty have no place when it comes to aging. With money and a good surgeon, you can look any way you want for a very long time. You have fifty-year-old women who could pass for thirty-five; sixty-year-old men, who look forty-five. But, not everyone has the resources to pay for a plastic surgeon or Botox. So, the privilege of having youth and beauty was reserved for the wealthy, for people of means. There was an entire world of people who were closed out of that existence. Then came the YF Cream. It stands for "Youth Fountain" as in the fountain of youth. It's relatively inexpensive, and it opened the door for everyone to the life reserved for the privileged. People fell in love with it. It was the number one selling product among all cosmetic products in the United States. Then, 'This Second' aired. It announced to the world that the price of youth was far more expensive than the cost to purchase a jar. People felt cheated. Becoming ill with autoimmune disease was not a price they were willing to pay. The plaintiffs and the jury are all living through the same emotions—the fear that comes from the thought of becoming sick, and anger toward the company that lured the consumer with promises of eternal youth and beauty."

"And the plaintiffs' bar pounced on that sentiment," said Jack, shaking his head.

"Yes. When that report aired, people felt betrayed, and the plaintiffs' lawyers got active fast. The White litigation was filed one day after 'This Second' aired, and that was followed by thousands of other cases that were filed the following week."

"But you are still selling the cream," said Shelly. "I was at the cosmetics counter at Neiman Marcus the other day and saw it."

"The FDA has not banned the cream, since there really is no scientific evidence that this cream causes autoimmune disease," said Susan. "Our lawyers have advised us to keep it in the market, because taking it off the shelves could send the wrong message to the jury. What's surprising is that our sales have not declined at all."

"How can that be?" asked Shelly.

"The researcher who was featured in 'This Second', Ulysses Ullman, said ceasing the use of the cream won't cure the disease, so people figured they'd continue to use it," said Susan. "The desire for youth is a powerful thing."

"What do we know about Ulysses Ullman?" asked Jack.

"He's local," said Susan. "He lives in Naples and has his research center in Ft. Myers, which isn't far from here. From what we can gather, the research center is funded by the plaintiffs' bar. We frankly had never heard of him until 'This Second' aired. He hadn't appeared in any lawsuits as an expert. He's become sort of a local celebrity now. He was written up as one of the most eligible bachelors in Naples. Word around town is he's a womanizer. He's often seen in clubs in town."

"We considered bringing a defamation action against the network and Ulysses Ullman, but decided against it," said Helen.

Jack nodded. "Good call. The jury would not react well to Pearl-Line going after Ulysses, since in their eyes, he blew the whistle on Pearl-Line. Also, truth is an absolute defense against a defamation claim, and Ulysses will point to verdicts against Pearl-Line as proof that what he said is true."

Helen nodded. "That was our conclusion."

Jack asked, "What's the current state of the litigation?"

"We have several adverse verdicts so far. The biggest one was in Madison County, Illinois for $35 million for Isabella White. That was also the first verdict to come in. We have over one hundred thousand other actions pending throughout the country. We can't take repeated hits like this," said Helen.

"Appeals," said Jack.

"Yes, we do appeal adverse verdicts, but appeals do not offer much of a solution. There aren't a lot of bases to obtain a reversal. These are relatively simple verdicts that are not heavily reliant on expert reports. Plaintiffs argue that they got sick after using the YF Cream, and they have medical doctors submitting medical reports confirming their medical condition. That's enough to get to the jury. There isn't a lot that an appellate court can point to and say there was reversible error. The problem is, we have no way out.

Our lawyers and jury consultants believe that we will take many, many more adverse verdicts at the trial court level."

"So, defending these cases on the merits won't get you anywhere," said Jack.

"That's right," said Helen. "Which is the reason you are here. We have about a month before the next round of cases gets to the jury. We have a bit of a breather, and we would like to focus during this time on developing a global solution to this litigation."

"Did you form a separate corporation that manufactures the YF Cream?" asked Jack.

Helen shook her head. "I know where you are going. Unfortunately, no. It's made by the parent company, Pearl-Line. So, we can't isolate the litigation to a single corporate subsidiary."

"Have you considered bankruptcy, chapter 11?" asked Jack.

"It's not something we have any interest in exploring at this stage, although, if we keep taking hits like this, chapter 11 is inevitably where we'll wind up," said Helen.

"I understand the hesitation, but a bankruptcy does not mean the company will go under. You can operate the company while in bankruptcy, and then use it as a vehicle to remove the one hundred thousand cases out of state court and into federal court and have them centralized. Also, every single case that's currently pending against Pearl-Line will be automatically stayed."

Helen and Susan stared at Jack, listening to every word. "Please explain," said Helen.

"We can accomplish two goals. First, we temporarily stop all lawsuits in their tracks. Then we get these cases out of state court and centralize all of them in a federal district court. There's a section in the United States Code that requires that all personal injury or wrongful death actions against a company in bankruptcy must be tried in the federal district court where the bankruptcy case is pending. If Pearl-Line were to file for chapter 11, then all of these cases can be pulled out of state court and centralized."

"What will that accomplish?" asked Susan.

"Several things. It will give you a breather from the litigation. Second, it'll buy you time to let science catch up to dispel the notion that this cream causes autoimmune disease. Most importantly, it provides you with a centralized forum where you can try and come up with a global settlement. Pay a sum of money into a trust that can pay plaintiffs who can demonstrate they have this illness."

"Has this been done before?" asked Helen.

"Yes. It's been done in many mass tort cases. A variation of that strategy is also very common in the asbestos context," said Jack.

Helen nodded. "That certainly is interesting, but it's not an option. Pearl-Line's success has been driven by its reputation. Filing for bankruptcy will destroy the brand."

"Tell us a little more about the adverse verdict you took in Madison," said Bob.

"As we said, it was the first case filed after 'This Second' aired," said Susan. "The plaintiff was suffering from autoimmune disease. She had a doctor who testified about her medical condition and the pain and suffering she's living through. The jury bought it hook, line and sinker. The jury returned a verdict for $35 million, and we settled it for $25 million and dropped the appeal. We were advised by our lawyers that an appeal would not be successful, so we focused on looking to settle for a lesser amount. We were pleasantly surprised when the plaintiff's lawyer informed us that his client would accept the settlement on the condition that payment be made within 24 hours."

Jack furrowed his eyebrows. "You got a hefty discount on a verdict that everyone seems to think would have been upheld on appeal. Why?" asked Jack.

"We don't know what their thinking was. We were just happy to get the reduction," said Susan.

Helen put down her coffee. "Now that you understand the seriousness of our problem, I would like to discuss the terms of your engagement. As we said, we have about a month before the next round of cases finishes trial and goes to the jury. We are talking about three thousand cases. After that, the remaining one hundred thousand plus cases go to trial before the end of this year. It doesn't take much to figure out that we will be in crisis mode in about a month. We want you to come up with a global solution to this litigation that does not involve bankruptcy."

Helen looked into Jack's eyes. "We have a lot of exceptional products liability lawyers around the country defending Pearl-Line. They are defending the company through conventional defense strategies, but we can't hold off the plaintiffs for long. If we are going to survive this litigation, we'll need unconventional thinking, creativity. We asked you to come here based on your reputation and what you have accomplished in your relatively young career. And, you have already displayed your ability to look at things from a different perspective—your bankruptcy strategy was a good example of that, even though that solution will not work for us."

Jack nodded to show he understood.

Helen continued. "Because we are so short on time, I'm asking you and your team to spend a full week here, to focus solely on this litigation and to propose a solution. I understand that we may be taking you away from your other clients, but we don't want you to be distracted with other matters. We're willing to pay you for that. We'll pay you double your normal hourly fees for every hour you are here in Naples. If after one week, if you are unable to propose a strategy that has promise, the engagement will terminate. If you develop a strategy that has some legs, then we'll extend the term of the engagement as necessary. There also will be a success fee component to this. If you are able to solve our problem, you'll be paid a success fee of five million dollars on top of your hourly fees."

Jack looked into Helen's eyes. "I understand the terms. But, I want to be up front with you. There is no formula for fixing this. If there were, mass tort cases wouldn't exist. So, to be perfectly frank, we probably are not going to solve your problem. I will not agree to let you pay double our normal fees only to have us come back here and tell you that we have no answers."

Helen looked dejected. "Are you turning down the engagement?" she asked.

Jack looked around the table at his colleagues and then turned back to Helen. "No. I just felt you are entitled to an honest reaction. We will take on the assignment, but you'll pay us our normal hourly rates. If we are able to deliver a solution, then you are free to pay us whatever success fee that you feel is appropriate, and five million dollars is more than fair."

Helen smiled. "This is the first time in my career where I've witnessed a lawyer turn down a premium offered up by a client, but OK. We'll do it your way. Thank you. Conventional thinking is not going to do the trick here. You need to do whatever it is that you do to deliver answers to your clients. At this point, all ideas are on the table."

"We'll need a war room," said Jack.

"We've reserved a conference room for you at the hotel. We've set up computers, printers, telephones. You're also welcome to use any of our rooms here," said Susan.

"We can start off at the hotel and see how that goes. Can you send us the litigation files from the White case?" asked Jack.

Helen stared at Jack for a few seconds. "Yes, we can, but as we said, we already settled that case. What would be the purpose of reviewing that file? Again, we've had plenty of lawyers analyze that case, and I don't think you reviewing the case file will yield anything worthwhile."

Jack smiled. "I wouldn't be reviewing it to solve that particular case."

"Then I don't understand," said Helen.

"You asked me to be unconventional. That's what I'm trying to do," said Jack smiling.

19.

Isabella drove to the brick building. Jenny was in the back, staring at her. She was only six, but her expression showed she knew something was terribly wrong. Isabella took Jenny's hand and climbed the steps to the second floor and knocked on the metal door. Patty opened it a crack and peeked out, and then she unlatched the chain to open it.

"What brings you here, rich lady? I heard about your win. Congratulations," said Patty.

Isabella stepped in with Jenny and closed the door. "Can we talk? Are you alone?"

"Yes, I can talk. I'm alone. What's going on? You look like you've seen a ghost," said Patty. "Also, why's there blood on the side of your head?"

"I need to talk to you. It's urgent," said Isabella, with tears streaming down her face.

"What? What's wrong?"

Isabella looked at Jenny and handed her the picture book and crayons. "Honey, will you go in the kitchen and draw? Mommy has to talk to her friend."

Jenny ran to the kitchen and opened the picture book.

Isabella turned to Patty. "You have to do something for me."

"Of course. Anything."

"If anyone comes asking, will you say that me and Jenny were with you all morning, just hanging out here?"

Patty took a step back. "Why?"

Isabella started sobbing. She tried to speak through the lumps in her throat. "It's Russ. I found him lying on the kitchen floor, bleeding."

"What did you say? Did you call an ambulance?" asked Patty.

"No. I got so scared, I just ran here."

"Why didn't you call an ambulance?"

"Because, I didn't want them to accuse me of killing him," said Isabella as she continued to sob.

"Why on earth would anyone think you would have killed Russ? Wait, did you get into a fight with Russ? Is that why you have blood on your head?"

Isabella didn't answer. She leaned into Patty, wanting to be held. Patty took a step back. "Wait, did you hurt Russ?" Patty asked.

Isabella didn't answer. "Oh no, how did this happen?" asked Patty.

"I don't wanna go to jail," Isabella said as she walked to the living room and sank into the couch with her face buried in her hands. "Who would be with Jenny?"

"Isabella, get a hold of yourself. If you don't want to go to jail, you need to think straight. Now, calm down and tell me what happened."

Isabella took in a few deep breaths and blew her nose into a tissue. She looked up. "He came at me. He wanted my money. He hit me."

Patty shook her head. "What did you do?"

"I grabbed a frying pan and hit him on his head. He fell. And, I ran."

Patty shook her head. "Oh dear."

Isabella sat up and looked into Patty's eyes. "You have to help me. If you'll tell the cops that I was with you all morning, then they can't prove I did it."

Patty pulled out two cigarettes and lit them both. She handed one to Isabella, and she willingly took it.

"You're asking me for a lot, Isabella. I know that fucking bum was hitting you, and he deserves to die, but if they find out that I lied to help you come up with an alibi, I can get into a mess of trouble."

Isabella nodded, knowing fully well where this conversation was headed. "I know I'm asking you for a lot, but if I go to jail, who'll take care of Jenny? She needs me."

"OK. You know you're gonna have to pay me."

Isabella looked into Patty's eyes.

"I mean, you know I can get in trouble," Patty said again.

"How much?"

"I want a million dollars," said Patty.

Isabella sat staring at her, thinking through what Patty said.

Patty smiled. "That's the price, honey. We have to think of the police finding out about you paying me, so we'll call it a loan. You'll have to pay me in smaller amounts. You're going to pay me a hundred thousand dollars at first, and then pay me additional amounts as we go. I'll tell you how much to pay me. Like I said, we'll call it a loan, but you and I'll know that I'll never pay you back."

Isabella nodded.

"One other thing. You'll have to tell me everything."

"About Russ? I already told you."

"No, my dear. I want to hear about the lawsuit against Pearl-Line. I want to know everything."

Isabella stared at Patty for a few seconds. "Why do you want to hear about that?"

The smile on Patty's face vanished. She let out a puff of smoke and then leaned toward Isabella. "I saw Peter and David talking about the lawsuit before you sued Pearl-Line. I think you planned the whole thing with them."

Isabella wasn't crying anymore. "What difference does it make to you, what we planned?"

Patty's smile returned. "Because the money you are going to pay me won't be enough to last a lifetime. Now, Pearl-Line. That's another story. That one will last."

20.

Sara stood in the doorway of their dark bedroom. She watched Peter sleep, and he looked peaceful. She couldn't remember the last time she saw him look so relaxed. They were up late last night, celebrating the settlement check. They were rich overnight, and everything was going to be different from now on. They had to toast what they had accomplished. By the time David and his wife left, Peter was passed out on the sofa. It took everything in her five-foot two-inch frame to help him into bed. She remembered running her finger down the scar on the side of his face. It was the only blemish on his otherwise perfect face. She found it sexy.

She thought about the settlement money. It was just yesterday when they couldn't pay the bills. They were nobodies in the legal profession. They survived on occasional slip and fall cases and real estate closings. But the closings dried up with the implosion of the real estate market, and the competition for slip and fall cases was fierce. But Peter changed their lives with this one case. Peter had gone out and taken what he wanted, like he had always done.

When she met Peter in law school, she didn't think about life in near poverty. When you are young, you don't think about life beyond today. It was never part of the thought process. She was taken by his physical beauty, his strong frame that stood six-feet tall; the long, wavy blond hair was prettier than hers. More than anything, she found his focus intriguing. His intensity didn't translate into being a good student; it affected how he dealt with life in general. If he wanted something, it would consume him, and he'd find a way to get it. She remembered taking their final exam in the final year of law school. Peter prepared for the exam hard, because he had to. Failing that exam meant he would not graduate. He thought he did OK, until he read his notes and realized that he had gotten half the exam wrong. He said he'd find a way to fix it. When the grades were posted, Peter jumped for joy as he received a passing grade. He never told her how he did it, but she guessed that he found a way to break into the professor's office to change his answers.

She didn't know anything about Peter's background. He never talked about his childhood, where he grew up, or anything about his family. He was a loner, and that made him even more attractive to her. They didn't worry about the future. She fell in love with him, and with their freshly minted law degrees, they figured they'd find a way to live. Little did they know that getting a Juris Doctor degree through a night program at a two-bit law school did not translate into riches. All they had accumulated were student loans they couldn't repay and countless rejections from law firms no one had ever heard of. Even after they passed the bar exam after a few tries, jobs didn't come knocking. Their only option was to open their own law firm—Cantor & Cantor. It barely paid the bills, until the Greene case. After that, they had nothing. She sensed Peter was getting angry. His focus on finding a way to make money became all consuming. He didn't sleep at night. He didn't eat. He didn't speak to her. Then, he heard about "the plan" from someone. He never told her who this person was, but she didn't care. They were off to the races, and it paid off. Now, Peter Cantor slept like a baby, without a worry in the world. She stared at the man with the focus who went out and got what he and she needed. And, she loved him for it.

Peter opened his eyes. He rubbed his face with his hands as he sat up. Thin rays of light streamed in through the Venetian blinds. He stared at the white mug of coffee with the chip on the brim that she'd left on the nightstand. He reached for it and took a sip, and then turn to her.

"Good morning," she said.

Peter didn't respond. He sipped his coffee again and then leaned against the headboard and closed his eyes.

"Hungry?" she asked.

"Yeah."

"Good. I've got everything ready to go. Eggs and bacon, pancakes and home fries. Everything'll be ready soon."

"When did you get up?" he asked.

"A little while ago."

Peter rubbed his neck and yawned.

"How do you feel?" she asked.

"Like shit."

"I don't mean that. I mean about being rich."

Peter looked up and smiled. "I told you this would work."

"Yes, you did, Peter."

He stood and walked to her. He grabbed her by the waist and picked her up. She wrapped her arms around his neck and kissed him hard. He brought her to the bed and ripped her shirt open. She felt his hands all over her, and she loved it. After he finished, he laid on top of her with his sweaty body. She hugged him and hoped that he'd stay with her. But he rolled off her and pulled on his shorts.

"Let's go eat," he said and walked out of the room.

Sara laid quietly on the bed, naked and wanting. She felt a teardrop slide down the side of her face. It wasn't that she expected him to stay with her a little longer. He always got up right after. There was never any intimacy that followed sex. It's just that she had hoped things might be different now that they were rich. She was wrong. But, she smiled anyway. She thought back to the White trial. She was scared to death when Pearl-Line's lawyers filed the summary judgment motion. The entire strategy would have been flushed down the toilet if they had lost the motion. But Peter never even winced. After Pearl-Line's lawyers argued the motion, Peter slowly walked to the podium with confidence. He looked at the judge and told her a story that left her with no choice but to deny Pearl-Line's motion.

"Your honor should deny Pearl-Line's motion for one simple reason. A company guilty of making millions of people sick in the name of making a profit should not be allowed to walk free based on a technicality. I ask your honor to look at my client. She didn't ask to be here. She had a wonderful life, with a loving husband and a beautiful daughter. Her life was turned upside down by Pearl-Line's promise of ever-lasting beauty. Now, she sits here in pain, not able to enjoy her moments with her family, because Pearl-Line decided it wanted Ms. White's twenty dollars. They talk about the reliability of Ulysses Ullman's interview, but what does that have anything to do with anything? Let's look at the facts before the court. Isabella was a healthy young woman. Within a year and a half after using the YF Cream, she developed this horrible disease. Pearl-Line says there is no causation. But, they can't deny the facts that are in front of the court. It is for the jury to decide whether or not YF Cream caused her illness. Your honor cannot answer that question today and deprive my client of her right to have the jury weigh the evidence."

She remembered her hands trembling as the judge sat and stared at Peter and then at Pearl-Line's lawyers. The judge wrote down something on her notepad, and then she looked up again.

"I am prepared to rule from the bench. Pearl-Line's motion is denied. Mr. Cantor is right. He has presented sufficient evidence of causation for the matter to be decided by the jury. Pearl-Line's motion to exclude Ulysses Ullman's opinions is also denied."

The judge didn't even give an explanation for her rulings, but she didn't have to. Everyone knew the appellate court would affirm, even if Pearl-Line had a legitimate basis for an appeal. Peter had won, and Sara wanted to run to him and kiss him, right there in the middle of the courtroom. After that day, winning was just a formality. She loved him for what he had done; for the way he always got what he wanted.

She threw on a T-shirt and stepped out into the kitchen. Peter sat at the table. Sara started the stove and cooked the bacon and eggs and heated up the home fries as he watched. She filled his plate and then sat down across from him. She watched him dig his fork into the scrambled eggs.

"How is it?" she asked.

"Just what I needed," he said as he looked up from his plate and smiled at her.

"I have a plan," she said with a smile.

"What's that?"

"I think we should go and have a nice lunch in St. Louis and then go and see Vivian."

Peter looked up and put down his fork.

"Why are we seeing Vivian?"

"Because she's going to show us our new home."

Peter stared at her for a few seconds, and then nodded.

"I've already called her. She's got some beautiful homes picked out."

"What do you think we'll clear after taxes?" he asked.

"Oh, I don't know. Maybe five million?"

"Fucking government! That's all we get from eight million dollars?"

"Five million dollars is a lot of money, Peter. We can buy our dream home in St. Louis with cash and still have money left over."

"Yeah, but everything costs money. What we have isn't going to last forever."

Sara walked around the table and sat down next to him. "Why can't you just enjoy what we have right now? Why do you have to ruin everything by worrying about what we might need five years from now?"

Peter stared at Sara for a while. "We'll need to bring another lawsuit."

"We can't, Peter. That was the deal. Just one time."

"Who made that decision?"

"All of us. It's too risky."

Peter put down his coffee. "We did it once, we can do it again. The table's been set already. All we have to do is repeat what we did with Isabella. We probably won't even have to go to trial. They've already lost, and nothing's changed. Going to trial against us won't result in a defense verdict. They know that already. They'll settle right off the bat. They have no choice."

"I don't want to discuss this, Peter. We agreed to do it once and then move on to something else. We can't risk someone catching on to what we did. The others are not going to go along with you."

"I don't need them anymore. They've done their job. All I need is David, and he'll play ball. We keep more of the money this way."

"Peter, I'm not going to discuss this with you anymore. I'm going to eat, take a shower and then let Vivian show us houses."

"Yes, we'll go and look at houses, but remember, the houses you want to go see cost money to maintain. You think the five million dollars will be enough to buy the house and all the other shit we are going to want to fill it with? How long do you think this money will carry us? A year? Two years? Then what?"

Sara didn't respond.

"You don't know where I came from," he said, staring into her eyes. "I came from the streets with nothing. I had to steal to have the things I wanted."

Sara sat in confusion. Peter had never before discussed his past. She didn't know why he was suddenly shedding light on his life before she knew him.

"Why are you telling me this?"

"Because you need to know that's who I am. If I want something, I find a way to get it. What we did with Pearl-Line is no different from when I used to break into houses with Manny."

"Who's Manny? What are you talking about?"

"Sara, I came from the streets. To survive on the streets, you need friends, and Manny was my friend. We helped each other, and we found a way to survive."

"How does this have anything to do with what we are discussing?"

Peter chuckled. "It has everything to do with what we are discussing because you need to know who I am. I came from nothing and I stole, robbed and even killed to make it out of there. Look around at the shithole we live in. This is what I escaped the streets for, and I've decided that this isn't good enough. We are not staying. We found a way to get out through Pearl-Line, just like the way I found a way to get out of the streets. I am not coming back here, Sara."

Sara stared at Peter, lost for words.

Peter laughed. "Don't worry. This is a lot less risky than sticking a knife in someone's throat."

21.

She couldn't recall ever seeing the sky so blue. The leaves on the palm trees danced to the gentle breeze from the ocean. Tessa stood on the sidewalk, staring at the row of Bentleys, Jaguars, Porsches and Ferraris parked along Fifth Avenue South. As much as she appreciated the warmth of the bright sun, she knew she didn't belong there. The only reason she came down to Naples was because Jack asked her.

Tessa grew up in a different world from where she was standing. She was born and raised in Astoria, Queens. Her mother left long before she was old enough to remember, and her father raised her on his own. They never had much money, but her father earned enough playing the violin to give them a roof over their heads and three meals a day. They had everything they ever needed, and she grew up happy, loving the life she was given. To her, life was about following your dreams. Nothing more and nothing less.

She ignored noises about attending the highest ranked college when she graduated as the valedictorian of her high school. Her dream was to play the violin. So, she enrolled at Julliard to study music. She willingly accepted the lessons from her father that life is precious and it should be filled with what's truly important. If music was important to her, then she should fill her life with music. No amount of money or fame can replace that. So, why was she standing on a street in downtown Naples, instead of her home, looking for the letter from the Philharmonic? She smiled as she remembered the night of the audition; that he came to watch her perform. She was taken by him the moment she saw him. He was different. But, it was more than just physical attraction. She remembered the way he was with Jas, the way he held Stevie's hand. He didn't have to make Jas's problems his own, but he did. There was nothing for him to gain by helping her and her son, but he chose to take on the burden. Jas and Stevie needed help, and he, a stranger, walked into their lives to let them believe that life can be better.

Tessa closed her eyes. Something about him made her long for him, long for the words that he spoke. But most of all, she respected his intense desire to solve other people's problems. And that desire wasn't driven by money—just the way he turned down the premium on his fees that Helen had offered. She didn't know what kind of a lawyer he was, other than being told by everyone at Thurman & Miller that he was the best. Helen Tsang seemed to like him. The fact that she hired him to solve this massive problem told the story of what she thought of him. He willingly took on the challenge. He seemed genuinely focused on finding a way to deliver what the client needed.

There was no one at home right now who could tell her if she had gotten a letter from the New York Philharmonic. She wanted to run home to see. But she didn't want to leave Jack. He had an insurmountable challenge, and she couldn't bring herself to leave him to face the task alone without helping him in any way she could. She knew him for only a few days and already she felt a loyalty to him that she couldn't understand. Her feelings for him confused her. Yes, there had been men in her life, but she never allowed them to distract her from her music. She smiled at the thought that a letter from the Philharmonic could be waiting for her at home, yet she chose to stay here with Jack.

22.

They sat in the living room, with half-filled tumblers of single malt Scotch. David accidentally knocked over a pile of paper sitting on the coffee table as he crossed his leg.

"Don't worry about that," said Peter. "That's the old file. It's going to storage anyway. In fact, we should just burn it."

They laughed.

"So, I got a visit from a new client today," said Peter.

"Congratulations," said David. "I didn't know you were open for more business?"

"Not just me. You too. We're all in business."

David had a puzzled look.

Peter took a sip from his glass. "How long do you think the money we won will last you?"

"Long enough."

"No, not long enough. I heard you just picked up a Mercedes, David. We'll all piss through the money in no time, and soon, there'll be nothing left of Pearl-Line," said Peter.

David shook his head. "No, Peter. We made a lot of money. We can't get greedy."

Sara sat quietly, listening and watching Peter work on him.

"We made our money," said David. "You know the saying. Pigs get fat. Hogs get slaughtered."

Peter stared at David for a few seconds, then took a sip from his glass. "Think about it, David. We turned Pearl-Line into the goose that lays the golden egg. Now, everyone's out there, taking their pound of flesh from the company. We did all the work to make this possible. You, me, Sara. We took all the risks. None of those other assholes did any work or took any risks. Yet, here we are, sitting on our asses while everyone else makes their millions off the work we did. Pearl-Line will be gone in no time. I'm not going to let that happen before we get what we deserve."

Peter put down his glass. "Do you see this piece of shit house we are sitting in? I was on the brink of losing this house. Imagine that; that I couldn't even afford to live in this shithole. You think I can make a living doing slip and fall cases? David, how much did you make last year? A hundred grand? Two hundred? After your expenses, malpractice insurance, what do you bring home to that lovely wife of yours?"

Sara watched David staring at Peter without responding.

"We all can live on this money and make a little more, living the life of a nobody. And we'll eventually wind up right back here in this shithole. But, by then, we would be too late. Pearl-Line will be gone. I don't know about you, but I want a lot more than this. I don't want to worry about money ever again. We have them by the balls. All we have to do is file the complaint and negotiate a settlement. We won't even have to show up in court. I already have a client who actually may have autoimmune disease. All you have to do is prepare medical records and stick in the right dates. Are you in?"

David cleared his throat but didn't say anything. Peter picked up his glass and took a sip. "There are other doctors around, David. I'm just trying to stay loyal."

Sara picked up her glass and held it up high. "I suppose we can do one more."

Peter smiled and brought his glass up and tapped it against Sara's glass. They both looked at David. He reluctantly picked up his glass, but before he brought it to meet the others, he said, "But this is the last one."

Peter smiled. "We'll discuss that after we cash the next check."

23.

Jack stared out of the large window that looked out over a row of palm trees. His mind wandered back and forth between the Pearl-Line litigation and Angela. He remembered the text. It angered him that he couldn't take his mind off of that night. *Why torture myself? Just let it go.* Those words constantly filled his thoughts, but they had little effect. Jack looked away from the palm trees outside and stared at the glass window. He saw the reflection of himself. He looked small against the large glass, almost frail. There was a time when he was confident about who he was. Angela told him she loved him. She told him she loved his chiseled face, the deep-set eyes that saw through to her soul. Those words felt empty as he sat alone, wondering how things had gone so wrong. The knock made him turn toward the door.

"Hi Jack,"

Tessa stood in the doorway. "Am I disturbing you? I'm early for the meeting," she said.

"No, come in," said Jack as he motioned for her to take a seat.

"Is there anything you would like for me to do for the meeting?" she asked.

"Nothing comes to mind. This'll be a free-wheeling meeting. We just need to get creative, and that includes you."

"What do you mean?" Tessa asked.

"No one here has the answer for the client. We'll need to make one up and hope that it works. A law degree doesn't give me or anyone else the exclusive access to creativity. You can help to solve this problem as much as me or anyone else here. Don't feel like you are here as an assistant."

Tessa nodded.

"I mean that," said Jack. "The client has a lot of very good lawyers here who haven't been able to solve its problem. You are as qualified as anyone else here who may be able to solve this riddle."

"OK," said Tessa.

Jack smiled at her. "Have you heard from the Philharmonic?"

Tessa shook her head. "No, well, I don't know. It would have come by mail, and there isn't anyone home to check."

"I'm sorry to take you away from that. I'm sure you're anxious to know if you've made it to the next step."

"Yes, I'm anxious, but it'll be waiting for me when I get home."

"Hey guys," said Bob, as he walked into the conference room. Shelly and Henry trailed him. Bob found a seat next to Tessa and smiled at her.

"Hi," she said, as she shifted her chair a bit to give Bob more room.

"Alright, boss. What would you like to discuss?" Bob asked as he turned to Jack.

Bob's question made Jack focus. He felt his brain kick into gear. "I don't have this figured out, but we need to think like a problem solver, and not as a lawyer providing legal analysis. Law is irrelevant here. The client has plenty of lawyers working on the legal merits of the litigation. We need to come up with a silver bullet that'll kill this. That doesn't mean winning a case, because that won't do anything for the other hundred thousand cases out there. It has to be broader than that."

Bob shook his head. "You assume there is a silver bullet. We've been doing this a long time, Jack. There's no way to kill a mass tort litigation like this. There are a hundred thousand cases out there. The only option available to the client is to defend each case to verdict, but come up with a different way to defend each case."

"Like how?" asked Jack.

"I guess that's the million-dollar question," said Bob. "Many great legal minds haven't been able to figure this out."

Jack stood and walked to the window. "So, we should just pack it up and go home? Is that what you're saying?"

"No, I'm not saying that," said Bob. "I just don't think there is an answer."

Jack turned back to the group sitting around the table. "Let's forget about the lawsuits. Let's take a step back. What's the original source of the litigation?"

"The YF Cream," said Shelly.

"No," said Jack. Then, he paused for a long while. "If you think about it, the answer is pretty simple."

Everyone looked around at each other in confusion. "What are you saying?" asked Bob.

"Everything started with the Ulysses Ullman interview on 'This Second,'" said Jack.

Everyone sat quietly, waiting for Jack to continue.

"Remember what the client said?" he asked.

"People are angry," said Tessa.

"That's right. Everyone's angry, which is making the jury find for the plaintiff. 'This Second' report took away something that was important to people, and they are angry that Pearl-Line took away their ability to enjoy their dream product without the fear of getting sick. Will convincing the populous that the YF Cream does not cause autoimmune disease take away the anger?"

"Of course," said Shelly.

"That's the hard part," said Bob. "We have a month to convince the world that this cream doesn't cause autoimmune disease, when the entire world is convinced that it does. Even if we can get credible laboratory research completed within a month, it's just a matter of who the jury wants to believe. This is the same problem that Pearl-Line has been facing at trial, and the client's already lost that battle."

Jack smiled. "I guess that's been the problem. The Pearl-Line defense team has been focused on winning the litigation by trying to win each case with evidence that contradicts the plaintiff's evidence. It may win some here and there, but most of these cases are destined for a plaintiff verdict, because the jury doesn't care about evidence. No, we cannot fight this with competing expert reports on whether this cream causes this disease. We have to attack the source of the anger—Ulysses Ullman."

"Isn't that what Pearl-Line's lawyers have been trying to do in these lawsuits? Trying to attack his research with competing experts?" asked Shelly.

"No, I don't mean attack him legally," said Jack. "I mean attack him in a way that the populous will understand."

"A second report from 'This Second' that acknowledges that Ulysses was wrong?" asked Tessa.

Jack smiled. "I don't know if we need a second report, but a public demonstration that he is a fraud should do the trick."

"How do we do that?" asked Bob.

"We need to find proof that his research was fraudulent. The kind of proof people can understand."

Jack sat back down. He looked into everyone's eyes and continued. "That's the task. We need to find a way to prove that Ulysses is a liar and that his entire interview on 'This Second' was a fiction that was intended to influence public sentiment. We basically have to remove the Ulysses Ullman interview from people's minds, and we accomplish that by turning him into a fraud."

Everyone sat in silence, thinking through what Jack said.

"Do you see where I'm going with this?" asked Jack. "If you think about it, the way to solve this problem isn't difficult to figure out at all. We attack the source."

Bob nodded. "Yes, I understand. The hard part is finding the proof."

Jack smiled. "Yes. That is the hard part. I want everyone to think about how we're going to achieve this. There's not much more we can accomplish right now, other than to just think. Let's break here and meet back up for dinner."

"What if we can't prove that it was a scam?" asked Tessa.

"Then Pearl-Line will have to go to plan B."

"What's that?" asked Bob.

"Bankruptcy."

Silence filled the room for a few seconds. Bob turned toward Tessa and placed his hand on her shoulder. "Feel like hitting the beach?"

"Sitting in the hotel's not going to make us think any better," said Shelly as she stood.

"A girl after my own heart," said Bob.

Henry stood. "I can't. I have some things to take care of. Sorry."

"Suit yourself," said Bob. "Tessa?"

Tessa looked over at Jack, without responding.

"You should go. The beaches here are beautiful," said Jack. "Susan Ines is bringing over the White files this afternoon, so I'll need to stick around."

"I can wait for the files," said Tessa.

Jack smiled. "Thanks, but I would like to go over the files when they get here. You guys go ahead."

Bob furrowed his eyebrows. "You just got through telling us that defending these cases is not the answer. What do you want to look at the White files for?"

"You're probably right," said Jack. "But, you have to start somewhere. Why not start with the first case that was filed after the interview?"

Bob stood and walked toward the door. "Suit yourself. I'm going to the beach because being in a beautiful surrounding helps me to think."

"Have fun," said Jack.

Bob looked back at everyone and said, "I love my job; to be paid for hanging out at the beach." He opened the door. "Let's meet in the lobby in 15 minutes."

Shelly and Henry followed Bob out of the conference room. Tessa remained seated in her chair.

"What's wrong?" asked Jack.

"I don't need to go to the beach, Jack. I can stay here and help you."

Jack looked at her. "There really isn't much for us to do right now, but you are welcome to stay back."

Tessa smiled. "When will the boxes arrive?"

"I don't know. Susan called about an hour ago and said their in-house legal team was still organizing the files. I suspect we won't see them for at least a couple of hours."

"So, you're just going to sit here for two hours?" she asked.

"No," said Jack. "You and I are going to see if the pecan pie at the hotel restaurant can match up to Uncle Pepe's.

24.

Peter took a sip of his Scotch and set the glass down on his kitchen counter. He thought back to the jury verdict in the White case. He smiled. Everything had played out to perfection. His phone ringing brought him back to the moment. The caller ID said "unknown."

"Yeah," he said into the phone.

"It's me," said the familiar voice. "You are not going to believe this. I'm on the team that Pearl-Line hired to deal with this litigation."

"What? What are you talking about?"

"Pearl-Line hired Jack Hatchet to find a way to stop this litigation, and I happen to work at his law firm. And, he put me on the team."

"Well, that is some coincidence, but I don't give a shit who they hired. No one can stop this runaway train."

"You're probably right, but Jack Hatchet has a reputation for solving big problems. He got me a little worried today when he told us to look for a way to go after Ulysses."

"What? How the fuck did he figure that out already?"

"Well, Ulysses did start all of this with his interview, so I guess we shouldn't be so surprised that Jack's going to go after the source."

"Shit."

"Don't worry. He may know to go after Ulysses, but I don't know what he thinks he's going to find. The point is, I'll know real time as to whatever strategy he pursues. We got lucky."

"Yeah, no doubt. It's better to be lucky than smart, or whatever the saying is."

"Well, we happen to be both. Have you mailed me the check? I really need the money."

"The accounting firm I hired sent you a check for a hundred grand. You'll get the rest over time as we discussed."

"Understood."

25.

The phone rang repeatedly. Henry held onto the receiver, knowing that she would answer, sooner or later. He made sure to disconnect the answering machine before he left so that she'd have to answer the phone. She picked up after the fifteenth ring.

"Hello," she said with her weak voice.

"How're you feeling?" he asked.

"The same. We got another letter from the collection agency. I can't believe you did this to us."

Henry gripped the phone tighter as his heartbeat quickened. "I said I'll fix it. I just need a little time."

She didn't answer.

"Did you see your therapist today?"

"Yes."

"Good. Thank you." His eyes began to well up. "I love you," he said.

"I would like to go back to bed."

"OK. I'll call you tomorrow." He heard her hang up. Henry opened his luggage and pulled out a bottle of Johnny Walker. He poured a glass and downed it in one gulp. It soothed his mind. He poured another glass and then called the collection agency. He was connected to a guy named Joe who was responsible for his file.

"It's Henry Lane. Stop sending letters to my house. My wife sees them and she gets upset. If you need to communicate with me, just pick up the phone and call my cell phone."

"Just make sure we get paid, and you won't have to worry about us sending any more letters."

"Go fuck yourself!" yelled Henry. The man hung up. Henry refilled his glass and then leaned back against the couch and closed his eyes.

26.

They sat at the outdoor table, surrounded by flowers of all colors. Tessa stared into Jack's eyes. He looked away from her and stared down at the half-eaten pecan pie, like a schoolboy who was too shy to acknowledge a girl with a crush. His dark hair fell to cover a part of his face and his deep-set eyes. She wondered what he was thinking about. They sat quietly for a few minutes, neither feeling the need to fill the silence with chit chat. She thought back to the time when she first saw him. She expected the famous Jack Hatchet to be different—aggressive, temperamental, unattractive. He was completely the opposite. For Tessa, Jack Hatchet's fame meant little. She appreciated that he was gentle, thoughtful. She was drawn to his face that always looked like he was deep in thought. He often looked away into the distance. She could tell he was troubled by something, trying to work things out in his mind, but she didn't know what. She just knew it wasn't her place to ask.

"So, how does the pie compare to uncle Pepe's?" she asked, breaking the silence.

Jack looked up. "Nowhere close."

Tessa laughed. "I thought you might say that."

Jack smiled.

"So, what makes you such a great lawyer?"

Jack laughed quietly. "You assume I am a great lawyer."

"That's what I was told."

"Making money for the law firm doesn't equate to being a great lawyer. I'm not sure I know what it means to be a great lawyer. What I do know is that I believe I can help my clients, and sometimes I succeed at that."

"You don't like to talk about yourself," said Tessa.

Jack shook his head. "I never thought of it that way, but I guess that's right."

"You are not going to answer me?"

Jack met Tessa's eyes. "No, because I don't know the answer. Anyway, whatever I may have accomplished in the past means nothing for Pearl-Line. Helen and Susan will judge me and us based on what we deliver for them on this assignment. That's why I don't spend a lot of time asking whether I'm good, bad or average." Jack looked down again. "I have one objective right now, and that's to solve Pearl-Line's problem. I think we have an angle, and whether we are able to make something of it is all that matters."

Tessa nodded. "You seem determined."

Jack nodded. "Yes. I guess you can say that."

"How do you know Pearl-Line's cream doesn't cause autoimmune disease?"

Jack stared at her. "I don't, but Pearl-Line shouldn't have to prove a negative, just because someone made an accusation. The legal system would fall apart if that were the standard. The accuser has to present credible proof that the cream causes autoimmune disease and I've yet to see anything to suggest that it does."

Tessa creased her eyebrows. "I don't understand. What about all these people suing Pearl-Line claiming that it does?"

"Autoimmune disease is not an uncommon illness. The fact that these people may have also used the YF Cream doesn't show anything. But that's all Ulysses said during his interview."

Tessa shook her head to show that she wasn't following. "What if he's not a fraud? What makes you so sure that he is?"

"If you look at his analysis, I think there is a good chance that he made this whole thing up." Jack pointed to the half-eaten pecan pie sitting in front of Tessa. "Do you believe that pecan pie is poisonous?"

"It doesn't taste very good, but I wouldn't say it's poisonous," said Tessa, smiling.

"How do you know that?"

Tessa laughed. "That it doesn't taste good?"

"No, that it's not poisonous."

"Because people eat pecan pie all the time, and no one has died from eating it."

"But, other than that observation, you have no other basis to prove that it's not poisonous."

Tessa didn't answer.

"Isn't it true that every person who's ever eaten pecan pie in human history eventually died?" asked Jack.

Tessa laughed. "Yes, I suppose that is true."

"So, why can't we argue that pecan pie is poisonous?"

"Because everyone dies at some point for reasons having nothing to do with pecan pie."

Jack smiled. "That's right. Ulysses's research proves nothing more than what I just said about pecan pie. There is a large population of people who suffer from autoimmune disease. This disease was around long before the YF Cream was introduced to the market. The fact that certain women who use this cream contracted autoimmune disease does not mean that the cream causes the disease."

"But he said the women began suffering from this illness a few years after they started using the cream."

Jack nodded. "Yes, he did say that, but that could be a lie too. How hard do you think it is to find a doctor who's willing to fabricate a medical report?"

"Would a doctor really do that?"

"Have you ever heard of B readers? Silica?"

"No."

"There was a spike in tort litigation where hundreds of thousands of claimants began suing companies that were in the minerals business for illnesses supposedly resulting from inhaling silica dust. The claimants had medical professionals who read their X-rays and concluded that the victims were suffering from various forms of lung disease. After a thorough investigation by some good lawyers, they were able to figure out that these supposed medical professionals were essentially paid to provide false X-ray readings. This fraud was reported in a thorough opinion written by a federal district court judge. Once that decision came down, the number of silica cases fell off the cliff. So, to answer your question, the fact that there may be medical reports supporting Ulysses's views doesn't necessarily mean a whole lot."

Tessa stared at Jack, thinking through what he said.

Jack continued. "I don't know if the YF Cream causes autoimmune disease, but what I do know is that Ulysses Ullman's conclusion that there is a causal link between this cream and this disease is as far-fetched as saying pecan pie is poisonous."

Jack's phone buzzed. He held up his finger as he answered. After a few seconds, he put the phone down. "Susan's on her way with the files from the White litigation."

"Why did you want to review those files?" Tessa asked.

"I just found it curious that that lawsuit was filed one day after Ulysses's interview aired on 'This Second.'"

"Didn't Susan say thousands were filed very shortly after it aired?"

"Yes, but even after an explosive report like that, I would think plaintiffs' firms would need at least a week to find plaintiffs and prepare skeletal complaints against Pearl-Line. But filing a lawsuit just one day after 'This Second' aired is a bit curious."

Tessa nodded.

"We have nothing to lose, but a lot to gain by educating ourselves. We have to start somewhere, so why not at the beginning?"

27.

Jack opened the door to the conference room. He saw Susan pouring a cup of coffee, as two men lined up boxes of documents on the conference table. The tension and stress on her face were apparent. She walked over to Jack and pointed to the boxes. "They're organized sequentially. The first box contains the complaint, answer, motion papers and the like. The following boxes contain medical records and other documents from discovery, as well as deposition transcripts. Those boxes over there are the trial transcripts. Everything happened real fast in this case. As the court became bombarded with a large number of YF Cream cases, the judge in Madison County entered an order for all YF Cream cases, and pretty much everything is on a rocket docket. Discovery, motion practice, everything gets done in a matter of months, and then you are in trial."

Susan picked up her coffee and took a seat at the head of the table.

"Will Helen be joining us?" Jack asked as he poured a cup of coffee.

Susan let out a sigh. "Unfortunately, no. She's meeting with the board this afternoon."

"Giving them an update?"

Susan shook her head. "No, just defending her job."

Jack looked up from his coffee. "Excuse me?"

"The board is blaming Helen and me for what the company's going through, but she's getting the brunt of it."

"That's ridiculous," said Jack.

Susan nodded in agreement. "They need a scapegoat, and they found two—me and Helen."

"Did you or she have anything to do with creating this product?" asked Jack, noticing that Tessa was still standing by the door. He motioned for her to take a seat. She nodded and then sat down on the other side of the table.

"Of course not," said Susan. "They aren't saying we're responsible for putting the cream in the market. They're blaming us for not being prepared for a litigation of this magnitude and not being able to manage it."

Jack shook his head. "This litigation has nothing to do with being ready. No one could have anticipated the interview on 'This Second' that started this circus."

"It's not about being fair, Jack. This was the hand we were dealt, and I don't think there's anything she or I can do to change the way they see things. So, all we can do is fight to save the company. Unless we can find a way out of this, this litigation will bring down the company. At the end of the day, it doesn't much matter who's blaming whom. Helen and I will either be heroes or scapegoats depending on what happens to this litigation. We've hired the best of the best law firms around the country, and nothing's changed. This situation is killing us, and we are desperate. That's why you're here. You are our Hail Mary. If you can't come up with something, it's chapter 11."

Jack shook his head. "It's a shame that people have to expend their energy on pointing fingers, rather than focusing on finding a solution."

Susan laughed to herself. "It is what it is. I suppose if we get to the point where we can't handle dealing with the blame game, we could just resign and walk away. I'm not ready to do that. Helen feels the same way. She wants to see this through. She sees this as a challenge. She really doesn't care who caused the problem or who is being blamed. She'll do everything within her power to get the company out of this mess. If she succeeds, she'll gladly resign at that point, but not before."

Jack nodded to show he understood.

"You really are our last hope, Jack."

"You are putting a lot of pressure on us," said Jack.

Susan didn't laugh at Jack's attempt to bring levity to the conversation. "Yes, we are putting a lot of pressure on you. You may as well feel the stress we are living with."

She stood and picked up her purse. "Helen would like to know if you'll have anything to report in the morning."

Jack walked to her. "Nothing fully baked yet, but we should have something to discuss."

Susan smiled and hugged him. "We'll meet at Pearl-Line for breakfast. Will 9 a.m. work?"

"We'll be there at 9."

Jack closed the door behind Susan. He looked at Tessa, still sitting at the table. "Is everything OK?" he asked.

Tessa turned to him. "Yes."

"You didn't say a word the entire time she was here."

"There wasn't anything I could say that would've contributed anything," she said as she stared down.

"Don't assume that. Remember what I said before. No lawyer has a leg up on you. The strategy to go after Ulysses Ullman isn't based on some legal theory. It's based on simple logic. Take down the guy who started this mess, and the people who have been fooled by him will clean up the mess for you. Now, we just have to find a way to take him down. You are as capable as me or anyone else in helping to find a way."

Tessa nodded.

Jack smiled. "I'm going to start going through the files. I made dinner reservations at an Italian restaurant down the street for seven thirty. Will you let the others know?"

"Of course. I left my phone in my room. I'll email them," she said as she left the conference room.

Jack refilled his coffee cup and pulled out the complaint from the first box. He read through the factual allegations and the repeated references to Ulysses's interview on "This Second". There were three counts in the complaint. One count sought money damages for personal injury arising from

Pearl-Line's defective cream. The second count sought money damages for failure to warn of the injuries the cream causes and the third count sought money damages for intentional infliction of emotional harm. Jack then turned to the final page of the complaint where he read through the "Prayers for Relief." The date of the complaint caught his eye—February 2. He stared at it for a second and then turned to the first page of the complaint, which had the filed stamped date of February 4. He then turned back to the factual background section of the complaint and reread the discussion of the interview on "This Second". Jack called Tessa.

"Tessa, it's Jack. Do you remember when 'This Second' aired?"

"It aired on February 3. Why?"

"I need for you to confirm that and then do some internet searches on some people. Can you help me?"

"Sure. I'll come right down."

Jack pulled Pearl-Line's motion papers seeking summary judgment. There was no mention of the date when "This Second" aired.

"Hi Jack."

Jack looked up and saw Tessa. "Thanks for coming down." He pointed to the laptop sitting on the table. "After you confirm the date when 'This Second' aired, see if you can find out if there is any connection between Ulysses Ullman and Peter Cantor or his law firm, Cantor and Cantor."

Tessa nodded and sat down in front of the computer. "What's going on?"

Jack looked over at her and saw her typing away. "The complaint was signed on February 2 and makes reference to Ulysses's interview, which aired on February 3."

Tessa stopped typing and turned to Jack.

"It may be a simple typo, or it may be something else," said Jack.

"You think Cantor knew about the interview before it aired?" Tessa asked.

Jack didn't answer. He returned to the summary judgment motion papers. Tessa turned back to the computer and began typing.

She looked over at Jack. "Ulysses's interview aired on February 3. Every news report on the internet confirms it."

"Thanks. See what you can find out about Cantor."

"Jack, I'm not finding a whole lot on Cantor. All I'm seeing are articles on the White verdict, but not a whole lot on him or his firm before the White lawsuit or any connection to Ulysses."

"Keep looking," said Jack as he picked up his cell phone and began dialing the number for Thurman & Miller's head of operations.

"Who're you calling?"

Jack held up a finger. "Hey Charlie, it's Jack. Listen, do me a favor. Find out which of our partners has a relationship with the TCB Network. I need to find out when the Ulysses Ullman interview on 'This Second' was originally scheduled to be broadcasted. It aired on February 3, but I'm trying to see if it was supposed to air at an earlier date."

Jack ended the call and looked at Tessa. She nodded and returned to the computer.

They sat quietly for hours. Jack went through the files as Tessa sat in front of the computer screen, clicking through the various articles. Jack's phone rang. He answered.

"Yeah."

"Jack, it's Charlie. Tomas Long is the relationship partner for TCB. He called the general counsel. He got some push back, but said he'd try and find out. The production guys apparently don't like to share that type of information with the legal department. Not sure why they should care, but it may be internal politics. I'll let you know if we get anything."

"OK," said Jack as he set his phone down.

He turned to Tessa. "We don't yet know if it was originally scheduled to air earlier. We're trying to get the information, but TCB may not give it up," said Jack. "What time is it?" he asked.

Tessa checked her watch. "It's seven. We'd better get ready to meet the others."

"Why don't you go ahead. I'm almost done getting through this box. I'll meet you at the restaurant."

Jack watched her nod and walk out of the room. He turned back to Pearl-Line's summary judgment motion papers. Pearl-Line's motion focused on attacking Ulysses's interview. It argued that his research failed to satisfy the *Daubert* standard for expert opinions established by the Supreme Court, because it provided no explanation of what controls were put in place to isolate the cream from other potential causes of autoimmune disease, and lacked any information as to whether the sample size for the study was of sufficient size. It argued that the opinion did not follow peer reviewed methodology accepted in the industry, and should be thrown out. The summary judgment motion went on to argue that since White's entire claim was premised on Ulysses's opinions, once those opinions are rejected, the claims had to be dismissed as a matter of law. Jack wasn't surprised the court denied Pearl-Line's summary judgment motion. Pearl-Line had failed to address the plaintiffs' simple argument that Isabella was diagnosed with autoimmune disease approximately a year and a half after she began using the YF Cream. Even if the *Daubert* motion had been granted and his opinions were excluded from the jury, to defeat Pearl-Line's motion, all that the plaintiff had to do was raise a factual dispute that the jury would have to decide. That Isabella suffered autoimmune disease after she began using the YF Cream was just enough to raise a factual dispute that simply could not be decided by looking solely at the law. The attack on Ulysses's opinions was a sideshow that would not have cured the fundamental problem with Pearl-Line's motion. Jack shook his head and wondered why a good law firm would file such a weak motion. Then he remembered that thousands of lawsuits were filed after the first week, and figured the defense lawyers were scrambling, leaving them no ability to think through the defense strategy. Such was life. The best of law firms couldn't maintain the quality of their lawyering when they were spread too thin and strapped for time.

Jack checked his watch. It was nearing seven thirty, but he didn't want to stop. He wanted to see if there was anything else in the files that would support his speculation that maybe Ulysses's interview was a setup. He reached for the second box.

28.

Tessa stared at herself in the mirror. She never cared much about the way she looked. Yes, people always told her she was pretty, but she didn't pay much attention to what they said. Her mind started to drift off to her father and the day she learned of her father's cancer. From that day on, she was consumed with fear that she might lose him. She cried night and day, and she prayed that God help him find a way to survive the horrible illness. She was afraid of how she could move on without him; how she could live with such sorrow. But, in the end when he said his final goodbye, she smiled into his eyes. She thought about his life. She was proud of the way he lived, and the way he spent his final moments. He raised her alone after her mother left them, while making a living with his music. He opened her eyes to the beauty of the melody, what it can do to a person's soul. He taught her to stay true to her passion, the way he lived his. To the very last day, he played his songs, and everyone loved him for it. Those profound memories defined who he was, and who she had become. How she looked in the mirror showed nothing about who she was.

Tessa pulled on a black skirt and a red blouse. She didn't have many outfits to choose from, so the decision was easy. She tied her hair back in a ponytail and took the elevator to the lobby. She saw Bob and Henry waiting. Bob waved at her with a smile. She walked up to them. "Hi, how was the beach?"

"Absolutely beautiful. You should've joined us," Bob said.

"Hey Shelly," said Henry, looking past Tessa. Tessa turned to see Shelly, dressed in a tight white dress with her wavy blond hair falling to her shoulders.

Bob whistled. "What an outfit," he said smiling. "I'm sitting next to you."

"You look very nice," said Shelly, looking at Tessa. "Then again, you'd look beautiful in boxer shorts and a T-shirt."

Tessa smiled.

"Where's Jack?" asked Henry.

"He was going through the White files. He said he'll meet us at the restaurant," said Tessa.

Bob shook his head. "Typical Jack. Let's go."

They stepped out of the hotel and jumped in a taxi. Tessa stared out at the ornate lampposts and the tall palm trees that lined the street. She lost herself in the warm ambiance of the small shops, art galleries, and the quaint architecture of the buildings that stood on both sides of the road. The taxi came to a stop in front of the restaurant. It was filled with people, young and old. They were led to a round table near the window facing the beautiful street.

"Should we wait for Jack?" asked Tessa as others took their seats.

Bob laughed. "You don't know Jack like I do. We're not going to see him tonight. By morning, he'll have this whole thing figured out."

"Then why are we here, if he doesn't need us?" asked Tessa.

"Oh, don't worry. He needs us. He'll have things for us to do. He just doesn't need us to come up with the strategy," said Bob. "Let's order some wine," he said, flipping through the wine list.

The waitress poured a taste of the cabernet sauvignon into the large wine glass. Bob swirled it around, stared at the color for a few seconds and then stuck his nose into the glass. He drank it slowly and then looked at the waitress with a smile.

"Very nice. You should open another bottle. We'll go through this quick," he said.

She poured a glass for everyone and then set the near empty bottle in the center of the table.

"I'll decant the next one," she said as she walked off.

"Good thing Pearl-Line's paying for this wine. It's been a while since I could drink wine this nice," said Bob as he slowly sipped the wine.

"You are a partner at Thurman and you can't afford this wine?" asked Shelly as she brought the glass to her lips.

"You have no idea," said Bob.

"Tell us, Bob," said Shelly. "I really want to hear how a partner at Thurman can't afford a bottle of Cakebread. At least I have an excuse."

The waitress brought over the decanter and refilled Bob's glass.

"Having two ex-wives is very expensive," he said. "What's your excuse? Don't we pay you well enough?"

Shelly put down her glass. "Well, actually, no. I have a lot of expenses and I have an elderly mother who I care for. I have student loans for college, law school and medical school. And most importantly, I have very expensive tastes. So, Mr. Bob the partner, if there's something you can do to help a struggling associate, I'd be much obliged."

Shelly picked up her glass and held it out toward Bob. "Here's to Bob getting me a raise."

Bob smiled and tapped his glass against Shelly's. "You're probably asking the wrong guy, but hey, I'll talk to Jack."

"I'm just playing with you, Bob."

Shelly turned to Tessa and Henry. "You guys should've come to the beach with us today. It was beautiful."

"We're here for a week," said Bob. "They'll have other opportunities. Tessa, how was your afternoon with Jack today?"

Tessa put her glass down. "I think he found something that caught his interest."

Bob leaned in closer to her. "What did he find?"

"He saw that the White complaint is dated one day before Ulysses Ullman was interviewed on 'This Second.'"

Bob sighed. "That's it? It's probably a typo."

Tessa didn't respond. Bob turned to Shelly and Henry. "Have you guys thought about the mess Pearl-Line's in? Any ideas worth discussing?"

Shelly shook her head. "It's an impossible task, Bob. We've seen these mass tort cases before. You can't stop them."

Henry turned to Bob and said, "I agree with Shelly."

Bob picked up his wine glass. "Looks like this is going to be a short trip. We might as well enjoy Naples while we're here. Who is up for going to a club after dinner?"

"Ooh, that sounds like fun," said Shelly. She looked over at Henry, looking for a reaction.

"Yeah, that sounds good," he said.

Bob leaned closer to Tessa. "How about you?"

"Thank you, but Jack asked me to do some internet searches about Cantor and Cantor. I should go back and finish that."

Shelly furrowed her eyebrows. "You can finish that in the morning. We'll just go for a short while."

"Why does he want you to research Cantor?" asked Henry.

"He wants to see if there's a connection between Ulysses and the Cantor firm. It makes sense to check since Jack's trying to see if the Cantors knew Ulysses was going to be interviewed. If they did, then it would support the theory that Ulysses's interview was a setup to help the Cantor firm," said Tessa.

Henry laughed while shaking his head. "Wow, that's some theory."

"You know, I sort of agree with Henry. This is a little crazy," said Bob.

Shelly laughed and sipped her wine.

Tessa didn't respond. It bothered her that Jack's own colleagues were ridiculing his theory. It wasn't as if they offered any better ideas. The table fell silent as the food arrived. Tessa ate a forkful of the thin spaghetti with meatballs and sipped the red wine. She hadn't realized how hungry she was. The wine was wonderful and it blended perfectly with the food. She found herself relaxing a bit and enjoying the moment. Bob started telling one funny story after another about the various cases he had worked on with Jack. Everyone laughed. Tessa started to feel as if she were one of them; a part of the team. As the evening wore on, Tessa noticed Henry downing several glasses of Scotch. She saw Shelly sitting close to Bob, constantly looking for excuses to lean into him.

As they wrapped up dinner, Bob said, "Time to head to the club."

"I thought I'd bring a plate of pasta back for Jack. I doubt he would've eaten," said Tessa.

"Meet us after," said Shelly. "You can't expect me to go alone with these two clowns."

Tessa smiled. "OK. I'll meet you there."

She called over the waitress. "Could you make a plate of gnocchi to go for me?" she asked.

Tessa saw the conference room door was open. Jack sat at the end of the long conference table, flipping through pages of documents resting in front of him. He looked up when she knocked on the door.

"Hey there," he said, smiling.

"I brought you some dinner."

"I lost track of time. What time is it?"

"You don't wear a watch?"

Jack laughed. "No, not when I'm working."

"Why?"

"Because time becomes irrelevant when I'm trying to learn something."

"Don't you miss appointments, like tonight?"

"I suppose that's right."

Tessa placed the brown bag on the table. "It's still hot, so you should eat," she said.

"Thank you."

"Is there anything you would like for me to do?"

Jack opened the brown bag. "No. You can continue the research in the morning. Where's everyone else?"

"They went to a place called the White Tequila. They asked me to meet them there. Would you like to go?"

"Why don't you go ahead. I want to get through these boxes."

"Can I ask you something?" asked Tessa.

Jack looked up. "Yes. What?"

"Why are you doing this yourself? Why don't you have others go through these boxes? Isn't that why you have a team of lawyers here?"

Jack nodded. "It's always been my problem. I'm terrible at delegating. I can't let others do the leg work, because I want to understand the details."

Jack ate a forkful of the gnocchi. "Excellent," he said as he pulled the document in front of him closer.

Tessa saw Jack getting sucked into whatever he was reading.

"I'm going to go now," she said.

Jack looked up. "OK. Enjoy. There will be work to do tomorrow."

Tessa gave him a smile and headed out.

29.

Tessa sat at the bar and saw Shelly dancing with Bob. He had his hands all over her, but she didn't seem to mind. Bob had his hands on her hips and pulled her closer, and she buried her face into his neck. Tessa now understood why Bob had two ex-wives. They began kissing, and Tessa turned away from them. Henry was holding a glass of Scotch. "Henry, are you OK?" Tessa asked.

Henry looked up. "Yeah, I'm good. I should head back to the hotel."

Bob and Shelly joined them at the bar as Henry was putting his drink down.

"You guys stay. I'll go find a taxi," said Henry as he stumbled off the stool.

Bob grabbed Henry's arm to prevent him from falling. "Let me help you." Bob walked with Henry out to the street.

"How do you feel?" Tessa asked Shelly.

"I'm fine. Why do you ask?"

"I just want to make sure you aren't drinking too much."

Shelly smiled. "Don't you worry your pretty self. I know how to handle him."

Tessa smiled.

Shelly suddenly stared across the bar.

"Tessa, look," said Shelly as she pointed with her eyes.

Tessa turned. "What?"

"It's him. Ulysses Ullman. Over there."

Tessa looked across the bar and saw him.

"You sure? You think that's him?"

"Yes, that's him. I remember his face from the interview."

Shelly turned to Tessa. "I think he's coming over here. If he comes over here, don't tell him who we are or why we are here." Tessa nodded.

Ulysses came up to them. "Hello," he said, smiling.

"Hi," said Shelly. Tessa smiled at him.

"I haven't seen you ladies here before."

"We're from New York, visiting," said Shelly.

"Good time to be here," he said. He pointed toward Shelly's glass. "What're you ladies drinking?"

"I'm drinking a cosmo," said Shelly.

Tessa smiled. "I'm just drinking water."

"Now, we can't have that. He waved his hand at the bartender.

"Two cosmos," he said.

Tessa was about to protest, but Shelly put her hand on Tessa's wrist. "Just one drink, Tessa."

Tessa turned to Shelly and nodded.

Ulysses moved a little closer to Tessa and put his hand on her shoulder. "I'm Ulysses Ullman," he said, smiling into her eyes.

Shelly put on a look of surprise. "I thought you were him. In fact, that's what I was telling Tessa just before you came over here. It's so nice to meet you."

"Likewise," said Ulysses with a big smile.

"Would you like to dance?" asked Ulysses, staring at Tessa.

Before Tessa could respond, Shelly said, "We unfortunately have to head back. My boyfriend's coming," said Shelly, pointing with her chin toward Bob.

Bob approached the group, staring at Ulysses.

Ulysses turned to Bob.

"Hi," he said.

Bob looked at him and smiled. "Hi." He turned to Tessa. "We need to go."

"Wait, wait, wait," Ulysses said. "We just met. The night is young."

Bob smiled. "Tessa?"

Tessa got off the barstool and took a step toward Bob. Ulysses grabbed her arm. He pulled out a business card.

"Tessa, give me a call if you would like a little tour of Naples," he said, smiling.

Tessa nodded and took the card.

The taxi pulled up to the hotel. "Let's see if Jack's still awake," said Bob as he walked briskly toward the hotel entrance. They walked quickly to the conference room and the light was still on. Tessa could see Bob was upset about something, but she had no idea what. Jack was in the conference room, pouring through a document.

"Hey, Jack," said Bob as they walked in.

Jack looked up. "Hi."

"You are not going to believe what happened," said Bob.

Jack leaned back, waiting for Bob to continue.

Bob said, "We saw Ulysses Ullman at the White Tequila."

"Makes sense. The client did say he hangs out at clubs. There aren't very many options in Naples," said Jack.

"Well, I guess we were at the right place. He came over to hang out with Shelly and Tessa," said Bob.

Jack went back to his document. "I guess he has good taste."

"I pulled them away from him as soon as I saw what was happening."

Jack looked up. "Why?"

Bob shook his head. "What do you mean, why? He's an expert on the other side. We shouldn't be speaking with him."

"In which case is he an expert for the other side?" asked Jack.

Bob thought for a moment without answering.

Jack stood. "Look, he obviously is tied in with the plaintiffs' bar, but as far as we know, he's not acting as an expert witness in any case against Pearl-Line. He's basically just a guy who appeared on TV and said some things that helped the plaintiffs. There's nothing improper about us speaking with him. How'd you leave things with him?"

Tessa pulled out his business card. "He gave it to me as we were leaving."

"Did you tell him anything about what we're doing here?" Jack asked.

Tessa shook her head no.

"I told him we were here just visiting from New York," said Shelly.

Jack smiled. "Good. We have our options open."

30.

Jack sipped the coffee and walked toward the large window. The sun lit up the tops of the palm trees. He hadn't slept all night. The White files had consumed him, and by the time he finished reviewing everything, it was getting light out. He had an hour before he had to be at Pearl-Line. Jack put down his empty cup and headed for his room. He walked past the reception desk and saw Tessa in shorts and a T-shirt. She walked up to him. "Were you up all night?"

"I wanted to finish getting through the files. What were you doing?"

"I just went for a run on the beach. It's so beautiful."

"If you want company, I'll run with you tomorrow," said Jack.

Tessa smiled. "OK, but I warn you. I won't slow down for you."

"We'll see if this old man can keep up."

Tessa rolled her eyes. "Old man…" she muttered as she shook her head and turned away from him. "I'll see you at the meeting."

Jack watched her walk off to the elevator. She warmed him for reasons he could not explain—the way she spoke, the way she smiled, the things she would say. Jack went up to his room. The cool shower brought his mind back to Pearl-Line. He knew there weren't enough facts to support his theory about Ulysses, but he had to go back to the beginning. Deciding to pursue this angle against Ulysses wasn't hatched from creative thinking. When all of the options were considered, this was the only one left that could possibly end the litigation for the company. For that reason, Jack felt he had no choice but to dig, to see if he could find something. The date of the White complaint was the first building block. The rest of the litigation files offered nothing more. He had to find more blocks. Their encounter with Ulysses at the club gave him an opening, but could they get him to talk? His mind rested on that thought. Fatigue started to set in. He was too tired to get over the hump of what's next? So, he put that thought to the side. It would stay there until his mind cleared up. Thoughts of Angela entered his mind. He shook his head, not wanting to live through that night again.

He heard his phone ringing as he stepped out of the bathroom. He saw it was Angela.

"Hi," he said into the phone. "How're you feeling?"

"I'm fine. Thank you for taking care of me after I fell."

"It's good to know you're OK."

"Jack, I know I've been bad to you, and I know you deserve better."

Jack didn't know what to say.

She continued. "But we both know we've grown apart. And it doesn't matter how we got here. I just think it's time we go our own way."

Jack nodded as his eyes welled up. He could hear Angela crying through the phone. "I understand. And I appreciate that we are finally talking."

"Thank you," she said.

"We'll work out the details when I return to New York."

"Oh, I didn't know you were away."

"I'm traveling on business. I should be back in a week or two."

"OK. Travel safely," said Angela as she ended the call.

Jack felt his heart sinking into his gut, as the failure of his marriage was no longer a question. But he also felt a sense of relief. Now he knew where he and she stood, and despite the deep pain he felt in his heart, they both now had a way forward to a different life. Better or worse, they both would be able to enter that new world without uncertainties or guilt. They'd be free.

31.

Jack pulled on his khakis and a white polo shirt. He walked to the lobby and sat down on a couch, waiting for others to join him. A woman walked past him and smiled. "I love your hair," she said. Jack turned to her and watched her smile at him as she got in the elevator. He hadn't had time to cut his hair in a month, and it had grown out longer than the way he normally kept it. He wondered what it might be like to be in a world where a complete stranger's hair merited a comment. From the day he entered law, his mind had been running nonstop, from one case to another, being consumed by having to find a solution to a problem. He thought back to his college days, which seemed like an eternity ago. Life was a lot simpler back then. There were no problems to solve, no price to pay for taking the wrong step. The promise and the excitement of the future masked pretty much anything that went wrong during those days. Things were different now. Nothing was simple. The consequences of failure or success affected the existence of companies and the many lives that are tied to those companies. The decisions he made determined the fate of cases. Yes, it was a heavy burden to carry, but he wouldn't have it any other way. He had to be the person who made the final call. He had to be held responsible for the decisions he made. He didn't want the luxury of the safety that comes with following someone else's lead. The only way he could make the right decision was knowing that the outcome, good or bad, would be his to own. Jack saw the others approaching. It was time to go.

"Where's Henry?" Jack asked.

Bob leaned in close to Jack. "He's going to have to meet us there. He had a late night."

Jack shook his head. "Let's go," he said and headed for the door.

The Pearl-Line receptionist directed them to the conference room. Helen and Susan stood when they walked in. A man stood behind them. He looked to be in his late forties.

"Good morning," said Jack as he shook Helen's hand.

"This is Mike Helm from our litigation group," said Susan. "He joined us recently to help us keep track of the surge in litigation."

Mike stepped toward Jack. "Nice to meet you. I've heard a lot about you."

Jack nodded. He took a seat with a cup of coffee, and the others did the same. Susan spoke in a low voice. "We were just served with another complaint by the Cantor firm. This will be a problem."

"Why is this any more significant than the other cases?" asked Jack.

"Because Peter Cantor and his wife Sara seem to be the most organized among the plaintiffs' firms. They know how to get to trial quickly. They already have all the discovery they need from Pearl-Line because of the White case, and the only discovery left would be against the plaintiff for her medical records. Cantor can request a quick trial, and he'll likely get it. We were hoping for a bit of a reprieve, but this may take away whatever breathing room we thought we had…" Susan's voice trailed off.

Helen leaned forward. "I know we think we have a month to come up with a solution, but the pressure is mounting here. The board will need something to make them believe we have a semblance of a strategy to deal with this litigation. Some of them are openly asking if we have to consider bankruptcy to fulfill their fiduciary duties to the company. They're concerned about the company becoming insolvent. I don't know where they are getting these ideas, but they're not holding back in expressing their concerns. They can pull the plug on what we are trying to do here at any point."

The conference room door opened, and Henry walked in. He quietly took a seat next to Shelly. His face was pale and his hair was disheveled. Jack could smell the alcohol reeking from him.

"I don't have any answers yet, but I have a half-baked idea," said Jack, turning his attention back to Helen.

Helen leaned forward. "Baked, half-baked. I'm not particular. I'm all ears."

"The only way we're going to solve this is by going to the source of the public outrage over the YF Cream. We all know that this fiasco started with Ulysses Ullman. If we can find a way to demonstrate that Ulysses is a fraud, that will defuse the anger, which is what's driving the jury."

Mike laughed. "How do you plan on accomplishing that? Dr. Ullman has not been personally retained in any case against us, so what would he have to gain by putting out a fraudulent report? This'll wind up a witch hunt."

Helen turned to Mike. "Please let Jack finish." She turned back to Jack. "Go ahead."

Mike leaned back, shaking his head. Jack stared at Mike for a second and then continued. "As Mike said, this could very well turn into a witch hunt, and it may take us nowhere. But, this is the only angle we have to stop this thing. Whether or not the theory works is, frankly, irrelevant, since this is the only way to get you what you want—permanent peace."

Helen looked confused. Jack continued. "This is a situation where the answer to the problem is obvious. The task is figuring out how we get to the answer. If we think about it, there's only one way to stop the one hundred thousand cases against Pearl-Line. If the Ulysses Ullman interview never happened, then the problem goes away. Since we can't go back in time and change the past, what we are left with is to discredit his report, to demonstrate that his report was part of a fraud. There's no legal mechanism to halt mass tort litigation, other than through bankruptcy, which you have already rejected. So, that leaves us with just one option. We have to find a way to discredit Ulysses Ullman, the man who started all of this."

Helen nodded. "OK, I understand the logic of what you're saying, but as Mike says, on what basis would we go after him? We couldn't just blindly accuse him of putting out a false report."

"I wouldn't say it's blind," said Jack. "We've all seen his interview. It's pathetically unscientific. So, why did he go through the trouble of being interviewed on 'This Second' to air his unscientific conclusions? It's not as if he's dedicated his life to finding a cure for autoimmune disease. What did he have to gain? I understand that his research center is funded by the plaintiffs' bar, so that may provide a part of the explanation. But, I come back to the first question. Why? It targets a single company with research that has no scientific merit. I don't think it's all that farfetched to conclude that the report is part of a scam concocted by the plaintiffs' bar. Now, let's take it one step further down this line of thinking. Let's focus on the White case. What if the Cantors and Ulysses planted the YF Cream story to be aired on 'This Second' to put Pearl-Line in the line of fire? We all know that his interview aired on February 3."

Everyone nodded. Jack continued. "You've all read the White complaint. It repeatedly refers to the Ullman interview, but the complaint is dated February 2."

Jack handed the complaint to Helen. She immediately turned to the last page and stared at it for a few seconds. Mike and Susan looked over Helen's shoulder.

Jack waited until everyone looked up. "If the Cantor firm knew what Ulysses was going to do on TV before 'This Second' aired, isn't it plausible that Ulysses's interview was staged to make Pearl-Line vulnerable?"

Mike turned to Jack. "You are going to base your strategy on what likely is just a typo? How do we know that Isabella White wasn't planning on suing Pearl-Line before the Ullman interview? Maybe they saw the interview and decided to include Ulysses's findings, but forgot to change the date? There could be a hundred explanations for something like this. This doesn't prove anything."

Jack stood to refill his coffee. "You may be right, Mike. And maybe, in any other situation, we wouldn't spend a lot of time thinking about a date someone typed into a complaint. But, being that Ulysses Ullman has decided to do a huge favor for the plaintiffs' bar that could potentially take this company down, I don't think we have much of a choice but to make something out of this."

"Jack, this company is on the verge of collapse, and this is the best you can do? You are going to save this company by chasing a typo?" asked Mike as he shook his head in disbelief.

"Why didn't we notice this before?" asked Helen, looking at Susan. Susan shrugged.

"I don't think anyone really paid attention to the exact day the interview aired. I guess we didn't think it was particularly relevant to defending the action, so it never registered," she said.

Helen turned back to Jack. "I'm not sure I like what I'm hearing. I think you are telling me that there is no way to stop this unless we make Ulysses's opinions disappear."

Jack nodded. "That is exactly what I'm saying."

"How would you pursue this?"

"I need to think that through. I'll need to gather as much information as possible about Ulysses Ullman and the Cantor law firm; to see if we can make a connection between the two."

"How about an investigation firm?" Helen asked.

Jack nodded. "Yes, a good investigation firm will be needed, but in light of the time pressure we're under, we need to come up with something more. I have some ideas, but I want to think them through before we launch into this."

Mike stood. "This is pure lunacy. We're going to hire an investigation firm to pursue this cockamamie idea?"

Helen turned to Mike. "Do you have any better ideas?"

"We should be focusing our resources on defending these actions," he said, sitting back down.

"And what is it that you think we should be doing to defend these actions that we are not already doing?" Susan asked.

Mike looked away from Susan. "This will just be a waste of time and money," he said under his breath.

Helen turned back to Jack, although she spoke to the entire room. "If Jack's idea doesn't bear fruit, then we are in bankruptcy. The money and time we spend with Jack's team doesn't concern me very much when we are talking about preventing the demise of this company. Jack, go ahead and think through the strategy. Hire an investigation firm that you trust. Let's talk tomorrow to see where you are."

Mike turned to Jack. "I would like to be involved in this. I want to know what the investigators are doing. I need to be kept in the loop."

Jack nodded. "OK. We'll get to work."

"One more thing," said Helen. "What we discussed in this room is not to go outside of the people here. If the public finds out that we are going after Ulysses, there could be some backlash. I can't risk the public relations fallout if people find out what we are doing. We would come across as acting out of desperation."

Jack nodded. "Helen, everything will be kept confidential. But, for the record, we *are* acting out of desperation."

32.

They stepped out into the bright sun. Jack walked up to Bob and Henry. "I would like to speak with you both when we get back to the hotel. Meet me in the conference room."

They both nodded and got in the car. The limousine pulled up to the hotel. Jack stepped out and marched inside. Bob and Henry quickened their pace to keep up.

"Close the door," said Jack as he entered the conference room.

Bob and Henry sat next to each other. Jack sat across from them.

"What happened?" asked Jack.

"I'm sorry I was late," said Henry, looking down.

"It was my fault," said Bob. "I shouldn't have kept him out so late."

Jack stared at Henry. "I don't have a problem with you enjoying yourself, but we are here to work. You should know better than to show up late for a meeting in your condition. We can't send a message that we are here on a client-paid vacation."

"I know, and I'm sorry," said Henry.

"I don't want to see this happen again," said Jack. "I have patience for a lot of things. This is not one of them. Go and sleep it off."

"I feel OK. I can work," said Henry.

"You won't do us or yourself any favors by trying to work now. Get some rest and we can meet back up later in the afternoon," said Jack.

Henry nodded and then walked out of the conference room.

Jack looked at Bob. "Has he said anything to you?"

"About what?"

"He doesn't seem right—to show up at a client meeting drunk."

Bob shook his head. "I think he's fine. I shouldn't have taken him to a club."

"No, he's not a kid. He should know better than to drink himself silly. I wonder if everything's OK at home."

"I'll speak with him," said Bob.

"Alright. Let him sleep it off first. Grab Shelly and Tessa and let's meet back after lunch. We've got to get to work," said Jack as he stood to pour a cup of coffee.

"Jack, I need to talk to you about something other than Pearl-Line," said Bob.

Jack turned. "What?"

"It's about Tessa."

Jack stared at Bob. "What about Tessa?"

Bob put on a smile. "I was talking to Shelly on the beach yesterday. She thinks Tessa may have a thing for you."

Jack turned away and laughed. "I don't think so, Bob," said Jack as he stared off for a second. "That's the furthest thing from my mind. Angela called me."

"And?"

"We are going to go our separate ways. We'll work out the details when I'm back in New York."

"I'm sorry, man," said Bob. "Well, at least now you have some clarity. That can't be a bad thing."

Jack nodded. "I can't say I'm happy. But I now feel like I can move forward. I feel accepting my failure is better than wondering whether I had failed, or even holding onto a glimmer of hope. Life is short. I have to live it based on reality. I can try and exist on hopes and dreams. But, that means I'll be standing still, with no control over my life. I may find comfort in believing things could turn out OK, but that fictional state would do nothing to tell me which road I need to take." Jack looked at Bob and smiled. "I've been here for too long. I need to start walking again."

Bob's eyes welled up as he brought Jack into an embrace.

Tessa saw Jack sitting at the table flipping through a document. She took a seat next to Shelly.

"We are all here," said Bob.

Jack looked up. "Hey guys."

"Where's Henry?" asked Shelly.

"I told him to sleep off the hangover," said Jack. "We need to gather as much information as we can about Ulysses and the Cantor firm. Bob, I think we should retain Monroe Investigation, Jesse Blair. What do you think?"

Bob nodded. "Jesse's good. Do you want me to call him?"

"Let's run it by Mike Helm first. He said he wants to be involved with the process."

"OK."

Jack looked over at Shelly and Tessa. "You understand that there's a limit to what an investigation firm can do, right?"

Shelly and Tessa sat without responding.

Jack continued. "They can gather publicly available information. They can dig around, but again, there's nothing they can get that'll help us prove that Ulysses is a fraud."

"Then why are we bothering to hire them?" asked Tessa.

"Because they can get us information that may give us clues. For example, they may be able to gather information that shows that Peter Cantor and Ulysses Ullman know each other. They may belong to the same professional organizations, bar associations. Whatever connection they may have, Jesse will find it. The key is to connect Ulysses with the Cantor firm to build our narrative."

"Let's say we get that information," said Bob. "As you say, that won't be enough to establish fraud. They probably do know each other. Cantor's a plaintiff's lawyer, and Ulysses conducts research for the plaintiffs' bar. It wouldn't surprise me at all if they ran into each other at some plaintiffs' bar convention."

Everyone turned to the door as they saw Henry walk in. "Hi, guys."

"Feel better?" asked Jack.

"Uh, yeah. Thanks, and sorry again for this morning."

Jack nodded. "Take a seat."

Jack turned to Tessa and Shelly. "I understand what you're saying, Bob, and that's where I think Tessa and Shelly can be of help."

Shelly furrowed her eyebrows. "How?"

"You guys met him and he gave you his business card. How would you feel about getting together with him? Get him to talk. Maybe he'll say something we can work with."

Bob shook his head. "You really think he'll just come out and tell them that he's a fraud?"

"No, but if they send the right message, like they are concerned about this disease because they had been using this cream, he may say something that could be revealing," said Jack.

"Even if he says something that in any way diminishes his conclusions, that wouldn't be enough to show fraud."

"I know, but if we have enough pieces to go on, and we are comfortable that our theory has some legs, I'm prepared to make the leap and call him a fraud publicly. He'll have to defend himself, and then he'll make mistakes. They always make mistakes."

Bob said, "He won't make mistakes if he isn't a fraud. You're assuming he *is* a fraud, and that's where we're taking a leap in logic. Also, do you think the judge's going to appreciate us getting information from Ulysses through trickery?"

"Yeah, I am assuming he is a fraud. As for the court, we'll cross that bridge if we get there. Right now, we're just trying to gather information."

"Shouldn't we have some basis to assume he is a fraud?" asked Henry.

Jack looked at him. "We don't have a basis. We're just following a hunch."

"I don't want to be a nay-sayer, but Mike Helm may be right. Should we really be spending our energy pursuing a hunch?" asked Henry.

"The short answer is yes, this is nothing more than a hunch. But, there's a real good reason for pursuing it. We don't have any other options. Defending these cases will not take us anywhere. The only way we're going to solve the problem is by proving my hunch. We have to go back to the beginning. Everything was triggered by Ulysses's interview. If we can disprove what he said, we get to rewrite the script. So, we are going to do everything we can to see if my hunch is right."

Henry didn't respond. Tessa looked at Jack. "So, what is it that you would like us to do?"

Jack looked at Shelly and Tessa. "You don't have to say yes, in which event we'll have to go another route. If you're willing to do it, you'll call Ulysses. We'll need to script out what you'll say in detail. What I'm envisioning is that you'll arrange to meet him. Maybe back at the White Tequila. I'm certain he'll do it. The idea is to get him to start talking about his research. You would try to open the door by telling him that you used the YF Cream, and that you're concerned about getting sick in light of what he said during his interview. I don't know if this'll yield anything, but it might."

Tessa nodded. "OK. I'll do it."

Shelly stared at Tessa for a second, and then turned to Jack. "Is this ethical? I am a lawyer. Can I really be doing this? Lying to him to get him to say something?"

Jack nodded. "We'll figure it out as we go, but I assure you, I will take full responsibility for any problems that may arise from this. You'll be acting under my direction."

Shelly smiled. "I guess we really are a full-service firm."

33.

The bartender squeezed the lime into the seltzer and slid the glass over to Jack.

"Thanks," said Jack as he took a sip out of the glass.

"Not a drinker, huh?" he said.

Jack smiled, "I do drink. I'm just not in that mode right now."

"When you're ready, you tell me and I'll pour you a nice glass of vodka martini. No one makes them as cold as me. I shake for a very long time."

Jack smiled. "Thanks. I do like them cold."

"My name is Roger. Roger Maguire." He held out his hand. Jack shook it.

"Jack."

"Nice to meet you. You from up north?"

"Yeah, how did you know?"

"You don't have much of a tan. Are you here on vacation?"

"No. I'm here for work."

"What kind of work?"

"I'm a lawyer. Dealing with some issues for a client."

"Not a bad place to come for work," he said smiling.

"I suppose."

"So, who's your client?"

"I'm here for Pearl-Line."

Roger shook his head. "Yeah? What're you doing for them?"

"Some stuff that I can't get into."

Roger nodded. "I understand. It's a shame what they're going through with all these lawsuits. They were our claim to fame—a home-grown company that's made it big."

Jack shook his head. "Yeah, nice company."

"That interview of Ulysses Ullman really screwed them," he said.

Jack looked up. "You saw the interview?"

"Yes sir. Everyone saw it. Who knew he'd make it so big."

"What do you mean?"

"Ulysses Ullman. He's pretty well known in the bar scene in Naples. I used to bartend at the White Tequila at the Mercato, and he used to come in, trying to meet women. Then, that show aired, and he's become an overnight big shot. A real celebrity. He's a talker too once he starts to drink. He'd tell me his life story—that he came to Naples to make some money doing plastic surgery, but he didn't want to work so hard. He then hooked up with some plaintiffs' lawyers and started his research center to do work for them."

Roger picked up the bottle of seltzer water and refilled Jack's glass. "Pearl-Line's a nice company. It kinda gave the city relevance. The company made us seem like we're more than just a nice beach town with great golf courses."

"You see Ulysses around anymore?"

"Not since I took this job here, but I bet he still hangs around the White Tequila. The guy never missed a night there."

"When did he usually show up there?"

"Around six or seven. He'd eat something at the bar and stare at all the pretty waitresses. He'd talk them up. The restaurant turns into a club later in the evening, and he'd stick around all night until he hooked up with someone."

"What do you know about his research center?"

"Not much. He never said much to me about it. But, I think he's come into some money recently."

"How do you know?"

"I still have friends at the White Tequila. He's supposedly throwing money around like there's no tomorrow. Rumor has it that he's buying a place in the Bay Colony Estates in Pelican Marsh."

"What's that?"

"Pelican Marsh is a large, gated community here in Naples. Bay Colony is a community within Pelican Marsh with its own golf course. Very, very exclusive. Houses go for millions. I assume he's got to have some real cash to live in a place like that."

Jack nodded. "Do you know where he currently lives?"

Roger shook his head. "Nah. He never told me."

"Interesting," said Jack.

"Why are you so curious about Ulysses?"

"No real reason. Famous people interest me."

34.

Tessa punched in "Cantor and Cantor Madison, Illinois." She sat for hours, scrolling down each hit, printing the stories she thought may be worth mentioning to Jack. A news article out of Madison, Illinois caught her eye. She read the story again.

"Here you go," said Jack as he put down a cup of coffee next to her. Tessa didn't take her eyes off the screen.

"How's it going?" he asked.

"Isabella White's husband was recently murdered in his home," she said as she picked up the coffee.

Jack pulled up a chair and read the article on the computer screen.

"Strange turn of events," said Jack.

"Isn't it? She gets a large settlement, and then her husband's murdered right after," said Tessa, scrolling down the article.

Jack stood and started to pace. "Any suspects yet?"

"No, but the murder weapon was a frying pan. They're speaking with Isabella, who supposedly was with a friend all morning. A woman named Patty Kullen. They're still investigating, so we should learn more as things develop."

Shelly and Bob walked into the conference room. Tessa looked up at Shelly, waiting to hear the news.

"He couldn't meet us tonight," Shelly said. "He said he has plans, but he said he's free on Friday. I gave him our cell phone numbers."

"Good," said Jack. "We have two days to work on our script. We can use the extra time."

35.

Patty tossed her cigarette out of the window and shut off the engine. She adjusted the rearview mirror to check her makeup. The red lipstick looked like blood against her pale skin. She pulled back a loose strand of her blond hair behind her ear and then leaned back. This was going to be a big moment for her, yet she wasn't nervous. She knew she held all the cards, and they couldn't call her bluff. For the first time in her life, she felt like things were going to change. She had been poor for too long. Funny how people talk about saving money, she thought. *If you make nothing, what's there to save?* Patty thought back to when she was a girl, growing up with her grandmother, because her mother was in prison and her father decided to run off with some bitch. She didn't even know where he was. He could be dead for all she knew. Her grandmother did her best to raise her, but living on social security in a shitty trailer home didn't make for a storybook childhood. Patty had one blessing. Boys thought she was pretty. She used that to make a few bucks. Let them touch her breasts, or stick their tongue in her mouth for a dollar. By eighteen, she was sleeping with married men to make a few dollars. All that ended when some vindictive jealous wife called the cops on her. She knew the guy who arrested her. He used to go to school with her. He stared into her eyes and said he'd try to help her if she'd promise that she would stop. He thought he was doing God's work, and it worked. As much as she hated her life, the thought of living in a prison cell seemed far worse. So, she limited her customers to just the handful of guys whom she knew would keep their mouths shut. That worked just fine for a while, but she wanted more. She needed more. But nothing changed. Working as a waitress at a diner and occasionally hooking up with a guy starved for affection meant only that she'd continue to live that pathetic life.

Today, Patty knew she could leave that world behind. She checked her face in the mirror. This meeting had nothing to do with her beauty, but feeling good about the way she looked gave her confidence. She stepped out of the car. The dark blue dress she bought at Neiman Marcus made her feel sophisticated. She turned and looked at her reflection against the car's window. She knew she was prettier when she was younger, but she didn't have the money to showcase her beauty back then. Yes, the wrinkles around the edges of her eyes were more visible, but she still had those beautiful blue eyes. Her breasts sagged, but they were still large, and the supportive bra underneath her dress held them up nicely. She was glad to get out of the waitress uniform, and she vowed to never wear it again. Patty walked up the cracked driveway and knocked on the door. Sara opened it.

"Hi Patty. Peter said you were coming by. You look so nice," she said as she gave her a hug.

Patty stepped into the house.

"Have a seat on the couch. Something to drink?"

"I'm fine, Sara. I'm a little crunched for time," said Patty as she sat down.

"Hey there Patty," said Peter as he walked into the living room.

Patty didn't get up. Peter sat across from her. Sara sat down next to him.

"So, you wanted to talk about Pearl-Line. I didn't think you had an illness, but we're here to help you if you've been using their cream," said Peter.

"I actually wasn't thinking about being a plaintiff," said Patty.

Peter furrowed his eyebrows. "Then, I'm not sure why you're here," he said as he turned to Sara.

"I'm here to negotiate my cut," said Patty.

"Excuse me?" asked Sara.

Patty laughed. "Oh please, stop playing dumb," she said staring at Sara and then turning to Peter.

"I know all about your scam. It all started when you met David at the diner. I knew something was up even back then."

Peter shook his head. "I don't know what you're talking about, Patty. The only thing I talked to David about that day was to see if I can hire him to be an expert in my lawsuit against Pearl-Line. There's no scam, Patty."

Patty smiled. "You are right, Peter. You were a little more careful when you were speaking with David. But, you see, someone who really, really needs me told me more."

Peter and Sara looked at each other and then turned back to Patty.

"Isabella told me everything, so let's just stop these games."

"I really think you've lost your mind, Patty," said Sara. "Isabella's husband just got murdered, and you are making up lies about what she told you?"

Patty stood. "I guess I have my answer," she said as she started for the door.

"What answer?" asked Peter.

"I'm getting on the next flight to Florida to meet with Pearl-Line," she said and walked out of the door.

"Wait!" Peter called out.

Patty turned and saw Peter standing in the doorway.

"Come back in," he said.

Patty did as asked. Peter closed the door and waited for Patty to sit back down on the couch.

"Alright. What did she tell you?"

Patty smiled. "Everything. Everything from Ulysses Ullman to what David did to her medical records."

"What is it that you want?" asked Peter.

"Peter, I told you. I want a cut of future winnings."

"What percentage?"

"I want half of your cut."

"That's not possible. I'm not going to do all the work and just hand over half."

Patty laughed. "Oh Peter, you are so predictable. You see, that half that you get to keep is better than going to prison."

Peter sat and stared at Patty without speaking. She knew she had him. He had no options. She didn't expect Peter to agree to give her half, but he would have to make her an offer. Patty stood.

"Peter, I'm sure this meeting came as a shock to you, so I'm not going to force an answer from you this second. I want you to give me a proposal by tomorrow. I've already bought my ticket to Ft. Myers. I hope not to have to use it." Patty stood and walked to the door. Peter didn't try to stop her this time.

"I look forward to our conversation tomorrow," she said as she walked out of the house.

36.

Jack saw her standing, staring out at the ocean. Not a soul was around her. He stood and watched her for a while, not wanting to disturb the tranquil sight. She must have sensed he was looking. Tessa turned to him and waved. He walked toward her.

"Good morning," she said.

"What were you looking at?"

"I saw two dolphins. They looked so carefree. There," she said, pointing.

"I see them."

Tessa stared at them in silence for a little longer and then turned to him. "Are you ready?"

"Yes."

Tessa pointed north. "Let's go that way."

Jack nodded. They ran next to each other. The beach was empty as the sun started to peek over the buildings along the shore. Tessa's pace quickened after a few minutes, and Jack kept up. He sensed that she wasn't spending a lot of time thinking about whether the pace was good for him. She just ran, almost expecting for him to keep up. At one point she turned to him and smiled, but her pace didn't let up. Jack began to feel his lungs burning, but he didn't want her to know. He picked up his pace to keep up with her.

"When should we turn back?" he asked as he slowed his pace.

Tessa laughed. "Tired?"

Jack smiled. She saw right through him. There was no point in trying to convince her he could keep up with her. He slowed to a jog. "Yes, I'm tired."

"OK. We can turn back."

They ran back at a slower jog. "I'm impressed," she said.

"At what? For making you slow down for me?"

"Not at all. You ran strong."

Jack laughed. "Thank you for the kind words, even though you're lying."

Tessa laughed and shook her head. They were nearing the path toward the hotel when Tessa stopped.

"What is it?"

She pointed up toward a tree in the distance. "See them?"

Jack stood next to her and squinted until he saw the two bald eagles sitting on a branch.

"I've read somewhere that bald eagles will find a mate and will spend the rest of their lives together," she said.

Her words took him away from the moment as thoughts of his own failures with Angela filled his head. Jack felt his heart tighten and he stood staring, not able to say anything. He felt her hand on his shoulder.

"What's wrong?"

Jack wanted to hide his pain. He thought he could overcome it. He forced a smile.

"Jack?"

He swallowed hard and then looked into her eyes.

"Are you OK?" she asked.

Jack nodded. She smiled with her eyes but didn't say anything. He sensed that she knew what he was going through, and he wanted her to know. He didn't know why, but he felt she needed to understand. Tessa held him with her eyes and did not let go. Her gentle smile warmed him. He took a deep breath.

"I once thought I had someone for life. I think she did too. But, things change, and I didn't do enough to hold on. To save it."

Tessa stared without speaking. Jack took in another deep breath. "I go through life fixing things, but the one thing that was most dear to me, I couldn't fix."

Tessa put her arms around him and brought him in to an embrace. She whispered, "I'm so sorry, Jack."

Jack closed his eyes. He felt her warmth numb the pain in his world. Her embrace shielded him from his vulnerability, from his thoughts, and he didn't want to let go of the comfort she gave him. "Thank you," he whispered. She didn't respond. There was nothing that needed to be said. He opened his eyes and looked into hers. She kissed him, somehow knowing that was what he needed. He didn't want her to let go. She took his hand and they walked to the hotel. His mind told him to stop, but his heart wouldn't let him. He held onto her hand, and she gripped his tighter. They walked to her room and kissed. He felt her delicate lips against his, her breasts against his chest. She pulled his shirt off and then removed hers. They fell to the floor, naked, dripping with sweat. For that moment, nothing else mattered. She had become everything.

37.

The sand felt good against his feet. It brought him to a simplicity he hadn't felt since he was a kid. He didn't want to think about Pearl-Line, Angela or anything else that took him away from this moment. The waves gently rolled in and out as birds strolled the beach looking for food. Jack sat on the sand and stuck his feet in the water. He closed his eyes and allowed the air to fill his lungs and the sun to warm his body. Thoughts of the delicate moments with Tessa made him smile. He didn't allow his mind to drift into questions about his feelings, what was to happen tomorrow. She told him not to think about those things. She told him that life didn't have to be about making promises. Jack checked his watch. The team would be gathering soon. He didn't want to leave this moment, but he had no choice. Jack stood, feeling the sand between his toes, and telling himself that he needed to come back to feel the sand again.

They were gathered in the conference room. Jack poured a cup of coffee and sat at the head of the long table. Tessa was on her laptop with a stack of paper resting next to the computer. Bob and Shelly stared at Jack. Henry strolled in and found a seat next to Tessa.

"Have we gone through the information Jesse sent us?" asked Jack.

"Yes," said Tessa as she reached for the pile of paper next to her. She started to flip through the pages.

"Ulysses Ullman was a plastic surgeon who came to Naples six years ago. He gave that up within a year. He opened up the Ullman Research

Center, which we know very little about, other than that it is funded by the plaintiffs' bar."

"So far consistent with what the bartender told me," said Jack.

"What?" asked Bob.

"I had a conversation with the bartender at the hotel bar, who's come across him when he used to bartend at the White Tequila. It looks like Ulysses may have come into a lot of money recently. He's supposedly purchased a multi-million dollar home here in Naples."

"According to Jesse, Ulysses's only current job is the Ullman Research Center," said Tessa.

Jack nodded. "OK, go on."

"We have information on where he went to college and medical school, but nothing before college."

"Nothing about where he grew up?" asked Bob.

"That information wasn't in the files Jesse sent," said Tessa, scanning the documents. She looked over at Henry.

"Did we receive anything else from Jesse?" she asked.

Henry shook his head. "No. I gave you everything he sent."

"I'll follow up with Jesse on that," said Bob. "I'm surprised he wouldn't have sent it with the other information."

Tessa continued, "There are no judgments against him. No criminal convictions. Consistent with what Jack heard from the bartender, he's under contract to buy a home in Naples, in Bay Colony Estates for three point seven million dollars."

"Is he financing it?" asked Jack.

"It doesn't say."

"Anything else?" asked Bob.

"No."

Jack asked, "What do we know about the Cantors?"

Tessa set aside the Ulysses Ullman pile and opened another file. "Peter Cantor spent much of his childhood at the Red Rose Orphanage in Gabrovo. It was conducted by the Rotary Club of Madison South. The orphanage records show that he left when he turned eighteen. There's no record of him for three years, and then he enrolled in Western Madison University. He attended night school at the Northern Law School in Illinois. Looks like that's where he met Sara Cantor. They graduated the same year."

"High school?" asked Bob.

"Madison Peak High School for Peter. Looks like Sara's from South Carolina. Marlboro Fox High School in Bennettsville."

"Anything on David Chen?" asked Bob.

"We haven't received that yet," said Henry.

"Henry or Bob, one of you guys should call Jesse and find out what the delay is on Ulysses's background and information on David Chen, though Chen's less of a priority," said Jack.

Henry nodded, "I'll take care of it. I'll call Jesse right after we finish here."

"Why are we less concerned about David Chen?" asked Shelly.

"We already have his connection to Peter, since both he and Peter operate out of Madison, and he was retained by Isabella as her expert. The missing link here is Ulysses and the Cantor firm," said Jack. "That is the critical piece of this. Let's follow up with Jesse on the missing information; the pre-college years for Ulysses."

"OK," said Henry.

"Let's discuss other facts we know," said Jack. "Isabella White's husband was murdered in their home with a frying pan. No suspects yet, although the police are talking to Isabella. She has an alibi—a woman named Patty Kullen who works as a waitress at a diner in Madison. Isabella has a young daughter, Jenny.

"How do those things tie into your theory?" asked Shelly.

"I don't know. I'm just throwing it out there—whatever facts we know. The task is to piece these things together, find other facts and see if we can make a story out of it."

Everyone nodded. Jack looked around the room. "The next step is for Tessa and Shelly to see what they can get out of Ulysses tomorrow tonight."

"And we're still comfortable that this is ethical?" asked Bob.

"I think we're OK. He's not a retained expert in any case I'm aware of, and he's not a party to the litigation. I'm sure someone will have a problem with the fact that we are deceiving him to get him to talk, but so be it."

Jack looked at Tessa and Shelly. "Are you guys still comfortable doing this tomorrow?"

They both nodded.

"Alright. Not much more we can do now. Let's meet back up this afternoon," said Jack.

Jack looked at Henry. "Please follow up with Jesse on Ulysses's background."

Henry looked up. "Yeah, I'm on it."

38.

TWENTY YEARS AGO

Henry waited impatiently on the parking lot, waiting for his brother to pull in. It was a hot day, and he preferred to be inside with air conditioning. This would be the last time he'd see his brother before his new parents took him to his new home. Henry hadn't seen his brother in over a month, but he always brought gifts when he visited.

Henry checked his watch, and his brother was almost an hour late. He felt the sweat dripping down the sides of his face as the sun beat down on him. As he began to turn to go back in the building to cool down, he heard the roar of a car engine. He turned and saw his brother's green Camaro pull into the lot. Henry could see two other people were in the car as it parked in front of him.

As the three men got out of the car, Henry could see blood on their shirts. He took a step back. "What happened? Why's there blood on you?"

His brother smiled. "Nothing to worry about, little brother. Meet my friends Manny and Ulysses. Sorry we're late. We had to take care of some business."

Manny and Ulysses nodded at Henry, but didn't say anything.

"I got something for you as a going away gift." His brother walked to the trunk and pulled out a box and handed it to Henry."

"What's this?"

"It's a down sleeping bag. I know you get cold, and I don't know how warm your new parents will keep the house. And there's an envelope with some money in the box."

"Dude, we gotta go," said Manny.

"Just another minute," said his brother. "What's going to be your new last name?"

"Lane. I'll be Henry Lane."

"That's a great name."

Henry didn't respond. He didn't know how he felt about getting a new last name.

"Keep in touch little brother. I'll keep an eye on you from time to time."

Peter Cantor took Henry into a hug and held him for a while. He looked into Henry's eyes and nodded. "Take care. Unlike me, you're a good kid. Let these people take care of you and go to school."

Henry felt his eyes welling up. "What about you? The blood?"

Peter held his brother's shoulders firmly. "Don't worry about me. I'm a survivor, and I do what I have to do to get what I need. I'll be fine."

Peter waved at Henry as he and his friends got in the car. They drove off without another word.

39.

PRESENT DAY

Henry closed the door to his room. He pulled out the thin stack of paper sitting in the FedEx envelope. Time was running out. Sooner or later, Jack was going to find out that Ulysses grew up in Madison. So what? He asked himself. That won't give Jack anything to prove his theory. Still, he had to find ways to throw roadblocks in Jack's way. Henry picked up the Hotel phone and dialed the number for Jesse.

"What's up, Henry?"

"Jesse, we need background information on Ulysses Ullman. The pre-college stuff."

"We sent that. That was in the files you should've gotten today," said Jesse.

Henry stared at the pages in his hand. "No, it wasn't in the stuff you sent. Can you resend it?"

"It's only a dozen pages. I'll put it in PDF and email it to you."

"No need. Just FedEx it," said Henry.

"You sure? You'll have it in thirty seconds if I email it."

"No, it's fine. My printer is on the fritz."

"OK," said Jesse.

Henry hung up. He took a deep breath. Jack's strategy was starting to worry him a bit, but he still felt things would work out fine. He couldn't figure out if Pearl-Line's decision to retain Thurman & Miller was a good thing or not. Yes, having access to Jack's strategy was helpful, but he wondered if he would have been better off not knowing. There was no way Jack was going to piece together what he and Peter had planned, but sitting in the war room with Jack added stress he did not need. Neither he nor Peter had anticipated that Pearl-Line would hire Henry's law firm, which was not known as a products liability defense firm. He never would have guessed that they'd hire Jack, who's a commercial litigator, with no real reputation in handling products liability cases. But, once they decided to hire Jack, it was just a matter of time before he would have put Henry on the team. Other than Shelly, there was no other associate who had any significant experience in mass tort cases. Yes, things were breaking the right way. He becoming a mole in Jack's camp wasn't even part of the plan. It was pure luck. Henry laughed. Whether or not being a mole was necessary for the plan to work, he was grateful that he would be able to blow up Jack's plan to send in Tessa and Shelly to meet with Ulysses. He pulled out his cell phone and dialed the number for Ulysses. He didn't want to take any chances by using the hotel phone. The plan was to always use the burner phones they picked up that couldn't be traced. The phone rang repeatedly. He gripped the phone tighter as sweat formed on his forehead. "Come on damn it, answer!"

Henry hung up and dialed the number for Peter Cantor. Peter answered right away. "Yes."

"Where the fuck is Ulysses? Why isn't he answering the phone? We need to deal with a situation!"

"How the hell do I know? I'm dealing with a problem here too."

"What?"

"Isabella talked."

"What? Talked to who?"

"Patty Kullen."

Henry remembered Tessa saying that Patty was Isabella's alibi.

"Go on," said Henry.

"Did you read the story about Isabella's husband getting murdered?"

"Yeah."

"Well, I think it was Isabella who smacked his head with the frying pan."

"Isabella?"

"Yeah, and she must've spilled her guts to Patty to get her to be her alibi."

"You have to be fucking kidding me!"

"I wish I were."

"She's fucking blackmailing you?"

"You got it."

"What are you going to do about it?"

"I'll deal with it."

"Alright. That sounds more serious than my problem. Deal with it fast."

"I will. What did you want to tell me?"

"My boss, Jack Hatchet is all over Ulysses. He's really digging in to his strategy to expose Ulysses to save Pearl-Line."

"You don't think that's a serious problem?" asked Peter.

"He's smart, but, he doesn't have anything of real substance right now, so we have nothing to worry about. He may be on the right track, but if we play our cards right, he won't get the proof he needs. Now, listen. A couple of women who came here with us ran into Ulysses at the White Tequila last night. He hit on them and gave them his card. They're going to meet up with him Friday night and try to con him into saying something. I tried calling Ulysses to warn him but he's not answering."

"Shit."

"Yeah. This can be a serious problem if we don't let Ulysses know. You need to try and get a hold of him. I'm with my team most of the time, so I can't be sure that I'll be alone to be able to call him. So, you have to call him and tell him to stay clear of the White Tequila for a while. I don't want that idiot saying something that's going to cause problems."

"This is getting too close," said Peter.

"Don't worry. Just be glad Pearl-Line hired the right law firm, which is the only reason I'm getting this information."

"We can keep Ulysses away from the White Tequila. That's not a problem. What's the strategy for dealing with Jack Hatchet?"

"We'll deal with Jack as we go. So long as Ulysses doesn't talk, Jack won't have anything to go on. He may be able to put Ulysses and you together at Madison, but that won't prove shit."

"What do you mean he'll put me and him together?"

"What I mean is he's hired an investigator who's gathered information that shows Ulysses growing up in Madison. That'll potentially create a connection between you and Ulysses, but that in of itself won't mean you guys are part of some conspiracy."

"Wait, wait, wait. Tell me again. How would he know to try and connect me to Ulysses?"

"Because your complaint talks about Ulysses's interview on 'This Second', but it's dated one day before his interview aired. He's thinking maybe you knew about the interview before it aired, which would support his theory that the interview was a setup to help you go after Pearl-Line."

"Shit."

"Yeah, shit is right. Go talk to Ulysses."

Henry heard Peter hang up. He dialed home. Elaine answered right away.

"Hello?"

"Hey, it's me. How're you doing?"

"I'm good. We got the check."

Henry smiled. "How much?"

"One hundred thousand dollars."

"Good."

"I can't believe they're paying you this much."

"Good consultants are hard to find."

"Promise me."

"Promise you what?"

"That you won't gamble it away again."

"I promise. This is more than enough to pay off all our debt and put money away for other things. Plus, this consulting gig will continue to pay every month, so we have no more worries about money. I'll be back soon, and we'll take a nice vacation. Some place really exotic."

"That'll be nice," she said as she laughed.

"OK. I'll call you tomorrow."

Henry hung up the phone. It was good to hear her laugh. But he knew that everything could come crashing down fast if he weren't careful. He had to think. Jack made progress on his theory, but all he had was just conjecture. He had nothing; no proof of anything. To prove his theory, he would have to get his hands on the secret that was tightly held between a small group of people who had no incentive to tell. Of course, Isabella already spoke, and that was a problem. But he was confident Peter would find a way to deal with Patty Kullen. He felt safe with the others. Peter, Sara and Ulysses were all key players in the game. And none of them had any reason to tell and dig their own grave. Jack could never piece everything together. Henry felt calmer. He poured a glass of whisky and downed it. The moment he took to convince himself that all was well worked. It would all work out fine. For now, let Jack learn the basic facts, but make sure Ulysses keeps his head down.

40.

Jack stared at the silver Tiffany pen. He rubbed his finger against the engraving, "To Jack, My Love, Always."

The pen Angela gave him when they first started dating brought back memories. She was a dancer for the Philadelphia Dance Company. He was a special guest of one of his clients who sat on the dance company's board. He didn't want to attend. He never really understood ballet, but his client insisted. Jack sat through the performance, and his client took him back stage. Angela was still in her leotard. She untied her blond hair and it fell beautifully on to her shoulders. She had deep, green eyes that grabbed onto Jack's and didn't let go. Her thin, delicate lips creased at the edges as she gave him a smile. There was an honest beauty about her that took him the moment he met her. It was obvious she knew what he was thinking as soon as their eyes met. There was a confidence about her. He could tell she was used to men falling for her. Jack sensed she had chosen him from all the many who were enraptured by her. It was the way she touched his arm, wanting to engage him in a conversation about something that he couldn't remember. They met at the hotel bar later that night. It was cold and snowing, but they were warm, shielded by the glass that looked out to the Avenue of the Arts. She gave him her phone number, and then everything started.

They fell in love before they even knew each other; they didn't know what made them laugh or cry; what made them tick; what was dear to their heart. Marriage came fast, and they were going to raise a family. She gave up dance, her passion, for the family that never came. Once the doctor said she couldn't conceive, life's goals changed. It was no longer about the family she could never have. She ran from that life. He tried to get her to go back to dance, but she had lost the desire. She wanted to fill her days with whatever excited her, whatever that could distract her. It was too painful for her to try and return to her reality. She never gave him a chance to bring her happiness, because he was a reminder of what she could never have. He was too blind to understand all this in the beginning. He thought he could fix things by surrounding her life with comfort. But she needed more—something he didn't know how to deliver. The knock on the door brought him back to the moment. He saw Bob standing in the doorway, and Jack smiled. For the first time in a long time, he was able to think about Angela and understand his emotions without pain or grief. He appreciated the memory of how they had met, how he loved her. Remembering the love and not the goodbye comforted him. He was starting to accept his life. Both the good and the bad were part of him, part of his past.

"Hey Bob."

"Why're you smiling?"

"Nothing. I was just thinking about something."

"I didn't mean to disturb you."

"You're not disturbing me. What's up?"

"Jack, I'm not comfortable with this whole strategy. We can get into a mess of trouble."

Jack nodded to show he understood.

"Look, we hired Monroe, why not have Jesse use his people for this?"

"We can't."

"Why not?"

"We don't have the time for Jesse to send in women who Ulysses may or may not go for, and more importantly, Mike Helm wants to know exactly what Monroe is doing and wants to participate in all of our conversations."

Bob looked puzzled. "So what? He *is* the client."

"I don't trust him."

"You don't trust him?"

"No."

"Why?"

"Do you know where he worked before joining Pearl-Line?"

"No."

"He was a partner at Bick & Carmen, the largest plaintiffs' firm in the country."

"Yeah, I knew he came from the plaintiffs' bar, but lots of companies hire lawyers from the other side to give them insight into what the bad guys are thinking."

"I understand, but the way he fought me on going after Ulysses, he over did it. I'm afraid he might be trying to protect him."

Bob brought his hand to his chin, thinking through what Jack said. "Yeah, I guess he did push back kinda hard. But, wouldn't Helen and Susan have vetted him before hiring him?"

Jack shook his head. "You think they administered a lie detector test before hiring him? People are better liars than we know, and as much as we'd hate to admit it, they are better liars than we are lawyers. They usually win that fight."

They turned as they heard footsteps.

"Hi," said Henry as he walked into the conference room.

Jack could smell the alcohol on Henry's breath. He stared at Henry for a few seconds and then stood. "Did you track down Jesse?"

"Yes. Somehow, Ulysses's background pages didn't make their way into the FedEx envelope. He's sending them by overnight mail."

"Why not have him send them by email?" asked Jack.

"Yeah, I can ask him to do that, but I didn't think we needed them this second," said Henry.

"I'm sure we'll get all this stuff if we subpoena Ulysses, but why don't you go ahead and ask Jesse to email them," said Jack. "I'm anxious to see where Ulysses came from."

Henry nodded. "OK. I'll go call him," he said and left the room.

Jack looked at Bob. "Before this trip, did you ever see Henry drink so much?"

Bob thought for a second. "Come to think of it, I don't think so."

Jack shook his head. "I wonder if things are OK at home."

"Let's not jump to the conclusion that there's anything wrong. The man needed a drink, just like I often do."

"I'm not jumping to anything. He hasn't stopped drinking since the moment we arrived here. He's shown up at meetings with the client with alcohol on his breath. I've never seen him act this way before this trip."

Bob looked at Jack without saying anything.

Jack continued, "Let's keep him away from clubs. We don't need him going on a binge and losing all sense. We can't take the risk of him saying anything about what we're trying to do."

Bob nodded.

"You think Shelly and Tessa are ready for tomorrow?" asked Bob. "I hope they are."

"Don't worry," said Jack. "What's the worst that can happen? They spend an evening having a drink with this guy and come back with no new information."

41.

Henry returned to his room and sat down on the couch. He didn't like the way Jack looked at him, and the way he sent him away as if he were a nobody. It was as if he knew something. He couldn't figure out what. And where did he get the idea of serving a subpoena on Ulysses? He wondered if Jack put together another piece of the puzzle. *No. No way. I'm being paranoid. There was no way he could have seen what was in my head. He's not a mind reader.* Henry's heart was beating fast. He reached for the bottle of whisky and poured a glass. The alcohol calmed him. He dialed the number for Peter again.

"Yeah," said Peter. Henry heard an edge to Peter's voice.

"Did you get a hold of Ulysses? They're going to send the girls in tomorrow night to meet him."

"I know, and yeah, I spoke with him. He told me he'll stay away. He also told me he thinks he saw someone who looks like you needing help to walk out of the White Tequila. What the hell are you doing?"

"I was there with the team. I couldn't just not go."

"I don't give a shit where you go, but this is a bad fucking time for you to be getting wasted."

"Look, a lot's changed over a short period of time. Everything was fine when I was at the club. Me having a drink has nothing to do with what's happening here."

"That's not the point. That asshole is coming after us. You need to stay dry so you can think clearly."

"I'm fine and am thinking clearly. I don't need you lecturing me."

He sensed Peter calming down a bit. "Look, just take it easy on the bottle," said Peter. "I've seen you when you lose your shit. I'm on edge because Ulysses is fucking bouncing off the walls. He went bat shit crazy when he heard that Jack was trying to set him up. He's talking about blowing out of town and disappearing with his money."

"That'll just be admitting to Jack that he's guilty."

"What do you mean?" asked Peter.

"Jack's talking about serving a subpoena on Ulysses. If he runs, it'll just prove to Jack that he's hiding something."

"What? What did you just say?"

"I think Jack might serve a subpoena on Ulysses."

"Fuck! He's gonna go nuts," said Peter.

"Don't tell him yet. Jack said he *might* serve a subpoena. No point in getting Ulysses worked up if Jack decides not to serve him."

"Shit," said Peter. "This is getting crazy."

"You just have to calm him down. We'll deal with the subpoena if they go through with it."

"Alright," said Peter.

"We'll get through this," said Henry. "We all have to stay calm. Jack doesn't have shit. All he's got are little tidbits he's trying to piece together, but he doesn't have any way to prove anything."

At that moment, it hit Henry. Maybe he had blindly convinced himself that he didn't have to worry when there in fact was a problem. There was more out there that Jack could use. Ulysses Ullman ran an unknown research center, yet he's throwing money around at bars and buying a multimillion-dollar house. Jack would want to find out where he got the money.

"Henry? You there?"

"Yeah, yeah. I'm here. Just thinking."

"Good. Keep thinking and get us out of this mess."

"Maybe Jack knows more than we think?"

"What are you saying? You just got through telling me I didn't have to worry, that Jack doesn't have enough to prove shit."

"He may have figured out more."

"Like what?"

"I don't know. He might be wondering where Ulysses got all the money he's been throwing around."

"He's throwing his money around because his research center got a large donation from my firm," said Peter. "You're being paranoid. The other firms with verdicts are also making donations. Maybe not as big as mine, but he's getting some serious cash."

Henry closed his eyes and nodded. "You're right. I am being paranoid, but I just want to be careful. What'll the records show if Jack subpoenas his financial records?"

"I'm sure it'll show money coming in from me and other firms as donations," said Peter.

"Is it normal for a law firm to send four million dollars to a research center?" asked Henry.

"Look, it doesn't take much to figure out that we wouldn't have gotten the White verdict without his research and what he did on TV. The firms in Mississippi and Pennsylvania are sending him big checks also."

"Talk to him and make sure he understands that explanation. He needs to be prepared to tell the right story about the money."

"Alright. I'll talk to him. You focus on getting Jack off our ass," said Peter.

"One other thing," said Henry. "I sense he's starting to keep things from me."

"Why do you say that?"

"I just saw him. He looked at me funny, and he seemed like he was holding back on telling me what was going on."

"What changed?"

"Nothing."

"Then why is he keeping shit from you?"

"I didn't say he was. Maybe I'm just being paranoid."

"Fix whatever the problem is. We need you to let us know his next moves."

"I will," said Henry.

Peter hung up the phone and stared at it for a while. He heard someone at the door and saw Sara stepping in.

"Where have you been?" he asked.

"I had to go and get groceries," she said as she put the brown bag on the counter. "What's wrong?" she asked.

"I don't like where this is headed."

"Can you clue me in on what you're talking about?"

"Jack Hatchet is focusing on Ulysses and is trying to set up a trap to have him talk to one of his people. I had to call Ulysses to warn him."

Sara shook her head. "Oh God. This is unraveling."

Peter stepped closer to her. "It is not unraveling. We just have to keep Ulysses out of sight for a while."

"What if they figure out what we did? Oh my God."

"They are not going to figure out anything. Don't worry. Where are we with Patty?"

Sara shook her head. "I'm still talking to her. Her demands are going up; not down. She wants a million in cash now, and a cut for all future cases."

Peter looked away from her. "She knows too much. We can't just pay her and think she'll go away."

"Well, we should have thought of that before we launched into this," said Sara.

Peter stared into Sara's eyes. "Look around us. This was the life we had, not being able to pay the mortgage to live in this shithole, and wondering where we are going to get money for the next decent meal. The law degrees we have are shit. This strategy is what has given us life. Don't start telling me that this was a bad idea!"

Sara looked away. Peter started to see red. This side of Sara drove him crazy. She was ready to spend the money the moment they got the White verdict, yet here she was, blaming him for even going down this path. He clenched his teeth and lowered his voice. "We are going to make this work. I will deal with Patty on my terms."

42.

Susan followed Helen down the hallway to the boardroom. She dreaded these meetings. The board used to meet only once a quarter to get updated on the company's performance. There was never bad news to report, and the meetings were short, pleasant. Ever since the start of the YF Cream litigation, the meetings became more frequent, at least twice a month, and sometimes more often, depending on what was happening in the courtrooms. The meetings had gone from seeking a status update on the litigation to outright finger-pointing at her and Helen. To the board, the company was paying a lot of money to have an in-house legal department, yet the lawyers had simply failed to prevent what was happening to the company. It was as if having a legal department somehow immunized the company from lawsuits. And because Helen and Susan had not been able to stem the litigation, they had failed to do their job. It was easy to come up with illogical blame, so long as the scapegoats didn't bother to push back.

Helen opened the bleached wood door and they stepped in. The six directors were seated around the mahogany table. Susan saw the chairman and chief executive officer, William Alexander, at the head of the table, wearing his pink golf shirt with black sunglasses on his bald head. A yellow cap and a leather golf glove rested next to him on the table. He obviously had just walked in straight from the golf course. He and the other board members just stared at her and Helen. None of them bothered to stand to greet them. Susan noticed two other men she did not recognize.

"Good afternoon," said Helen and walked toward the two men.

"I'm Helen Tsang, the General Counsel."

Susan followed Helen and introduced herself. The two men stood to shake their hands, and introduced themselves as Carl Keenan and Brian Ross. They said they were lawyers from the firm Fitzgerald & Minka. Helen turned to William with a confused look. He cleared his throat.

"Helen, the board decided to retain Carl and Brian to advise it of its fiduciary duties and to discuss next steps. Carl is an expert in corporate governance, and in light of where we are, and the simple fact that we apparently aren't able to manage this litigation, we felt we needed to get separate counsel to advise us on our duties. Brian is a bankruptcy lawyer."

Susan was speechless, even though she feared this day would come. She expected a reaction from Helen, but she just stood and stared. After a long while, she spoke. "I'm hopeful that our lawyers have a credible strategy to get us through this."

William leaned forward. "I hope so too, but the board cannot take any risks of personal liability, and Carl and Brian have given us some important advice on the steps we need to start taking. Carl? Would you mind bringing Helen and Susan up to speed?"

Helen cut in before Carl could speak. "You are protected by the business judgment rule defense. Every decision we've made has been based on a careful consideration of what's happening in the courtrooms, and on advice of counsel. You have the right to exercise your judgment to let Jack Hatchet solve this problem, without any risk of personal liability. The business judgment rule protects you from having made the worst possible decision, so long as you considered all relevant information before reaching your decision. The law protects you from making bad decisions. You can't be second-guessed. That's black letter law. You have no personal liability for pursuing a strategy that will save the company."

William stared at Helen for few seconds and then turned to Carl. "Go ahead, Carl."

Carl picked up his pen, even though he wasn't writing anything on his clean notepad. "Thanks, William. Let me first address the business judgment rule. Yes, it will protect the board, but it does not give the board the right to rubber stamp decisions or recommendations coming from others. The board has to consider all of the pertinent facts and circumstances before coming to a decision. Now, let's look at Pearl-Line, and the facts surrounding what this company's going through. Brian and I have reviewed the company's financials and received an update on the status of the litigation from Mike Helm. The company has some serious challenges. If the company continues to take the kind of hits it's been taking recently, it's just a matter of time before it becomes insolvent.

"Now, I'm sure you are aware that once a company becomes insolvent, the officers and directors continue to owe their fiduciary duties to the company. But because the company is insolvent, creditors have an interest in the company's assets—namely the plaintiffs who are suing the company as well as the company's lenders, suppliers, employees, contractors, you name it. Now, based on these facts, we've already advised the board that it needs to prepare and file for chapter 11 protection. The board is not at liberty to ignore that advice."

Helen held up her hand. "Carl, first of all, we have no lenders. If you've seen our financials, you are aware that we are far from being insolvent. We have over a billion dollars in cash and investments. We have no debt. We just have these baseless lawsuits relating to the YF Cream. And, if Jack Hatchet's strategy works, we will be able to put this litigation behind us."

Carl nodded, not to show he understood, but to signal that he had a response to Helen. "You say baseless lawsuits, but the plaintiffs have been winning. So, I think saying the cases are baseless ignores some important details of what we are dealing with here. As for whether the company is solvent, Pearl-Line can have all the cash in the world, but the way these cases are going, it's just a matter of time before it becomes insolvent. Just this week, the company got hit with multiple adverse verdicts that add up to over one hundred million dollars. No company can take those kinds of hits without financial ramifications. Even if it could, it's just a melting iceberg. I understand that we have thousands of cases going to trial in a matter of a month. The Company's billion dollars will be gone in a blink of an eye. Unless the company's profits exceed the amounts of the adverse judgments, and I know this company doesn't make one hundred million dollars a week in profits, it's just a matter of time before it becomes insolvent."

Carl looked around the room and then turned his attention back to Helen. "The problem we see is that the company currently is in what we call the 'zone of insolvency' or 'vicinity of insolvency.' What that means is the company is in financial distress, and it can see significant distress down the road based on all the facts that we know. Now, I know this theory of liability has not been recognized here in the US, but there are plenty of plaintiffs out there who will still go after boards of directors for failing to act when the company is in this state.

"This brings us to the advice we have given to the board. The company needs to start making plans to preserve its assets before all of its assets are paid out to the plaintiffs."

"And what would those plans be?" asked Helen.

"We need to get the company ready for a chapter 11 bankruptcy filing," said Brian who had remained quiet during Carl's presentation.

Helen stood. "But, we may have a way out. We are meeting with our lawyers tomorrow to hear their strategy that may solve this problem."

William leaned back in his chair. "Helen, calm down. We are not pulling the plug on your strategy yet. We just have to protect ourselves from breach of fiduciary duty claims for not doing the right thing for our shareholders and creditors by keeping it in the tort system indefinitely. That's why we've decided to file for bankruptcy protection."

Helen spread her arms to show her dismay. "Excuse me? What do you mean you've already made the decision to file? Why wasn't I made a part of that discussion?"

"Helen, the decision has to be made by the board. You know that. Besides, you are too emotionally charged about this and we didn't think you could add to the analysis," said William, avoiding eye contact with her.

Helen looked dejected, but spoke in a calm, strong voice. "William, you know this company can't survive a bankruptcy. The entire business is built up on the company's prestige. A chapter 11 filing will be its death knell. Whatever value the shares of this company has will be destroyed. There are a lot of people who invested with us who will be irreparably harmed if we were to file. There are retirement funds who invested, employees' options. How can we make that decision without at least giving Jack Hatchet a chance to solve the problem?"

Carl put down his pen. "We don't think there is any other solution. This is a delicate balancing act. We have to look out for both the shareholders and creditors. I've heard of Jack Hatchet and some of the brilliant work he's done, but even he couldn't pull the company out of this mess. With the public sentiment being what it is, there is no way he can deliver a victory in any of these cases, much less all of them."

"When are you planning on filing?" asked Susan.

"We have a team of our bankruptcy lawyers who will be arriving tomorrow," said Brian. "I suspect we will need a week to understand the company's operations, and another couple of weeks after that to prepare the necessary first day motion papers."

"What are first day motion papers?" asked Susan.

"They are the motions the bankruptcy court must hear on the first day after the filing of the bankruptcy petition. Motions that ask the bankruptcy court to let us maintain bank accounts, use cash, keep the lights on, make payroll, pay important vendors who we need to continue to run the business. Things like that," said Brian.

"That gives you approximately three weeks to solve this mess," said William.

Helen stood. "Got it," she said and left the room.

Susan caught up with her in her office. She saw Helen staring out of the window.

"Are you OK?" Susan asked.

Helen stood in silence for a long while and spoke without moving. "Please tell me Jack can save us."

Susan looked down. "I hope he can, but we all know it's a long shot. Maybe we should think about what those lawyers said. Maybe William is making the right call for everybody…" Susan's voice trailed off.

Helen turned to Susan. "William doesn't care about anyone other than himself. He cashed out his own shares years ago before you joined the company. He's got his millions stashed away. The only thing he'll lose are his options. He's doing this to protect his millions—not to protect shareholders, creditors or anyone else."

Susan nodded.

"We were required to publicly disclose William's sale of his shares under the securities laws. He didn't care that he was sending a message to the public that our own CEO doesn't believe in the value of our company. Shareholders reacted, as expected. Our PR group had a nightmare dealing with this. Thankfully, we were able to manage the fallout, because the company was doing so well. He knew that's how it would play out. Before we knew it, people forgot about what he did. He anticipated that too."

"What about the other directors? Why would they support a bankruptcy filing if they didn't believe it was the best solution for the company?" asked Susan.

"William obviously set them up. He hired his lawyers to lecture them about their fiduciary duties, and that they'd have to authorize the chapter 11 filing to fulfill their duties. Once they did that, the directors' hands were tied, because going against their advice would directly expose them to claims that they breached their fiduciary duties to the company. Our directors are wealthy people with assets to protect. They are all retired senior executives of public companies. To a large extent, they are on this board out of interest and to stay in the game. They didn't sign on to gamble away their life's savings. They are not going to go against the advice they've been given and jeopardize their mansions, yachts and golf memberships. You can't blame them."

Susan sat down on the chair next to the desk. Helen turned back to the window. "We have three weeks. If Jack fails, we are out of options."

43.

Susan put down her coffee and looked out at the bright sun rising from the east. The anxiety that engulfed her after the board meeting the day before was gone. The promise of a new day gave her hope. She picked up her briefcase. It was time to head to the hotel. She walked past Helen's office and saw her hanging up the phone.

"Are you ready?" asked Susan.

Helen looked up and smiled. "Yes."

They walked to the limousine. She saw Mike standing next to the driver. Helen asked, "Why didn't you tell me you met with the lawyers William hired?"

Mike looked puzzled. "What's there to tell? William asked me to give them an update on the litigation."

"We'll discuss this later, but I want you to tell me everything that's going on at the company, especially if it involves William," said Helen as she stepped into the car.

Susan sat next to her. Mike found a seat on the other side of the circular seating area in the car.

"Jack will lay out the plan for us when we get there," said Susan.

"Are you optimistic?" asked Helen.

Susan looked down for a minute and smiled. "I am. Don't ask me why. I just am."

"If you think about it, going after Ulysses really is the only option we have," said Helen.

Susan nodded. "It's amazing that we didn't think of it. It seems so obvious now."

"I wonder how he was able to see through everything to get to that conclusion so fast," said Helen.

Susan smiled. "Almost makes you feel foolish, doesn't it? Whether or not his strategy works, it does make sense, and it was sitting right in front of us the entire time."

"Let's just hope it works. How're you feeling?" asked Helen.

"A little anxious, but OK."

"I'm sorry I laid all of that on you yesterday."

Susan stared into her eyes. "We are in this together, Helen."

"I shouldn't have told you that William is just out for himself. I had no right to say that."

Susan put on a smile. "Helen, I don't agree with what William is trying to do, and I respect you for taking what he throws at you and staying the course for the good of the company. I want to stay positive. Jack will tell us something good this morning. I can feel it."

Helen nodded and looked out of the window. Susan leaned her head back, re-living the meeting with the board the day before. Would Jack deliver? Can this one man solve the problem that no one else could? She closed her eyes and hoped.

44.

Jack debated calling Susan to ask that Mike Helm not attend the meeting, but decided against it. He didn't know her relationship with Mike, and had no idea how she'd react to an accusation against one of her colleagues. Mike already knew the strategy—to attack Ulysses Ullman—but he had no details on how they were going to achieve it. Jack had to explain their plan, but he felt uneasy. Any leak of the plan to expose Ulysses, the Cantors or anyone else who may be involved would destroy this opportunity.

The team strolled in, including Henry, and found seats next to Jack. Helen, Susan and Mike followed. Jack could see the intensity in Helen's face. She had no time for small talk, and she launched right in.

"Jack, we had a bad meeting with the board yesterday. We now have a three-week deadline to solve this crisis, or we are in chapter 11."

"What happened?"

"The board retained a corporate governance attorney, Carl Keenan. The board members wanted guidance on their fiduciary duties when the company enters the zone of insolvency. Since we are supposedly in that zone already, according to Carl, the board has a duty to start making provisions to protect the interests of the company, which now include creditors. The board brought in Brian Ross, a bankruptcy lawyer, to get the company ready for a chapter 11 filing. He expects they will be ready to file in three weeks."

Jack nodded and waited for Helen to finish.

"So, unless your strategy works, it's game over for this company," said Helen.

"OK," said Jack. "Let's discuss the strategy."

Helen looked at Jack with a puzzled look. "You are not concerned about this deadline?" she asked. "We lost 25 percent of the time we thought we had."

"What would be the point of having a reaction to the deadline? We know we have one. We have to make it work," said Jack without expression.

Helen nodded to show she understood. "OK. Walk us through the strategy. I assume you have more detail?"

"Yes. Our strategy to undermine Ulysses Ullman has not changed. We are continuing our analysis to find a connection between Ulysses and the Cantor law firm. As Mike knows, we've hired Monroe Investigations to assist us. The analysis is ongoing."

"That's not a whole lot different from what you told us yesterday," said Susan.

Jack leaned forward. "Yes. What has changed is we will be sending in Tessa and Shelly to meet with Ulysses this evening."

Helen looked puzzled. "I don't understand."

"The goal is to get him to start talking about his interview. We'll see what we learn and take it from there."

Helen nodded. "This is not something I expected. When will we get a report?"

"I hope tomorrow. I will call in the morning if we have something to report and we can schedule a meeting at that point. I do have a request."

"Yes?" asked Helen.

"Please ask your lawyers to serve a subpoena on Ulysses Ullman, because I would like to take his deposition."

"What for?" asked Mike.

Jack looked at Mike. "If I'm going to go after Ulysses, I want to get his story under oath to lock him in. It'll give me more ideas to chip away at him."

Mike rolled his eyes. "I'll take care of it," he said.

"After that, I would like to serve a deposition notice on Peter Cantor and Sara Cantor," said Jack.

Mike laughed. "And how are you going to manage that? They are the counsel of record for Emma Pierce. No judge is going to let you examine the plaintiff's lawyers."

Jack nodded. "That depends on what we are able to get out of Ulysses."

"And what would that be?" asked Mike.

"You'll know soon enough," said Jack. He looked over at Helen and saw that she was smiling.

45.

The second glass of wine went down nicely, especially after the apple martini. Patty glanced at the mirror behind the bar and saw the reflection of herself. She was pleased. Annie at the hair salon had done her hair just right. She straightened out the curls. The straight hair made her look younger. An older man offered to buy her a drink but she declined. She wanted someone young, strong, handsome. The young man in the corner table smiled at her, but he was sitting with someone. It's not going to happen tonight, she thought. The bar was mostly filled with couples and guys over the hill. She would go home alone tonight, but she was OK with that. She had drunk too much anyway. Drinking had come easy ever since her talk with Isabella. It was no longer to escape the miseries of her existence. It was to enjoy the moment and to remind herself that she was alive. The fruits of the Pearl-Line litigation and the little game she had played with Isabella had given her the ability to live carefree. Peter was next, and then life would be perfect.

She thought about where she would go in the morning—Neiman Marcus, Saks. She would have to drive to St. Louis, but she didn't mind, especially with her new Mercedes. The bartender asked if she wanted another. She shook her head no and asked for the check.

The streets were slick from the rain. She opened her umbrella and began her walk toward her car. The clicking of the heels of her new Manolos echoed through the empty street. She liked the sound. Every step was a reminder that she was wearing them. She would start a collection. Manolos were first. Next, maybe Jimmy Choo, Gucci. As she got closer to her car, she could make out a figure off in the distance a few feet away from the driver's side door. She wondered if he was the man who smiled at her at the bar, but as she got closer, she could see he was a lot larger. He wore a hooded jacket that made it difficult to see his eyes. All she could make out was his pale cheekbones. He didn't move. A chill went down her back, and she became frightened. She slowed to a stop and saw the man start walking toward her. Her heart began to race. She turned and began walking away from him, back toward the bar. She looked over her shoulder and saw him following her. The heel on her right shoe got caught on a crack in the sidewalk and she fell. He was getting closer. She stood and pulled off her other shoe and began to run. She looked back again, and this time he was gone. She breathed a sigh of relief and then stopped. The rain continued to fall and she was drenched. She picked up her shoes and slowly began her walk back to her car, looking anxiously around to make sure he wasn't hiding. She pressed the remote and the car unlocked. As she reached for the door, a hand covered her mouth. She couldn't scream or breathe. The other arm went around her waist and she was pulled into a dark alley. She was thrown to the ground, into a puddle. Her dress was soaking wet. She looked up and saw the large man with the hood.

"Please, please don't hurt me. I can pay you."

The man pulled out a gun and aimed it at her head. Her heart stopped, and before she could scream, he pulled the trigger. Patty Kullen lied on the street and stared. She no longer knew what she was seeing. She felt something warm against the side of her face. Things began to fade until everything turned black. She died lying in a puddle of her own blood.

46.

The taxi drove up Tamiami Trail and made the right into the Mercato. Shelly and Tessa walked to the bar. The White Tequila was hopping. Men and women crowded around the large bar with young, shapely waitresses in black tights and pink satin tank tops rushing about with trays. They found a table in the outdoor seating area and ordered drinks. Another taxi pulled up and Bob stepped out. Tessa saw him smile and then walk to the other side of the bar. They knew it was a little risky to have Bob present, since Ulysses had met him the first night. But everyone thought he should be there to intervene should something unexpected happen. The plan was for him to keep his distance from Tessa and Shelly while keeping an eye on them. It was 8 p.m., and the dinner crowd seemed to be thinning out as the club goers started to pile in. They picked up their drinks and started to roam around the area near the dance floor, looking for Ulysses. They saw no sign of him.

"Let's go back to the bar," said Shelly. Shelly smiled at two men leaning against the crowded bar, and they moved aside. As she put her empty martini glass on the bar, an older man put his hand on hers.

"Let me buy you that drink," he said.

Shelly smiled. "Thank you."

"How would you like to be my next ex-wife?" he asked, waving over the bartender.

Tessa looked up at the older man. He looked to be in his late sixties, with a thick head of gray hair. He had sharp blue eyes and wrinkles in all the right places. She saw Shelly smiling at him.

Shelly said, "I would like a cosmo, please."

"Who's your pretty friend?" asked the man.

"This is Tessa. I'm Shelly. We are visiting from New York."

"Well, you came to the right place. My name is Tanner," he said, extending his hand toward her. Shelly shook it.

"Nice to meet you."

The bartender poured the cosmopolitan into a martini glass for Shelly and then looked over at Tanner. "How're you doing with your drink, Tanner. Need a refill?"

"You bet," said Tanner, pushing his empty martini glass toward the bartender.

"Looks like you're a regular here, Tanner," said Shelly.

He smiled. "Yeah, I come here a lot."

"You live down here full time?"

"Nah, just half the year. I live up in Ohio during the summer and parts of spring and fall. I'm down here to get away from the cold."

"Are you here alone or with friends?" asked Shelly.

He turned to look behind him and then turned back to Shelly. "They are all my friends. I don't have to call anyone to meet me here. They all know to come," he said. "But right now, I'd much rather be having a drink with you two ladies," he said, putting his hand on Shelly's.

"Well, Tanner. I was hoping you knew someone I was looking for," said Shelly, as she gently pulled her hand away.

"And who might that be?"

"Ulysses Ullman."

Tanner laughed. "What do you want with him?"

"We met him the other night and we agreed to meet here for a drink. Do you know him?" asked Shelly.

"Yeah, I know him. I've seen him around here a lot. More recently, he's been tossing a lot of money around at the waitresses, thinking that's going to get him something more than drinks."

"Are you friends with him?" asked Tessa.

Tanner shook his head and sipped his drink. "Nah. Don't like him much. He's a phony."

"Why do you say that?" asked Tessa.

"Because, he's changed. Don't get me wrong. He's always liked the ladies. But before, he was more down to earth. He was friendly, hung out with every-one. Then, he goes on that stupid TV program and thinks he's a hotshot now. I don't like people who change like that. People need to be grounded. Like me," said Tanner, smiling at Tessa.

"Do you know if he's coming here tonight?" Shelly asked.

"He used to come here every day, but I haven't seen him here the past couple of nights. I'm surprised he's not here."

"Maybe he had other plans," said Shelly.

Tanner shook his head. "The man never missed an evening here. Something must be up."

The music started to get louder, and Tessa saw people gathering at the dance floor behind the bar.

"Do you want to dance?" Tanner asked as he got off the stool.

Shelly shook her head. "No thanks, Tanner. I just wanted to have a drink. We should get back to the hotel. Will you be here tomorrow?"

Tanner sat back down. "Yeah, I'll be here, right in this spot. Come look for me."

"I will do that."

Shelly kissed Tanner on the cheek. "Thank you for the drink."

She and Tessa stepped out to the curb and a taxi pulled up. She could see Bob waving down another taxi. The two cars headed downtown and stopped in front of the hotel.

Bob caught up to Shelly in the lobby.

"What did you kiss that guy for?" he asked.

"I made a friend. He was helpful," she said.

"Next time, just talk. No physical contact."

"Are you jealous?"

"No, I'm not jealous. I just want to make sure you don't get yourself in trouble."

Shelly rolled her eyes and headed to the conference room. Tessa followed. Jack looked up from his notepad as they entered the room. Henry was next to him, going through a stack of paper.

"How'd it go?" Jack asked.

"Ulysses wasn't there. He stood us up," Shelly said.

Jack nodded. "Strange. How could he have known?"

"Let's not jump to conclusions," said Bob.

Shelly looked at Bob and then turned back to Jack. "We met a guy there. Tanner. He knows Ulysses. He said some interesting things."

Jack looked up at her. "Go on."

"He said Ulysses never missed an evening at the club and he was surprised not to see him there the past couple of nights. He also said he saw Ulysses throwing a lot of money around lately, and that he started to act differently ever since the interview."

"So, he had no idea on why Ulysses wasn't there?" asked Jack.

Shelly shook her head. "No. He was genuinely surprised that Ulysses hadn't shown up."

"How about the money?" asked Jack. "Did he say when he thinks Ulysses came into this money?"

"He just said recently. Nothing more specific," said Shelly.

Jack nodded.

"We did subpoena Ulysses's financial records, didn't we?" asked Bob as he looked at Jack.

"Yes. We served him with the subpoena today, and we'll take his deposition next week. Henry's been scouring the internet to see if he can find anything of interest about the Ullman Research Center." Jack looked over at Henry. "Find anything?"

Henry shook his head. "No, but I'm still looking. I've printed everything that may be of interest. I need to go through these," he said, looking at the pile in front of him. "I'm going to take these up to my room with me and review them there. I'm getting tired."

Jack nodded.

"I'll come down if I find anything. Otherwise, I'll see you guys in the morning," said Henry as he headed out of the conference room.

Henry placed the stack of paper on his desk. He dialed the number for Peter. He answered right away.

"Yeah," said Peter.

"They went ahead and subpoenaed Ulysses."

"I know. Ulysses called me right after he was served."

"They're trying to get Ulysses's financial records."

"I spoke to him about that, and the testimony he has to give when he's deposed," said Peter.

"Alright. Just make sure he's calm and able to tell his story."

"He gets it, but he is not calm. I told him he should take it easy with his spending to avoid attracting unneeded attention, but he said he didn't go through all this shit to hide his money. The purpose of what we did was to make money, and he wasn't about to go back to living the life of a researcher."

Henry leaned his head back against the couch. "Look, I get what he's saying. So long as he can stay calm, we're probably OK on this front."

"Like I said, he's going nuts and he's not calm. The fact that he's got answers to questions about his finances won't solve the problem that he doesn't want to sit through a deposition."

"He's just got to tell his story. He can do it," said Henry.

"I'll tell him that, but I know he's not going to buy it. He'll be afraid he's going to crack. He's already starting to blame you and me for getting him into this."

Henry sat without speaking for a long while. "What are we going to do?" he finally asked.

"I'll talk to him. I've got to convince him that he just has to be prepared, and he'll be fine."

Henry closed his eyes. "Yeah, but even if he survives the examination, Jack's going to depose you next."

"What the fuck is he doing?"

"He's coming after us."

"You are the brains of this thing. You think of something."

47.

The detective stood next to the dead body, surrounded by crime scene investigators rushing back and forth. His cell phone buzzed.

"Yeah."

"Isabella White came in."

"Did she give you anything?"

"No. She said she saw the news report, and decided to come down to the station to see what happened."

"What did you tell her?"

"Not much, considering I don't know anything. What'd you find?"

"Looks like it was a robbery. The assailant took everything of value from her purse. No witnesses. The bartender remembered her leaving around 1 a.m., but he said she left alone. There was a guy who tried to buy her a drink, but he hung around at the bar all night and closed it down. We don't have any leads."

"What should I do with Ms. White?"

"See if she'll stay voluntarily. I want to talk to her."

"About what?"

"I don't know, but two people associated with her are now dead."

"What are you thinking?"

"We know she came into a lot of money recently. From what we're hearing from her acquaintances, Mr. White was physically abusing her. Patty Kullen was Ms. White's only alibi, who happened to have received a large loan from her."

"I hear you. Makes you question the legitimacy of the alibi, but the fact that her only alibi was murdered doesn't fit the narrative."

"Unless Isabella had nothing to do with this murder, and this was a random incident."

"Time will tell."

48.

Tessa called Jack's room, but he didn't answer. She ran to the courtyard, then to the restaurant. She saw him at the bar, speaking with the bartender. Tessa sat down next to him.

"I have news."

Jack turned to her.

"I just read that Patty Kullen was found dead in an alley in Madison."

"The one who was the alibi for Isabella?"

Tessa nodded. "There's more. The investigators found that Patty had come into a lot of money recently. One hundred thousand dollars. She quit her job as a waitress at the diner where she used to work. The one hundred thousand dollars came from Isabella. Isabella gave her a check. The police are questioning Isabella again about her husband's death and naming Patty as her alibi. She claims that she loaned the money to Patty who was her friend. The implication here is that Isabella may have paid Patty to offer up the alibi."

Jack shook his head in disbelief. "She paid with a check? How stupid can these people be?"

"Should I fill everyone in on this? Should I tell everyone to meet in the conference room?"

Jack called over Roger. "Can you get us a couple of glasses of chardonnay?"

"Sure thing," he said and walked over to uncork a bottle of Simi Chardonnay.

Jack lowered his voice. "Have you tried calling Ulysses again?"

"Yes, but he's not answering."

Jack nodded. "Going forward, we keep our discussions among ourselves. Do not include anyone on our team or the client."

Tessa leaned in close to Jack. "What? Why?"

"I'm afraid someone may be feeding information to the other side."

"Who?"

"My initial instinct was Mike Helm, but now, I think it's someone on our team. Mike served the subpoena on Ulysses. He would have done everything he could to prevent us from serving the subpoena if he was working for him. It has to be someone on our team."

Tessa sat quietly.

"I have people at Thurman reviewing every email and call logs for Bob, Henry and Shelly going back to January."

"You can do that?"

Jack nodded. "Yes. We have the right to see every communication people make using the law firm's equipment. It belongs to the firm."

"At dinner when we first arrived here, Bob was complaining about his finances after going through two divorces. And Shelly sounded like she's struggling with student loans and having to care for her mother."

"Do you think it's one of them?"

"Well, I don't know, but I would think there's higher likelihood that people in need of money would get involved in something like this."

Jack nodded. "And, I know Henry is dealing with some financial issues. He was working on a case with me not too long ago, and asked me if I would speak with the payroll department to see if he can get an advance on his pay. I asked him why he needed an advance, and he admitted he had a bad day at the casinos in Atlantic City the prior weekend."

"So, if this is driven by money, it could be any one of them."

Jack nodded.

"How do you know you can trust me?" asked Tessa.

Jack looked into her eyes. "You are a girl from Astoria who's spent her entire life playing the violin. I'm not worried about you."

Roger came back with two wine glasses. "Anything else?"

"No, we're good."

Jack turned back to Tessa. "I want you to tell everyone to meet in the conference room. We'll report on Patty Kullen."

"OK," said Tessa

"I already have my guess as to who might be working for the bad guys."

"Who?" asked Tessa.

"You'll see for yourself at the meeting."

49.

Jack saw them seated around the conference table. He looked at Tessa. "Go ahead and tell everyone what you learned about Patty Kullen."

Tessa looked around the room. "I read reports today out of Madison that Patty Kullen was found dead in an alley. Patty was the woman who Isabella said she was with at the time Isabella's husband was killed. The investigators found a lot of money in Patty's bank account, and she recently quit her job as a waitress. The money came from Isabella, by check. The police are questioning Isabella about both deaths."

Henry leaned back. "Wow. Bizarre," he said.

Jack looked into his eyes and then at Bob and Shelly, trying to gauge their reaction. They showed nothing, other than surprise at the news.

Jack smiled. "So, looks like my hunch is right."

"I don't follow," said Bob.

"Isabella, the Cantor law firm and Ulysses Ullman concocted the entire story on 'This Second' to be able to go after Pearl-Line. Isabella then got caught up in her husband's death, and needed Patty to be her alibi. She told Patty about the Pearl-Line litigation, and Patty got greedy and wanted more money from the conspirators, so they had her killed."

Henry sat up. "Aren't we taking major leaps in logic here? Isn't it possible Isabella had Patty killed because Patty was blackmailing her to get more money out of her? If Isabella paid her to be her alibi, then Patty could've threatened that she'll run to the police unless Isabella paid her more."

Jack stared at Henry. "So, you think Isabella would kill her only alibi? Also, Patty already cashed the check from Isabella. If she was paid to be her alibi, then she too would be implicated in the crime. She would've had no ability to blackmail Isabella, because Patty running to the police would've meant both of them would wind up in prison. It's doubtful Patty would have blackmailed Isabella."

"These people were dumb enough to leave a trail by paying with a check that can easily be traced back to Isabella. I wouldn't put a lot of weight on Patty's ability to figure that out," said Bob.

Jack nodded and looked at Bob and then Henry. "I see your point Bob, but I have something that will fill the gap in my theory."

Henry sat up. "What?"

Jack smiled. "I don't want to unveil it yet."

"Why not?" asked Bob.

"I just need a little more time to confirm what I know." Jack turned to Henry. "Did we ever get the background pages about Ulysses?"

Henry's face turned red. "I didn't forward that email to you? I thought I did. I'll send it after this meeting."

Jack glanced at Tessa and noticed that she was staring at Henry. "OK. Let's break here."

Bob, Henry and Shelly made their way out of the conference room. Jack remained seated. Tessa walked over to him.

"Did you find your answer?" she asked.

"I don't know for sure, but I think I have my guy."

"Henry?"

Jack nodded. "I spoke with Jesse. He told Henry that he could send the background information on Ulysses by email, but Henry told him not to. Jesse sent the documents to me directly."

"Why would he have done that?"

"The obvious answer is he didn't want us to see the information, or he's trying to slow us down. Ulysses grew up in Madison, just like Peter."

Tessa looked shocked. "Are you going to confront him?"

Jack shook his head. "No. I think he can be more helpful if he thinks we don't know. Also, I want him to see at least some of the things we're planning. He'll be helpful in making the other side panic."

50.

Henry paced back and forth in his room. He was sweating through his shirt. His heart was pounding. The three shots of whisky did nothing to calm him. *What does he know? He said he had something to fill in the gap in his story. What is it? It all tied in to Patty Kullen, but what? How did she wind up dead? This was getting way out of control. Jack had pieced everything together.* It didn't matter how he did it, Henry thought as he paced the room. He had to find a way to stop him. Henry pulled out his phone and dialed the number for Peter.

"Hello," said Peter.

"We have a problem, Peter. We need to get Ulysses. Can you conference him in?"

"Yeah, hold on." A few seconds letter, Henry heard Peter's voice again.

"Ulysses, are you there?" asked Peter.

"Yeah, I'm on."

"Guys, we have a serious problem here," said Henry. "What the hell happened to Patty Kullen?"

"Why're you asking? What difference does it make?" asked Peter.

"Jack has somehow connected her death to what's going on with Pearl-Line. He thinks you had her killed because she was blackmailing you."

"He can think that if he wants, but he's wrong," said Peter. "The story is pretty simple. Isabella killed her husband. She needed an alibi, so she paid a chunk of money to Patty to be her alibi. Patty got greedy and tried to black-mail Isabella for more money, so the brilliant Isabella had her killed. That's how the story goes."

Henry shook his head. "Listen, Jack's no longer trying to figure out what happened. He's already scripted the story that connects you two with Isabella and Patty. He's now trying to find proof to back up what he's already pieced together. He thinks Patty found out about Pearl-Line and was killed because she tried to blackmail you."

Peter laughed. "I heard you the first time. His story doesn't work. Everything points to Isabella. He has no proof that Patty was blackmailing us."

"It's not that simple," said Henry. "Jack has something else. He told me he had something, but wouldn't tell me what it is. He must have something to show that Patty was blackmailing you."

"What are you guys talking about?" asked Ulysses. "What do you mean Isabella killed her husband? Who the hell is Patty Kullen?"

"Don't you read the fucking papers?" asked Peter.

"I do read the papers," said Ulysses. "You think the Naples papers will report on people dying in Illinois?"

"Guys, we don't have time for this shit," said Henry. "We need to come up with a strategy to stop Jack."

"There's no way he could've found out about Patty blackmailing us. She only spoke to me and Sara," said Peter. "She did not tell anyone else."

"What else can it be?" asked Henry. "He specifically said that Patty's death confirms his theory."

"You guys can debate this all day, but I'm done," said Ulysses. "I've had enough of this shit. They served me with a fucking subpoena. Now you are telling me that he's connecting us with murder. This is getting way, way beyond what I signed up for. I've got to disappear. I can't show up and let them depose me."

"You can't disappear!" said Peter.

"I am not going to let him interrogate me! I am not going to prison over this!"

"Listen! If you don't show up, that'll give him more ammunition to think you are guilty of what he's suspecting," said Peter. "No normal person with nothing to hide would just violate a subpoena. There's no other explanation for you not to show up and risk being sanctioned by the court. You have to show up."

"Everyone stop!" Henry yelled. "Just take a deep breath and let's think this through. The bottom line is we can't let Jack figure out what we did. We'll all wind up in prison. The subpoena is secondary. We have to come up with a strategy to stop him. We have to find a way to distract him from what he's doing for Pearl-Line."

"How're we going to do that?" asked Ulysses.

"I have an idea," said Henry. "We've been going about this all wrong. We've been letting him chase us. We have to stop running and turn the tables. We have to become the aggressor. We have to create a problem for him."

"I'm all ears," said Peter.

Henry smiled. "We are going to create a bigger problem for him to solve than the one he's dealing with for Pearl-Line. Peter, you have to make a call to Manny."

"Why the hell do you want to call Manny?" asked Ulysses. "That lunatic is only good for one thing, and that's for hurting people."

"You'll know soon enough," said Henry.

51.

Jack put down his coffee and continued to prepare the outline for Ulysses's deposition. Tessa and Shelly sat across from him, reviewing the additional information they received from Jesse. Jack's blood was pumping. He knew Ulysses would lie at his deposition, but that didn't matter. The purpose of the examination would not be to elicit truthful testimony. It would be to send a clear message to Ulysses that he sees through the conspiracy. Fear can do a lot of things to people. Once they start making mistakes, he would find an opening. He was going to gather the proof he needed to take down Ulysses, the Cantor firm and all others who were involved in the conspiracy. He knew he needed more, but he was getting close.

Bob was off to the side, organizing the various documents about Ulysses that they could use as exhibits at his deposition. Jack wanted to get Henry away from the team while they planned the next step. Even though he had nothing hard, he was convinced that Henry was involved. He sent Henry to Pearl-Line to meet with Mike Helm and to analyze the medical reports that had been produced by plaintiffs in all of the lawsuits. Jack told him he wanted to see if there was a parallel between the medical reports of the different plaintiffs. He didn't yet want to confront Henry about what his involvement with Ulysses might be. He wanted to keep his options open. If Henry was involved, letting him continue to operate under the belief that no one suspected anything could yield more information.

Tessa's cell phone rang. She answered. She turned to Jack and mouthed, "It's Ulysses."

"Hi Ulysses," she said. "So good to hear from you. Yes, that sounds great. I'm looking forward to it," she said as she wrote something down on her notepad. She shut off her phone and then looked at Jack.

"He wants to meet me tonight."

"Just you?" asked Jack.

Tessa nodded.

"Where?"

"At his home. He wants to cook for me."

Jack stared at her in silence.

"I can do it," said Tessa.

No one spoke.

"I said I'll do it. He's a womanizer. Not someone who's going to harm anyone. I won't let him touch me. I'll have a nice dinner with him, get the information we need, and then leave."

Bob stood. "This is getting out of hand. It's one thing to meet him in a public place, but to meet him in a private home alone? This is crazy. We shouldn't even be doing this. We should be acting like lawyers. That means suing people, or defending people who get sued. Instead, we are running around like fucking private investigators, trying to trick people into fessing up. Now we are going to send in Tessa to be alone with these people? Two people associated with these fucking clowns are already dead. We cannot do this. We should just alert the police."

"Alert them to what?" asked Jack. "What crime have they committed that we can prove?"

Bob said nothing.

Tessa stood. "I can do this, but this is for you to decide. I'm going for a walk. Just let me know what you want me to do." She left the room.

Jack stared off, thinking things through.

Bob shook his head. "Jack, I know how badly you want to solve this problem for the client, but don't even think about it. We can't take the risk of this asshole attacking her."

"Where is his house?" asked Jack, ignoring Bob.

Shelly reached for Tessa's notepad and read out the address.

"I thought he lived in Pelican Marsh," said Bob.

"No, that's where he bought his new house," said Shelly.

"Bob, we can get Snake and his team here to get us concealed listening devices. I want Tessa wired so we hear everything that goes on. He can also provide security who can jump in and grab her if something goes wrong," said Jack.

"Let's just stop," said Bob. "Even if you somehow convince me to go along with this, it's already three o'clock. What makes you think Snake'll drop whatever he's doing and come here to wire up Tessa?"

Jack looked at Bob. "He'll do what he needs to do to help us. You know he's a friend. This is an important opportunity. Our theory about Ulysses is starting to fall into place. There is no longer any doubt in my mind that Ulysses's interview was part of a scam that involves the Cantor firm. The only piece we are missing is an admission that YF Cream does not cause autoimmune disease. Tessa may be able to get what we need."

"This is a very bad idea," said Bob and walked out of the room.

Jack found Tessa standing on the beach, staring out into the Gulf.

"Hey," he said as he approached her.

Tessa turned to him and smiled.

"Are you sure you want to do this?"

Tessa nodded.

"There's a private investigator I know named Snake…"

Tessa cut him off, "Snake?"

"Well, yeah. That's what he goes by. He's a former cop. He went under-cover on a case and was instrumental in exposing an underground criminal syndicate. The kingpin called him a snake as he was getting handcuffed, and the name stuck. He actually liked it. To be honest, I don't even know his given name. He introduces himself as 'Snake.' In any case. I trust him with my own life. We've worked together on some important matters, and he's the best there is."

Tessa nodded. "What will he be doing for us?"

"I'm going to have his people wire you up so we can hear everything that happens in Ulysses's house. They'll also be nearby to grab you should anything go wrong."

Jack saw three men enter the conference room. The largest one, Snake, introduced himself to the team and then came over to hug Jack. "Good seeing you, old friend."

Jack smiled and shook Snake's hand. "This has to go perfectly. We can't risk anything."

"It'll be fine," said Snake.

The other two had human names—Tony and Lance. Lance was the tech guy. He immediately got to work. He asked Tessa to remove her shirt and began taping a small microphone beneath her collar bone, and ran the thin wire below her bra strap and down her side to her back. Jack explained the drill. Snake nodded along.

"We need to be absolutely certain that we can protect her should something go wrong," said Jack.

Snake opened his yellow sport coat to show the pistol resting in a holster.

"We're prepared for anything, but it won't come to that, if this is just a simple fraud situation. We'll have a speaker set up here for you to listen to everything that's said. Lance and Tony will be waiting in a van nearby, and they'll jump in if something goes wrong," said Snake.

"Is this legal?" asked Bob.

"No," said Jack. "Florida's a consent state, meaning all parties to the conversation must consent to being taped or wiretapped. We only have Tessa who's consenting."

"And we are still doing this?" asked Bob.

Jack nodded. "The listening device is just to make sure Tessa's safe. It's not to gather evidence. No one'll know what we're doing."

Bob threw up his hands. "So, you're saying that it's OK to do something illegal if you are not going to get caught?"

Jack didn't answer.

"She's ready," said Lance.

Jack looked at Tessa. "Can I speak with you for a minute?"

Before she could answer, Henry stepped into the conference room.

"What's going on?" he asked.

Jack stared at him for a few seconds.

"Tessa is meeting Ulysses tonight," he said.

"That's unexpected," Henry said. "I guess that's good news. Maybe we'll get something from him after all. Who are these guys?"

Jack responded before anyone could say anything. "Let's take a walk, Henry," he said as he pulled Henry out of the conference room and led him to an adjoining room.

"They're friends of mine who run a security outfit down here. They're here to help us."

"How? What are they going to do?"

"I'll fill you in later. I want you to give Bob a download on what you learned from reviewing the medical records. Do it in here. I need to speak with Tessa for a few minutes."

Henry nodded. Jack returned to the conference room.

"Bob, can you get a download from Henry?"

Bob looked confused. "Download of what?"

"Just go to the next room and have him fill you in on what Mike told him and the information he gathered on the medical records. And take your time."

"OK," Bob said as he slowly made his way to the door, seemingly confused at what Jack was doing.

"And Bob, don't go into details about what's going down tonight," said Jack.

Bob turned. "Why not?"

"I don't know the legality of what we're doing. I want to limit the number of people who are involved."

Bob shook his head. "Why didn't you extend the same courtesy to me?" he muttered as he walked out of the conference room.

52.

Henry spoke as quickly as he could, hoping to get back into the conference room. Bob nodded along.

"Looks like you got the details we need," said Bob.

"Can we head back to the conference room?" Henry asked.

Bob shook his head. "It's better that you not know what he's doing in there."

"What do you mean?"

"Jack doesn't want you to know what he's doing. Trust me, you'll thank him later. You've done your job for the day. Go get some rest," said Bob as he stood and walked out of the room.

Henry waited a minute and then walked to the closed door to the conference room where the team was meeting. He tried to hear what they were saying, but he heard nothing. He ran to his room and dialed the number for Peter .

"They're up to something," said Henry.

"What else is new. Our plan is foolproof."

"I know, but make sure we don't say anything. I think they may have her wired. I saw equipment in the conference room."

"OK."

Henry closed his phone. He was startled when he heard Jack's voice.

"Give me the phone."

53.

Jack handed the phone to Snake and turned to Henry.

"Tell me what's going on."

"Nothing's going on. I don't know what you are talking about. Why are you in my room?" asked Henry.

"I know you are involved with Ulysses's scam."

Henry laughed. "You must have lost your mind, Jack. Bob told me that I was done for the night, so I came up here to call my wife."

"Check the number he just dialed," Jack said to Snake.

Jack turned back to Henry.

"Why would you be telling your wife not to say anything because we have listening equipment?"

Henry shook his head, acting confused. "We are lawyers, and I didn't like the fact that we are playing with listening equipment. For all I know, you could be listening to conversations I'm having with my wife. Apparently, I wasn't too far off. I didn't want her to say anything personal."

"You are lying."

"You are chasing ghosts, Jack."

"Nothing," said Snake. "The phone doesn't show what number he dialed. There's no call history. It's a burner."

"See, Jack, you have no basis to accuse me of anything."

"Why do you have a burner phone? We caught you red handed, Henry."

Henry let out a deep breath. "You didn't catch me doing anything. I was talking to my wife, and you can't prove otherwise. I need to go and get some air."

Henry took a step toward the door.

"You are not going anywhere," said Jack.

"You can't force me to stay here!" said Henry. "This is illegal."

"I'm not forcing you to do anything," said Jack as he stepped away from Henry.

Henry tried to follow, and Snake stepped in front of him. His six-foot four-inch frame dwarfed Henry, whose head only reached Snake's chin.

"I don't think you want to walk out that door right now," said Snake, smiling.

54.

Jack walked into the conference room.

"What happened? Where's Henry?" asked Bob.

"We heard him call someone. We heard him warn someone to watch what they say and that we have her wired," said Jack.

"Oh my God!" said Shelly. "What does this mean?"

Bob had a blank look on his face with his mouth open.

"I've suspected that Henry was the mole giving information to Ulysses."

"How?" asked Bob.

"I'll explain later," said Jack.

"OK, but now we can call off sending in Tessa," said Bob.

Jack shook his head. "It's not that simple. The problem is we don't have anything hard. He'll deny everything, and all we have is him speaking with someone about having to watch what they say because of the equipment we have."

"It's pretty darn good circumstantial evidence, if you ask me," said Bob.

"So, we're going to spend the next six months trying to convince the DA's office to investigate this, while the company goes down?" asked Jack.

The room fell silent. Tessa stood. "I'm ready."

"Ready for what?" asked Bob.

"To go meet Ulysses."

Bob stared at her with wide eyes.

"OK, let's go," said Jack.

"We are all set up here. You can hear everything that'll be said when she gets in," said Lance. "Tony and I'll follow Tessa, who'll be driven by a taxi. We'll park near the house and jump in if something goes wrong."

"We don't take any chances guys," said Jack. "You hear something even remotely bad, you go in and get Tessa."

"Don't worry," said Tony.

Jack walked up to Tessa and looked into her eyes. "Are you sure you're OK with this?"

Tessa reached out and took Jack's hand and smiled into his eyes. Jack felt a rush of emotion go through him. He stared at her for a while and tried to force a smile.

"Be careful," he said.

"I'll be fine."

Tessa followed Lance and Tony out of the conference room. Jack stared at the empty doorway long after they left.

"I can't hear anything. Is everything working? Where are you?" asked Bob.

Jack heard Lance's voice through the speakers. "You can't hear anything because no one said anything. We just walked past the reception desk."

"Good, just checking," said Bob.

55.

The taxi turned left onto Bonita Beach Rd. The white van followed, with Lance driving. They turned right onto Imperial River Rd., and then left onto Tarpon Avenue. The taxi came to a stop in front of a small ranch that backed up to a canal. The house looked unkempt and had a "For Sale by Broker" sign on the front lawn. Lance parked fifty feet away from the taxi.

They watched her walk up to the house and ring the bell. She stood waiting for a few seconds. She opened the screen door and knocked on the door, and the door swung open. They watched her step in. They heard nothing.

"What's going on?" they heard Jack ask. "We don't hear anything."

"She just walked in. No one's said anything," said Lance.

"Not even a hello?" asked Jack.

"Let's give them a minute," said Lance.

"I don't like this," said Jack. "Get her out of there."

Lance and Tony jumped out of the van and ran to the house. They drew their pistols and opened the door. They walked into the small foyer that led to the living room. No one was in the room. On each side of the room was a hallway. "I'll go this way," said Tony as he walked down the left hallway. Lance took the right, which led to what looked like the master bedroom. No one was in the room. Lance saw the sliding glass door was open. He stared at the wooden dock beyond the door and a bunch of motor boats in the canal heading toward the Gulf. A moment later, Tony joined him. "Nothing," he said as he walked into the room.

"Did you get her?" they heard Jack ask.

"No," said Lance.

"What?"

"The house is empty. They must've subdued her and taken her out back. They must've taken off in a boat, because we didn't see anyone come out of the front."

"Find her!"

"There is no trace of her, Jack."

56.

"Where the fuck is she?" Jack screamed out as he ran into Henry's room.

Henry sat on the couch staring up at Jack. Snake was seated across from him.

"Where is she?" Jack asked again.

"I don't know what you are talking about, Jack."

Jack grabbed Henry by his collar and brought him to his feet.

"Do you really think I'm going to play by the rules when a person's life is in danger?"

"You are assuming I know anything, Jack. You are illegally keeping me locked up here, and now you are accusing me of taking Tessa. You are out of your mind."

Jack reached back and swung his fist at Henry and caught his temple. Henry stumbled to the floor, and then tried to get up. Snake put his large foot on Henry's back to keep him down.

"What is wrong with you? I don't know where she is," said Henry with gritted teeth.

"Yes, you do."

"Are you mad?"

"Yeah. I am mad, and I'm going to make your life a living hell. You are going to regret the day you decided to go down this path."

57.

Tessa opened her eyes. Everything looked blurry. She blinked her eyes a few times. Things started to come into focus. She tried to sit up, but she had no strength. "Where am I?" she asked.

No one answered. She blinked again and saw three men with black masks standing over her.

"Who are you?"

They just stood, staring and not answering. Tessa looked down and saw that her shirt had been ripped open. She could see the red marks where the tape that held the microphone and wire had been ripped off her. She closed her shirt and looked up.

"No one can hear you so don't bother screaming," said one of the men.

Her heart began to race as she started to regain her senses and fear started to set in. "What do you want with me?"

"Nothing right now," said the same man. "You'll be safe, so long as you cooperate. These two animals next to me haven't had a beautiful woman like you before. They'll get their chance if you don't cooperate."

Tessa felt tears filling her eyes and her throat tightening. "Why are you doing this?"

"You'll know soon enough."

58.

Henry felt his head throbbing from Jack's punch. He had to think. He made a serious mistake by calling Peter. The plan was always to limit the number of calls, but things were getting too hot. He had to let Peter know that she was wired and they were going to listen to everything. He didn't know what instructions were given to Manny and his guys who grabbed Tessa, and what they might say that could destroy their plan. But, he should have been more careful. How could he have been so stupid to let Jack hear him talk? Henry knew he didn't say enough to give Jack proof of anything, but he said enough for Jack to be convinced that Henry was part of the scam. There was no doubt in his mind that his cover was blown. He had to use Tessa as leverage. It was time to negotiate. He looked up at Jack.

"I don't know where Tessa is, but I know how to find her."

Jack took a step toward him. "If anything happens to her, I swear I will kill you with my own two hands."

"Do you want me to help you or are you just going to continue to throw these stupid threats at me?"

Jack stepped toward Henry. "I want to know what's going on. I want to know everything."

"Can I have a glass of water first?"

Jack nodded at Snake. He walked off and came back with a bottle of water from the mini-bar.

"Talk."

"Alright, Jack. I can help you find Tessa, but you have to give me something in return."

"Like what?"

"Drop what you are doing. Resign from your engagement with Pearl-Line and call it a day, and offer me something that'll give me assurance that you won't run to the cops to have me arrested after you get Tessa back."

"I'll give you that assurance."

"It's not that simple, Jack. I know you think you're smarter than everyone else in the world, but even stupid me is smart enough to know that your words don't mean shit. I need some insurance that you'll follow through with the deal, and your promise just isn't good enough."

"Do you know where she is?"

"I do not, but I can easily find out."

"You better make that call."

"Now why in the world would I do that?"

Snake stepped toward Henry and put handcuffs on Henry's wrists.

"I, I don't understand," said Henry. "What are you doing?"

Jack brought his face to within an inch of Henry's nose. "You just admitted to us that you are part of the conspiracy. Snake is a former Sherriff with the Collier County Sherriff's Office. It won't be very hard for him to call his old friends and make your life a living hell. Snake and I have a very short memory. You let us know where Tessa is, and we let you go. That's the deal."

Henry laughed. "You think you got it all figured out. The problem you have Jack is I'm not going to talk. I gave you an opportunity to save Tessa, but you just threw that out the window. See, if you arrest me, the orders are that Tessa dies. Just like Patty Kullen. So, Jack, you need to make a decision. You can continue to threaten me, or make me an offer to save Tessa's life"

Jack looked at Snake. "Where can we put him where he can't cause trouble while we work this out?"

"I'll have a car come pick him up. I have a place to hold him until we're ready for him."

59.

The black van with tinted windows drove off with Henry. Bob stared at Jack with a blank look. Shelly stood next to Bob.

Jack turned to them. "Now we know for certain that Henry's working for Ulysses and Peter. He knows how to find Tessa."

"How did you know he was involved?" asked Shelly.

"We checked the phone records back at the office. The calls he made gave us enough to suspect he was involved."

Bob cut in. "What calls?"

"Once Ulysses stood up Tessa and Shelly, I figured we had someone leaking information to the other side. I had the office review all communications in and out of the office for you, Shelly and Henry around the time 'This Second' aired. Henry was the only one with calls to untraceable numbers."

"Go on."

"He also purposely delayed getting us the background information about Ulysses, who grew up in Madison, Illinois. Everything was pointing to Henry being a mole. I needed to be sure, so Snake and I waited for him in his room. That's when we heard him talk."

"I can't believe Henry's really involved," said Bob, looking away and shaking his head. "Why would he do that?"

"I assume he was getting a kickback from Ulysses or the Cantors," said Jack.

"What are we doing with Henry? Shouldn't we involve the police?" asked Shelly.

Jack shook his head. "Snake has his guys holding Henry where he can't cause any more trouble. We can't call the police, because Henry claims Tessa will be killed if the police get involved."

"My God," said Shelly, covering her mouth with her hands.

"So, what are we going to do?" asked Bob. "We can't just sit here and do nothing. Why can't we get Henry to help us find Tessa?"

Lance and Tony walked into the conference room.

"How the hell did you lose her?" Snake asked.

"It happened really fast. She couldn't have been inside for more than a minute. I, I don't know what happened," said Lance.

Bob sat down, buried his face in his hands and shook his head. Shelly looked stunned, and stared off into the distance without speaking.

"Have we contacted the Sherriff's Office?" asked Tony.

Snake threw the cup of coffee he was holding against the wall. "We can't, you fucking idiot! They'll kill her if they find out the police are involved."

Bob looked up. "What do we have to do to get Henry to help us?"

"He wants us to drop what we are doing for Pearl-Line and release him," said Jack.

"We have no choice. We have to give him what he wants," said Bob.

"It's not that simple," said Jack. "We need to give him something that'll protect him if we break the deal after we get Tessa back."

"How are we going to do that?" asked Bob.

"I don't know. There are too many of us who know, and Henry will never get comfortable with whatever we promise him."

"We need to get Henry back here to find out what he wants," said Bob.

Jack shook his head. "There's nothing we can give him that'll be acceptable to him. He already has the one thing that'll force us to keep the promise. That's the threat of killing Tessa. Once he releases her, he has nothing. That's why we can't continue this discussion. There is nothing we can offer. We have to eliminate the leverage they have."

Snake's phone rang. He answered and just listened. He looked up at Jack.

"The house is in foreclosure. No one lives there. We're trying to track down the prior owner to see if he knows Ulysses. Looks like these guys lured Tessa to an empty house to avoid any connection to Ulysses. At this point, we have nothing to prove that Ulysses had anything to do with this."

"What about Henry?" asked Shelly.

"He's admitted nothing about Ulysses. All he's said is he could find out where Tessa is, but he's said nothing about Ulysses or the Cantors," said Jack.

Everyone stood in silence. Jack walked to the window and stared out at the dark sky. He thought about Tessa, and his heart ached. Capitulating to what Henry wanted achieved nothing. There was no way to deliver what Henry demanded. He had to play the game on his own terms. Henry knew Jack's goal was to get Tessa back. That was a vulnerability that Jack could never overcome. He couldn't negotiate with Henry with that glaring weakness. He had to level the playing field. He had to create a vulnerability for the other side that they could not shield with the threat against Tessa's life. Jack turned to the team.

"I have an idea," he said.

Everyone stared at him without speaking.

"I need to get on a plane to Madison, Illinois."

60.

Susan walked next to Helen into the conference room, wondering why Bob called them in the middle of the night for an emergency meeting. She expected to see Jack and was anxious for an explanation. Bob greeted them, and introduced them to Lance and Tony. She and Helen sat across from Bob.

"A lot has happened today. We now firmly believe the Ulysses Ullman interview was part of a conspiracy involving the Cantor law firm and,...one of our associates, Henry Lane."

Helen brought her hand to her mouth in shock.

"Did I hear you right?" asked Susan.

Bob nodded. "We just found out about Henry's involvement. Up until earlier today, we were trying to tie Peter Cantor to Ulysses Ullman. We sent Tessa Malino to meet with Ulysses, hoping to get him to admit that the YF Cream does not cause autoimmune disease. Unfortunately, they abducted her, and we are trying to find her. Henry claims he can find out where she is, but won't talk until we agree to back off on our work for Pearl-Line and give him some insurance that we won't report him to the police."

"Have we notified the Sherriff's Office?" asked Helen.

"We can't," said Bob. "Henry claims that whoever is holding Tessa will kill her if the police get involved. At this point, all we have is Henry, but he's not talking."

"God help us," said Susan.

"Where is Jack?" asked Helen.

"He is on his way to Madison, Illinois to meet with Isabella White. I don't know what he's planning, but he asked that you get Mike Helm to schedule an emergency hearing in the White case as soon as possible."

"I don't understand," said Helen. "We settled the White case. Why would he want a hearing on a case that's already settled?"

"Good question," said Bob. "I'm just relaying what Jack wants. Also, he asked that once you get a hearing date, you have your PR people contact as many outlets as you can and get them to court for that hearing."

"Why?" asked Helen.

"He's going to save Tessa's life and solve Pearl-Line's problem."

"How?" asked Helen.

"I have no idea," said Bob. "But, he had that look."

"What look is that?" asked Helen.

"A crazy man who has everything figured out."

61.

The small room was hot; too hot to breathe. She sat on the twin bed against the corner of the windowless room. She was told to knock on the door if she had to use the bathroom. The brown plastic tray with a sandwich and a glass of water sat on the floor where they left it. Tessa had no more tears to shed. All she had left was fear; the fear of not knowing what was happening. Would they kill her? She had not confronted death until her father passed. He had a chance to say good bye, and the way he left, he gave comfort to those still living. When her time came, she wanted to go like him—with love for the life she lived and those who came into it. She knew she didn't want to die where she was; not like this. Being locked up in this room made her realize how quickly things can end. She wasn't going to be able to script out the way she was going to leave this world. She was at the whim of the three men standing on the other side of the door. Are people looking for her? Who? How would they find her? She thought about Jack and that gave her some comfort. She believed he would look. He wouldn't just give up on her. It wasn't part of his makeup. He would dig until he found her. She wanted to believe her thoughts. "Where are you, Jack?" she mouthed the words. "Where are you?"

62.

Jack stared out of the oval window as the Gulf Stream hit the runway. He kept reliving the few moments before Tessa left—the way she smiled and took his hand, and the rush of emotion that went through his body. She didn't have to go, but she chose to go. She went for him. He knew it. A deep pang of guilt set in as he knew Tessa being taken was a calculated risk.

"How did you get this plane so fast?" asked Snake.

Jack turned to him. "The CEO of a company I represented recently has a house down here. He happened to be here when I called him. He loaned it to us."

Snake nodded, seemingly impressed with Jack's ties.

"So, what's the plan?"

"Henry's expecting for us to run away and drop everything about Ulysses Ullman. The problem is, Tessa will never go free so long as we do what Henry wants us to do. She's his only leverage, and short of him killing all of us, there's nothing we can give him that'll assure him that we won't notify the police when this is all over."

"I agree with you so far," said Snake.

"So, I'm going to do something different. I'm going to make Isabella help me find Tessa."

Snake looked confused. Jack turned back to the window. "Isabella's scared right now. She's afraid she's going to prison for the murder of Patty Kullen. I can use that fear as an angle to get information from her."

"What information can she give you that'll help us find Tessa?"

"The people who are holding Tessa answer to the Cantors, Ulysses or Henry. They have too many options right now. They hold all the leverage.

They expect us to run around and come up with a solution to an impossible problem. Now, we turn the tables. The world doesn't know about what they have done. Once we threaten to publicly expose them, with the help of Isabella, they'll be limited to two options—either let Tessa go for what I will offer them, or kill her and get nothing. I think they'll go for the first option. Tessa will be their only remaining leverage. They can't harm her."

"I hope you're right."

Jack closed his eyes. "Me too."

63.

Ulysses paced back and forth as he shouted into his phone. "This is way, way getting out of control, Peter. What the hell is going on?"

"Just stay calm. We can't think if we're panicking."

"Where the hell is Henry? He's disappeared from the face of the earth. He's not answering his phone. We were supposed to make a few bucks, and now, we are caught up in a kidnapping? Peter, this is not what I signed up for."

"You didn't complain about taking Tessa when Henry came up with the strategy, so shut up."

"What are we going to do with her?"

"I don't know yet. Unless Henry talked, no one knows who took her. No one can connect her to us. Manny and the guys holding her were told to wear masks, so she won't be able to identify them. So long as everyone sticks to the plan, we won't have to kill her."

"Kill? What do you mean, kill? Have you lost your mind? We're not a teenage gang anymore. I'm a fucking doctor now, and you're a lawyer. We can't solve problems like we used to when we were young."

"Forget what I said. We are not going to kill her. We need her as leverage."

Ulysses shook his head. "But you would kill her?"

Peter didn't answer.

"Peter, get that thought out of your head. I'm not going to prison over this."

"If things don't go right, we are all going to prison, regardless. But, don't worry. She's our leverage right now, and she's no good to us if she's dead."

Ulysses took a deep breath. "Alright. I'm going to pretend I didn't hear you say anything about killing anyone, but if you do anything crazy, I'm out.

Do you hear me? I'm out. Now, tell me you are not going to go off the deep end and do anything crazy."

"I am trying to get us out of this. I'll deal with it."

"God damn it, Peter! Tell me you are not going to do anything crazy!"

"I will do what I have to do to solve this problem."

64.

Isabella looked at Jenny, playing on the floor. She closed her eyes, wondering how things went so wrong so fast. It seemed like yesterday when she was in court with Peter, waiting for the verdict. He was confident that they would win. The jury came back quickly with the $35 million verdict. Life was going to be different from that moment on. Jenny was going to have a real home without Russ. She would be able to grow up without having to see her mother get slapped around. Jenny would have all the things that girls her age should have. A home, nice dresses, three square meals. But now, Isabella feared that she would wind up in jail for killing Russ. Jennie would be left all alone, with no one to take care of her. When she was so convinced that everything was going to be different, nothing had really changed.

She turned to the window and saw the white Camry pull into a parking spot. Two men got out and started to walk toward her apartment. Her heartbeat quickened. She wondered if she made a mistake in agreeing to talk to him. At the time he called, she thought there was nothing to lose and everything to gain. Now, she was doubting herself. She wondered if she should have had her defense lawyer with her, but Jack Hatchet insisted she meet him alone. It didn't matter now. She had to hear what he had to say, then go from there. The doorbell rang. She opened the door just a crack, even though she was expecting him.

"Good afternoon. I'm Jack Hatchet."

"Hi," said Isabella as she stepped back to let him in.

"Isn't he coming in?" she asked, pointing at the large man.

"No. Just me."

Isabella nodded and Jack closed the door.

"We can sit here to talk," she said as she walked over to a worn brown couch.

Jack sat down on a loveseat across from her.

"I'll get right to the point. As I told you, I'm a lawyer who can solve a lot of your problems."

Isabella nodded.

"Right now, you are the target of an investigation for the death of your friend Patty Kullen."

Isabella's heart sank. Even though she knew the police was asking questions about her death, no one had said it so bluntly. Her eyes began to well up. She didn't want to go to prison.

"There are people out there who are trying to frame you for her murder."

"I didn't do it. Why would I kill Patty? She was my friend." said Isabella through her tears.

"That's why I'm here. I can fix everything,"

Isabella sat up. "How?"

"The people who you think are helping you are in fact the ones who are behind the scam to send you to jail."

Isabella sat without speaking, shocked at what she was hearing.

"I have evidence that'll show that Ulysses Ullman, the people at the Cantor firm and others concocted a scam to get money out of Pearl-Line. I know you were part of that scam, whether or not you knew what you were doing."

Isabella stared at Jack in complete shock. How could he have figured it out? No one knew, except for Patty.

"Isabella, I'm not here to implicate you in the Pearl-Line scam. I'm here to help you, and you have to trust me on that."

Isabella didn't respond. She wondered if she could trust him. Thoughts raced around her head. She tried to stay focused.

"I also know you were just a pawn in this whole thing. Your lawyers, Peter and Sara Cantor, concocted the whole scam with others and used you to execute the plan. Now, what's happened is that your friend Patty somehow figured out what they were doing and she blackmailed them. They had Patty killed to silence her. But now, someone has to be held responsible for her death, and they figured you would be the perfect scapegoat."

Isabella brought her hand to her mouth in shock. It had never occurred to her that Peter could have been involved with Patty's death.

"Now, if you'll work with me, I can help you get through this mess. Will you work with me?"

Isabella sat motionless. She wasn't sure if Jack was lying to her to get her in trouble. He seemed genuine, but she didn't know if she could trust him. "Why should I work with you? If you can help me, then help me. Why do I have to do anything?"

"Because the only way I can help you is by you helping me. But there are two things I can promise you—you will not get in trouble for the Pearl-Line scam and you will not take the fall for Patty Kullen's death."

"What's in it for you?" Isabella asked.

"I work for Pearl-Line, and if I can nail Peter and Sara Cantor and their friends, I can save Pearl-Line."

Isabella nodded. "How do I know you're not tricking me?"

Jack leaned back. "I guess you won't know, but what options do you have? You do nothing and stay the course you're on, you take the risk of going to prison for the murder of Patty Kullen. You take your chance with me, you might be able to put all this behind you and go and live your life."

Isabella looked away. "I need to think about this."

"I'm sorry. I have no time. Either you commit now, or you're on your own."

Jack started to get up.

"No, wait."

Jack sat back down.

"What do I have to do?" Isabella asked, staring down at the floor.

Jack smiled. "I'm going to ask you some questions."

65.

"She'll do what we want."

"How'd you manage that?" Snake asked.

"I explained to her the difference between my way, which will keep her out of prison, and her way, which will get her framed for Patty Kullen's murder. She was smart enough to figure out that my way was better. She's going to testify in court about the Pearl-Line scam."

"Wasn't she part of the Pearl-Line scam? Wouldn't she wind up in prison for participating in the fraud?"

"She would never admit that she was part of the scam, nor do I need her to do that. I just need her to say enough to get people thinking that Ulysses and the Cantors masterminded the conspiracy and were behind Patty's murder."

Jack's phone rang.

"Jack, it's Bob."

"Did we get a hearing date?"

"We got it."

"When?"

"The judge will have a status conference tomorrow at 2 p.m."

"Good."

"We had local counsel lie to the judge's clerk. We told him that Peter Cantor consented to an emergency status conference. The clerk checked the judge's calendar, and she was free, so here we are."

"You made sure the Cantors know about the hearing, right?"

"Yes. Just like you said, we left a message that a hearing has been scheduled for tomorrow and that Peter or Sara needed to appear. I sure hope you know what you are doing. It's not good to lie to the court."

"I know what I'm doing."

"So, I'm clear, do you or don't you want them to show up at the hearing?"

"It really doesn't matter. Even if they don't show up, they'll send someone to listen in. Either way, I'll get my message to them."

"What if they do show up? Wouldn't they tell the court that we lied about them consenting to the hearing?"

"They may, but that'll just make the judge take a greater interest in what I have to say."

"Alright. You're the boss. We're flying out there tonight with Helen and Susan. They want to be there in court to see what you are going to do."

"Did they notify the media?"

"Yes. You'll have a full courtroom, even though no one knows what the hell you are doing."

"Good."

"I hope Tessa's OK."

Jack thought for a long while. He closed his eyes and shook his head. "Me too," he said in almost a whisper.

"What did you say?" asked Bob.

Jack opened his eyes and stared into the distance. "After tomorrow, they'll have no choice but to tell us how to find her."

66.

Sara closed the door behind her. She was exhausted from spending the day looking at houses. She walked to the kitchen and poured a glass of pinot grigio. The thought of sipping the cold wine excited her. She picked up the wine glass and held it up against the window. The wine looked as clear as water, and she wondered what colors wine lovers looked for in a glass of wine. She sipped it. No, the taste of the wine didn't live up to the anticipation. It was always that way. The blinking red light on her answering machine caught her eye. She pressed the play button, and heard the message that a hearing had been scheduled for the next day. Sara wrote down the message and then walked to the kitchen to grab the bottle. She didn't want to have to get up again to refill her glass. She settled into the sofa and leaned her head back against the cushion. The thoughts that used to torture her mind were long gone; no more concerns about finding the next client, paying the mortgage, or putting food on the table.

There were moments when her mind drifted to what Peter had said; the things he may have done when he was younger. She fought those thoughts by looking for ways to justify who he was at that time and the man he was today. It was a long time ago, she reminded herself. Besides, was she any better? She was part of the conspiracy that was intended to defraud millions out of Pearl-Line, and even put the company out of business. She willingly agreed to participate. *Why should it make a difference that he had taken a life? It was a nameless, faceless life.* Sara closed her eyes and thought about the beautiful mansions she saw in St. Louis; the coffered ceilings, the two-story foyer with marble floors, the wine cellar. She thought Peter would love the wine cellar. Too bad he didn't see the houses. The comfort of knowing she had money in the bank, the thoughts of calling one of those mansions her home and the cool wine on her lips brought her serenity. Her eyelids began to close and she drifted into sleep.

The sun shined in through the frosted glass door. She stood in front of the glass, watching her wine bend the rays of the sun in shapes she hadn't seen before. She thought she saw the colors of a rainbow in her glass, but it was fleeting. She tilted the glass in different ways, trying to find the colors again. A figure approaching her on the other side of the glass door startled her. It looked like a man. Maybe it was Peter? He began yelling, "Sara! Sara!" She didn't know why Peter was screaming her name. She was so comfortable in her new home. Why was he screaming her name?

"Sara!"

Sara opened her eyes and saw Peter staring at her. "Sara!"

Sara blinked her eyes to focus. "Yes, Peter."

"Did you take this call?" he asked, holding up a piece of paper.

Things were coming back in focus. Sara sat up and rubbed her face. "No. I just wrote down the message from the machine. What's wrong?"

"Pearl-Line scheduled a hearing for tomorrow afternoon."

Sara looked up at Peter in confusion. "So? It's not like we haven't had to attend court conferences before. Why are you so excited?"

Peter shook his head. "Because the hearing is for the White case, and we settled that case. This is what you wrote down. 'Court conference for White case.'"

"I wrote that?"

"Yeah."

"I still don't see what the big deal is."

"Sara, the big deal is that I think Henry got caught. Pearl-Line's now scheduled a hearing with the court. Don't you see? They may be coming after us. Shit! Shit! I gotta think."

"Why do you think Henry got caught? What are you saying?"

"Because after my last conversation with him, we haven't been able to reach him."

Sara's heart began to race. She brought her hand to her mouth, suddenly fearing for the worst. "My God, what do we do?"

Peter stood and began pacing. "One thing's for sure. We can't be in that courtroom, in case they have something that can prove what we did."

"We have to send someone," said Sara.

"We can send Mark Boyle. He owes me because I covered for him last time. I'll pay him his hourly fee for just showing up."

"What are you going to tell him to do?"

"I'll tell him to just take notes about whatever happens. And if they try to accuse us of doing anything improper, he'll object and say something to stop the hearing."

"Do you really think they figured it out?"

"I don't know, but we still have Tessa. She's our ticket out."

67.

Jack looked behind him and saw the gallery, filled with reporters. He saw Helen and Susan and his team staring at him intently. Judge Scarlet Wood sat on the bench with a perplexed look. He knew she was confused, and he waited for her to ask.

"Mr. Hatchet, I thought Mr. Cantor consented to this hearing. Why isn't he here?"

"Mr. Cantor was advised of the hearing, but I believe we can proceed without him, your honor."

"I'm not following you Mr. Hatchet."

"Everything will become clear shortly."

"I'm waiting, Mr. Hatchet."

Jack turned around and nodded at Isabella. She stood and made her way to the witness stand.

"What is this, Mr. Hatchet? We are not going to listen to witness testimony today."

Isabella stopped in her tracks.

"Your honor, Ms. White is here for your benefit."

"I don't understand."

"I'm here to reveal to the court what I have uncovered regarding the Pearl-Line litigation. I ask the court to indulge me for ten minutes, and after that, your honor will decide if she will hear the remainder of my story and what Ms. White has to say, or throw me out of the courtroom."

"You have a deal Mr. Hatchet, and based on what I have seen so far, you will be lucky to be just thrown out of here. If I conclude your side made misrepresentations to the court or Mr. Cantor, I will hold you in contempt.

I hope you brought a toothbrush. Now, before I let Ms. White get on the stand, I want to know exactly what you are trying to accomplish here for a case that's already been settled."

Jack nodded at Isabella, and she returned to her seat in the gallery. Jack continued. "Your honor, I represent Pearl-Line, the company that has been named as a defendant in over one hundred thousand lawsuits throughout the United States. There likely will be many more cases in the future. Pearl-Line has been defending these cases the best it can, but as the court knows, its efforts have been met with futility. I understand that your honor's role here isn't to help Pearl-Line for the sake of helping it. But, I do hope that once the court sees what I present here today, that your honor will feel a need to correct the wrong that's been committed against Pearl-Line and the entire judicial system as a whole."

Judge Wood sat, staring at Jack without saying anything.

Jack continued. "The Pearl-Line litigation has highlighted the blemish in our judicial system. It has shown that decisions that lead to victory or loss may be made based on public sentiment rather than what the evidence may show. We have questions of science and medicine being answered in a courtroom and the media, and not in the laboratory where those answers should be sought and found. That is our system, and a small group of people who understand the system came up with a criminal plot to exploit it. They put in motion a series of events that have brought a company to its near demise, while they collect their millions under the guise of pursuing justice. Your honor, Ms. White and I are here today to expose this criminal conspiracy.

"So, your honor must be asking, how did they do it? The litigation against Pearl-Line was given birth by a thirty-minute news report involving Ulysses Ullman, where he dreamt up a fictional report about the YF Cream causing autoimmune disease. That interview tugged at the emotions of the American public. That report denied the masses of the right to enjoy everlasting youth and beauty for a price they can afford. The price of illness was not one they were willing to pay. And from that, they found anger and resentment. How dare they give me something so important, without disclosing the actual price one has to pay? So, they turned against Pearl-Line, and demanded compensation. But, this courtroom saw the quality of the evidence trying to create a causal connection between the YF Cream and autoimmune disease. There was no medical evidence. But, the play on the public's emotion was all that was needed to start this criminal attack on Pearl-Line."

Jack paused and gauged Judge Wood's reaction. He had spoken for more than ten minutes, and she sat quietly, waiting for Jack to continue. Jack turned back to look at the gallery to see if anyone was going to object. He swallowed hard and turned back to face the judge.

"I'm here to bulldoze over the house of cards that has been built by Ulysses Ullman and the Cantor firm. Ms. White was the first plaintiff to sue Pearl-Line, represented by Peter and Sara Cantor. She will testify to the truth and tell you what happened before the Ulysses Ullman interview and after that interview."

Jack nodded at Isabella. She walked to the witness stand and sat, staring at him, appearing nervous and confused.

"Are you ready Ms. White?" asked Jack.

Judge Wood raised her hand before Isabella could respond. "This is highly irregular Mr. Hatchet, but you have gotten my attention. Just to be clear, whatever Ms. White says on the witness stand will not be evidence. There is no jury here, and Mr. Cantor is not here to cross examine. So, I'll indulge you only because you have captured my interest. Go on."

"Judge, shall I swear her in?" asked the bailiff.

Judge Wood thought for a few seconds. "There is no jury here, but I do want her to swear to the truth of what she is going to say. Go ahead. Please swear in the witness."

The bailiff moved to the witness box and asked Isabella to raise her right hand. He swore her in and then returned to the side of the courtroom.

"Ms. White, please tell the courtroom how you met the Cantor law firm."

"I was at my doctor's office because I had headaches."

"Objection!" someone shouted from the gallery.

An older man made his way to the podium. Jack let out a sigh of relief. He needed someone to stop the hearing. Isabella was not going to go much further than to testify that Peter suggested to her that the cream may be the cause of her illness. She was not prepared to incriminate herself. That was the deal. But, he thought she had said just enough to convince the Cantors that she had more to say about the fraud."

Judge Wood stared at the older man. "Identify yourself, sir."

"Your honor, my name is Mark Boyle. I'm co-counsel with Mr. and Ms. Cantor for Ms. White. I just learned about this hearing, to which we never consented. Mr. Hatchet here never communicated with us about this hearing, your honor. His people just left a message on Mr. Cantor's answering machine. Again, Mr. Cantor never consented to this hearing. It is outrageous that he is standing here to make these accusations without alerting his adversary, who has the right to respond to these frivolous charges."

The judge turned to Jack. "Mr. Hatchet, you just got through telling me that Mr. Cantor consented to this hearing, but chose not to attend. What is going on here?"

"That was my understanding, your honor. If your honor would give me a few minutes for me to speak with Mr. Boyle, I expect to be able to straighten out whatever questions the court may have. But frankly, your honor, I don't believe the presence of Mr. Cantor here is particularly relevant. This hearing isn't about the interests of a particular plaintiff. It's about a criminal conspiracy orchestrated by a handful of individuals that has made a mockery of the judicial system. I believe, as an officer of the court, that I have an obligation to present our findings to you. Even if the Cantors were present today, it remains for the judicial system and the criminal justice system to decide what they will do with the information Ms. White and I intend on presenting to the court."

Judge Wood looked up at the ceiling and then looked back down at Jack. "I want to take a fifteen-minute recess. And when I return, I want a full explanation."

"All rise!"

Judge Wood disappeared into the door behind the bench. The courtroom filled with voices, while the marshals stood by the wooden gate to hold back the reporters from approaching Jack. Jack saw Helen and Susan staring at him in shock. Boyle stepped up to Jack.

"What the fuck do you guys think you are doing?" Boyle asked.

Jack stared into his eyes. "You have no idea what you have gotten yourself involved in. If you are part of the Cantors' scam, then I'm going to nail you just the way I'm going to nail Peter and Sara. If you are not, and you were dumb enough to come here voluntarily to represent their interests, I will give you a chance to walk away and avoid winding up in prison with your co-counsel."

Boyle was silent. Jack wasn't sure if he was part of the conspiracy, but he didn't care. It was irrelevant to the big picture. Boyle looked scared. Whatever money the Cantors were paying him wouldn't be worth risking his law license or a prison sentence. That wasn't hard to predict. Regardless of his role in the scam, he was there to stop the flow of information. Jack knew Boyle would have no choice but to agree to adjourn the hearing. Jack predicted this moment would come, and it was critical to finding Tessa. He had guessed right. Jack put his hand on Boyle's shoulder.

"Mark, I don't believe you are part of the scam, so I'm going to do you a favor. I'm going to suspend the hearing at this point and give you time to figure out what's going on. I will ask that we adjourn until tomorrow. That will give you time to decide if you want to be part of the conspiracy or walk away."

Boyle nodded.

"All rise!"

Judge Wood returned to the bench. Before she could say anything, Jack spoke.

"Your honor, there apparently has been some miscommunication somewhere in the chain. Mr. Boyle and I spoke, and we agreed to a short adjournment of this proceeding so that we may be able to get to the bottom of everything. I believe Mr. Boyle consents."

Jack looked over at Boyle.

Boyle walked to the podium. "Your honor, Mr. Hatchet is correct. I just need a little time to find out exactly who on my, I mean, uh, Mr. Cantor's side received notice of this hearing. I believe a short adjournment will be very helpful."

Judge Wood nodded. "OK, gentlemen. When would you like to return?"

Jack stood back up. "I believe a one-day adjournment would serve our needs."

"We agree, your honor," said Boyle.

"Very well. One day gentlemen. I want to complete whatever it is we are doing by tomorrow. Come back here by 2 p.m." Judge Wood turned to Jack. "Mr. Hatchet, I've been on the bench for eighteen years, and a practicing lawyer before that for twenty, and frankly, I've never quite experienced anything like this."

"I hope it will be memorable, your honor," said Jack.

"I don't think you have to worry about that, Mr. Hatchet."

68.

The thrill of the high revving engine of his Jaguar XKR didn't excite Ulysses as it had the day before. He jumped in his car the moment Peter called. Peter was scared, and so was he. He had known Peter since he left the orphanage in Madison, and he could never remember Peter being afraid of anything. He was always the aggressor. Nobody got in his way. Peter always had it his way. But today, he was different. His voice shook at times, and he seemed uncertain. The weakness Peter exhibited made Ulysses feel exposed. He felt naked, alone. Peter asked him to meet in Atlanta, and that he not take the plane. He wanted no trace of them being at the same location. It made sense, thought Ulysses, especially after Henry disappeared into thin air. He wiped the perspiration from his forehead. He drove on, even though he hadn't slept much the night before. He was too scared to be tired. He felt like he was running for his life. Things changed so fast. He was rolling in millions just a day before. Today, he felt like a fugitive. The nine-hour drive felt like an eternity. He only stopped to get gas and to refill his coffee mug. The city limits sign for Atlanta, Georgia made his heart pound. He tried to calm himself. No one was after him yet. He swallowed hard and made his way to the Marriott on Peachtree Center Avenue. Ulysses avoided the valet and found a spot in the guest parking lot. He walked in to the lobby and was about to call Peter's cell phone, when he decided he needed to calm down. He went to the hotel bar and ordered a Scotch. He needed the drink to stop the tremor in his hands. He downed the glass and then dialed Peter's number.

Peter answered and gave him his room number. Ulysses paid the bill with cash and took the elevator up. Sara was sitting on the couch with a tissue.

"Have a seat," said Peter as he emptied a small bottle of Johnny Walker into a glass.

"Still nothing from Henry?" asked Ulysses.

"Still nothing," said Peter. "I've been calling him. They must have him." Ulysses shook his head.

"We have other problems," said Peter.

"What?"

"That fuck, Jack Hatchet, got to Isabella and was about to have her spill her guts in court earlier today. Mark Boyle intervened just in time."

Ulysses's eyes opened wide. "How did he get to Isabella?"

"I don't know. Boyle wouldn't talk to me, other than to say that he thinks he stopped everything in time. He doesn't want to have anything to do with us anymore. We are on our own…" Peter's voice trailed off.

"I don't understand," said Ulysses, sitting up. "We took Tessa so he'll be forced to do what we want and disappear. How did that turn into him blowing the whistle on us?"

"That fuck set us up! He knew we would have someone in court, and knew we would stop him. Now, he's got the threat of finishing his story in court and is holding that over our heads. He just created leverage he did not have. He fucking turned the table on us," said Peter.

Ulysses sat without responding, staring at Peter.

"Don't you see? Before, we had him by the balls because we have Tessa. He called our bluff. He bet that we wouldn't harm her, and then he made a credible threat that he is going to go public on us. He went far enough to get the judge's interest and to scare the crap out of Boyle, and then he stopped just in time to give us an opportunity to let Tessa go in exchange for dropping whatever he was going to do in court. This shit is all over the news and internet. He just created a bargaining chip that he didn't have before. He's also given us a deadline until tomorrow. That doesn't give us a lot of time to fix this."

"How did he give us a deadline of tomorrow?"

"Because the hearing's been adjourned until tomorrow. That means he'll finish exposing our conspiracy when he returns to court."

Ulysses sat up. "And how are we going to fix this?"

Peter stared into Ulysses's eyes for a second and then downed the whisky in his glass. "We have to kill him. That's the only way."

"What? You really would kill him?" asked Sara, visibly shaking.

"From now on, we do things my way. Fucking Henry's been useless. I'm going to fix this the same way I fixed the Patty Kullen problem," said Peter.

"Oh my God," said Ulysses.

"Everyone just shut up!" said Peter. "We're all in this together, and there's a way to get through all this. If we do nothing, Jack'll go forward with the hearing tomorrow, and we'll all wind up in jail. He knows we're not going to harm Tessa, because she's the only chip we have. We have no choice but to negotiate with him. That means we offer to give up Tessa in exchange for an opportunity to kill him. Once we kill Jack and Isabella, no one would be able to expose us; at least with any sort of proof."

"Why would Jack sacrifice himself?" asked Ulysses.

"He won't. We're going to tell him we want to exchange Tessa for Henry, and when we get Jack in our sight, we're going to have him killed."

"Oh my God," said Sara as she stood and walked into the bedroom in tears.

Peter didn't react to Sara leaving. "Manny and the guys holding Tessa are wearing masks, so Tessa doesn't know who her kidnappers are and she has no proof to tie her kidnapping to us. Henry's the only one who knows we were involved with taking her, and he's not going to tell them what we did and incriminate himself. It's really simple. We offer to exchange Tessa for Henry, and when we get them to meet us, we kill Jack. Then we go after Isabella."

"Wouldn't people think we would have had something to do with their deaths, considering what Jack and Isabella were trying to do?"

"They will, but with what proof? There's no perfect way to solve this. This is the best that we have."

"How do we know Henry didn't already spill his guts?" asked Ulysses. "All of this would be for nothing. We are just digging our graves deeper and deeper. The police may already be after us."

"I don't think Jack would've gone through the trouble of doing what he did in court if he had run to the police. There would be a nation-wide search for us, but I haven't heard anything. The plan was always to get Jack to stop what he's doing in exchange for Tessa. I assume Henry stuck to the plan and told Jack that we'd kill Tessa if he goes to the police," said Peter.

Ulysses shook his head. "This is getting completely out of control."

Peter nodded. "Yeah, that about sums it up. But, what choice do we have? Bottom line, we have to take care of Jack and Isabella."

Ulysses sat quietly for a few minutes, then stood. "Peter. I didn't sign up for this. No one said anything about killing people. We were supposed to make a few bucks and move on. Now we're talking about murder. I'm out."

"Shut the fuck up and sit down!" Peter screamed.

Ulysses plumped back down in the chair.

"Get your head out of your ass, Ulysses. You want to go to prison? Is that what you want? If this thing gets blown open, we will serve time for fraud, conspiracy, murder, and a bunch of other crimes. Jack will blow this thing open tomorrow. He's daring us to do nothing, and then you can bet your ass that every cop under the sun will be after us. You say you didn't sign up for murder? I didn't sign up to live in a fucking jail cell for the rest of my life!"

Peter stood and opened another bottle of Jack Daniels and poured it into his glass. "Killing these people is nothing, Ulysses. I have no problem with killing anyone, so long as I have a way out. If we do nothing and let Jack do his shit, we are fucked. My way is the only way. You want out? The answer is no. You are in this to the end, whether you like it or not."

Ulysses sat silently; his heart ready to jump out of his chest.

"It's just two more lives, Ulysses. Jack Hatchet and then Isabella. It's not like you are not already implicated in Patty's murder," said Peter.

"Oh, dear God," said Ulysses as he buried his face in his hands.

"God has nothing to do with this, Ulysses. We have no other option than to do this. Start praying to the devil. That's all we've got left."

69.

Jack and Snake walked in to the hotel conference room they rented in St. Louis. Shelly and Bob stood.

Bob said, "Jack, you really stirred the pot. Every major news outlet had a story about what you said in court. And you hadn't even offered up any proof of the conspiracy."

Jack nodded. "The media doesn't care."

"You literally came up with a crazy hunch and you made the facts fill the holes to make the story real. Helen and Susan saw it too. They were more shocked than excited that you are going to solve their problem."

They walked to the large conference table and sat. "I got a call from the office," said Jack. "Someone called the receptionist and requested that I be ready for a phone call at midnight tonight."

"Who'll be calling?" asked Bob.

"It'll be either the Cantors or Ulysses, probably with a disguised voice. This is when negotiations begin."

Bob looked puzzled. "You expected him to call, didn't you?"

Jack nodded.

"You purposely ended the court hearing today," said Shelly.

Jack turned to Shelly. "Yes."

She nodded. "You wanted them to call you so you can cut a deal with them."

Jack nodded. "Yes. That was the plan all along. We're going to negotiate. We drop everything and they let Tessa go."

Jack's cell phone rang right on time. He pressed the speakerphone symbol on his phone to answer.

"Yes."

"Jack Hatchet?" asked a voice that sounded mechanical and unrecognizable.

"Speaking."

"You want your girlfriend back?"

"Who is this?" asked Jack.

The man laughed, but didn't respond.

"Can I call you Peter, or do you prefer Ulysses?" asked Jack.

"Don't think you're so smart, asshole."

"What do you want?"

"You know what I want. Just tell me how you're going to solve this little problem you created."

"Release Tessa and I'll cancel tomorrow's hearing and drop what I'm doing for Pearl-Line," said Jack.

"I need something else."

"What?"

"I want you to release Henry Lane."

Jack looked up at Snake. Snake nodded.

"OK. We'll let him go."

"Not so easy. You are going to cancel tomorrow's hearing. You and Henry are going to go to the Half Moon Beach in Naples at 11 tomorrow night and start walking up north. If everything looks clear, I will find you on the beach and you'll get her back in exchange for Henry. If I see police anywhere near the beach, the deal is off and she dies."

Snake mouthed the word "No."

Jack ignored him. "We'll be there at 11."

"Good. You have to deliver Henry personally, otherwise, no deal." He ended the call.

Snake shook his head. "I don't like this at all. That's a very wide beach with lots brush in random spots where people can hide. He wants you to walk the length of the beach so you're completely exposed, and he can take you out at any point. I can't stake out a location to protect you, since we won't know where they'll have Tessa positioned. The best I can do is track your location through my phone from the street so I can get to you once you locate Tessa."

Bob stood. "This is nuts. They're setting you up to kill you, Jack. You are the guy who knows the whole story to take them down, and the only way they think they can escape this is by killing you. We can't let you just walk into this trap."

"We have no other option," said Jack. "It's the only way we're going to get Tessa back." Jack turned to Snake. "We need to alert the Sheriff's Office."

Snake nodded. "I still have people there. When do you want to alert them?"

"I want them positioned nearby and ready to go. Once I see Tessa's safe, I'll send you a text, and then you can call them in. You need to give them a heads up so they'll be ready, but you've got to make sure they don't move in too soon and give these guys a reason to kill Tessa. How quickly can you get men on the beach, once I get Tessa?"

"That's the problem," said Snake. "He hasn't given you a location on where he'll meet you, which means we won't know where to position the deputies to get to you. If they can't move in until after you see Tessa, at best, it'll take fifteen, twenty minutes for them to get to you. We need a lot of luck on our side. I think this is a very bad idea. We should rethink this."

Jack shook his head. "We can rethink all we want, but there are no alternatives. I understand the risks. We are going to do this."

Snake shook his head. "Jack, you are ignoring one important detail."

"What's that?"

"You are assuming they're not going to shoot you the second you step onto the beach. This deal makes no sense for them unless they kill you. They are not dumb enough to believe you'll take Tessa and keep your word that you won't run to the police. The second you and Henry step on the beach, they will shoot you both."

"No," said Jack. "They want to kill *me*. Not Henry."

Snake looked confused. Bob grabbed Jack's arm. "Did you hear what Snake just said? They are not even going to wait for you to walk up the beach. They are going to kill you both the first moment they see you."

Jack stared at Bob for a long while. "I'll be safe so long as I'm with Henry, and if they don't know who's who."

"What makes you so sure they give a shit about Henry?" asked Snake.

"I had Jesse run a check on Henry once we figured out he was involved. He spent a few years at the Red Rose Orphanage in Madison. He was adopted by Hannah and Larry Lane. Do you know what his name was before he was adopted?" asked Jack. Everyone stared at him in silence. "Cantor," said Jack.

Snake nodded. "Let's go. We have work to do."

70.

Ulysses stared hard at Peter as he brought a duffle bag out to the sitting area. Peter pulled out a rifle and a pistol and began loading them. He handled the weapons with ease, opening the cartridge and loading the bullets.

"Where did you get that?" he asked.

Peter looked up. "It's not hard to find guns anywhere. You just have to know where to look."

"Did you kill her yourself?" asked Ulysses.

"Patty?"

"Yeah."

Peter stuffed the weapons back into the duffle bag. "One hundred bucks."

"What?"

"That's what it cost to find a guy willing to pull the trigger."

"Is that who you're using for Isabella?"

Peter stared at Ulysses. "Stop saying 'you.' It's 'we.' Don't try and detach yourself from this."

Ulysses downed his Scotch and felt it burn his throat. "What if this guy gets caught?"

"That's not today's problem. We first take out Jack. We worry about Isabella tomorrow."

"Are you going to kill Jack yourself?"

Peter laughed. "I would love to, but it'll have to be Manny. He's got a better shot from a distance."

Ulysses shook his head. "I don't like this at all."

"Tough shit," said Peter. "Give me your car keys."

Ulysses reached into his pocket and pulled out the keys to the Jaguar.

"I don't understand why you have to go yourself when you have Manny there already."

Peter stared at Ulysses. "I need to make sure it gets done. Manny has nothing vested in this other than the hundred grand we'll be paying him. He'll run at the slightest sign of trouble."

"I don't want my Jaguar anywhere near the beach. They'll trace the plates," said Ulysses.

"Don't worry. Manny's picked up a stolen car that'll be waiting for me. I'll drop your car off at your house."

Ulysses nodded. "What do you want me to do here while you're gone?"

"Stay with Sara. Make sure she doesn't do anything crazy."

Ulysses watched Peter pick up his bag and walk to the adjoining room. He opened the door. "Sara," he called out to her. "I'm going," he said.

Ulysses didn't hear Sara respond.

Peter started for the door and then stopped. He turned and looked into Ulysses's eyes and laughed.

"What's so funny?"

"You."

"What?"

"You're afraid I'm going to kill you."

Ulysses's heart dropped. He couldn't respond.

"If you do anything stupid like running to the police to extricate yourself, I will kill you."

71.

She awoke at the sound of the man's voice. The bright light hurt her eyes. She didn't know how long she'd slept. She sat up.

"It's time to go," the man with the mask said.

"Where?"

"You cooperate, you may go free today."

Tessa swallowed hard and stood.

"But, if you don't cooperate, you will die."

Tessa nodded at the man and walked out of the room. The other two men with masks waited in the living room.

"Where am I?" she asked.

They didn't answer. One of the men tied a gag around her mouth and then put a black bag over her head. He then tied her hands behind her back. She tried to stay calm, hoping that the nightmare would end soon. They pulled her by her arm out of wherever they were. She heard a car door open and she got in with the help of the man holding her. The engine started and they were on the move. She didn't sense anyone was in the back seat with her. The car came to a stop. She heard the driver's side door open and someone get in and close the door. Then the rear door opened and someone else got in. She felt someone's hand on her breast.

"I finally get to check out these nice tits," said the man next to her. It was the same voice as the man who was driving before. They apparently had changed drivers.

Tessa tried to scream, but all she could manage was a muffled moan.

"We don't have time for that crap," said the man driving. She hadn't heard his voice before.

The man took his hand off her. "Give me the sequence again?" she heard him ask.

"I'm going to hide the car at the northern tip of the beach. There's a small lot there where hotel workers usually park. I'm going to take her to the beach. You'll go to your position and wait. When I see them, I'm going to leave her on the beach and join you. She won't be able to warn them. When they get close enough, you shoot him. Make sure you don't hit my brother. Once he goes down, we grab our guy and get to the car as quickly as we can, and then we take off to Bonita Springs."

Tessa tried to think. He said don't hit his brother. They were going to kill Jack and grab his brother. Who were the two men in the car? One of the men had to be Peter Cantor. Who was the other one? He couldn't be Ulysses. She heard Ulysses's voice at the White Tequila. This man had a lower pitched voice. Who was the brother? Why would the brother be with Jack? Tessa tried to think. Jack had suspected Henry was working for the other side. Could it be? Could Henry be Peter's brother?

"What about the girl?"

"We take her with us until we talk to my brother."

"Then what?"

"I don't know. We'll figure it out."

"Easy enough."

Tessa tried to register their conversation through the chaos of her fears. They were going to kill Jack, and in all likelihood, her too. The brief moment when she thought she'd be released was now just a distant memory. She was going to die tonight with Jack. There must be a way to stop them, she thought, but she felt helpless. With her hands tied, a gag in her mouth and a bag over her head, what could she do? She could do nothing to stop them. All she could hope for was that Jack had something planned. He couldn't possibly have thought he could just walk up to these guys and expect them to release her. Hope started to set in. She would not accept death, she thought. Not like this. It was time to stop thinking about fear or death. It was time to hope that she and Jack will find a way to survive this…somehow.

72.

Henry sat quietly in the corner with his hands in handcuffs behind his back. He saw Jack speaking with a few men, who probably were Snake's guys. He didn't know what was happening, and a good part of him didn't care. The agony of living was overwhelming. Wanting out was winning the battle. He had lost everything he owned, and the plan to get everything back failed. He thought about how he got here. Winning came so easily at first. But all it took was a few losses in a row. He had to find a way to win, and that thought was what did him in. He hocked their retirement, exhausted their credit cards to win back what he had lost. But, he kept on losing.

He thought it was over for him, until he came up with the idea. Having seen how the jury works, all he needed to do was to convince Susan LaColla to tell the story to the world. That wasn't hard. He knew the story would be so shocking, that she would jump at the chance to report it. It took a thirty-minute meeting with Ulysses for her to agree to take on the story. It was working perfectly until Jack stepped in. Henry thought he could pull it off even then, but now he was certain he was wrong. The plan was falling apart, piece by piece. Jack Hatchet won the fight. He had lost.

He wanted to make everything right for Elaine, but now, he knew he had failed miserably. The pain in his chest brought tears to his eyes. There was nothing left to be done now. Once they released his handcuffs, he would reach for the nearest gun and eat a bullet. Elaine would collect his life insurance, which would cover his debt and give his family a comfortable life. That was the only way out.

He saw Jack take a seat next to him.

"We are going to go for a ride, and it may be the last ride you or I take," he said.

Henry stared at him.

"I'm going to exchange you for Tessa on Half Moon Beach."

Henry kept staring, not responding.

"I suspect you won't answer me, but I have to ask. Why? Why did you do it?"

Henry pulled away from Jack's eyes and looked at the floor.

"You had everything going for you, Henry. You were a rising star at the firm. Where you could have gone with your future was for you to decide. It was all up to you. You were the only one who could have gotten in the way of what you were capable of achieving, and you chose to throw a roadblock in your own path. You have a loving wife and a daughter at home. Why would you throw all that away?"

Henry continued to stare down without responding.

"I know everything, Henry. I know you are Peter's brother."

Henry looked up at Jack for a few seconds and then looked down again.

"I know about the orphanage, the adoption. Your connection with Ulysses from Madison. There is nothing left to hide. You didn't have to wind up here, Henry. You threw it all away," said Jack as he stood to leave.

"I had nothing, Jack," said Henry, still staring at the floor.

Jack sat back down.

"I needed a quick fix. The worst thing that could have happened to me was to have early success at the tables. The excitement and adrenaline that come with that first big win is something you never forget. Then, came the losing. A bad roll of the dice or a lousy hand. I needed another shot to win back what rightfully belonged to me. I lost again. I would win here and there, but I lost far more often. But it was the occasional winning that kept me in the game. Soon, I had drained my bank account. Then came the credit cards. And then came loans, secured by our retirement money. Elaine found out about it. She was already suffering from her depression, and I made our lives worse."

Jack sat quietly, staring at Henry.

"You wanted to know what happened," said Henry under his breath. "Now you know."

"I had no idea, Henry."

"Not everyone can live a storybook life like you, Jack. Not everyone has the patience to build a life like you. For a lot of us, we don't have the stamina to walk a path to success. We want everything, but aren't willing to put in the work or the time needed to build a life. I thought by getting a law degree and a good job, I'd learn patience, and begin to appreciate the piece-by-piece construction of my life. I was wrong. I couldn't. People like me are not capable of coming up with a plan to put some money away each year, invest right, and then do it all over again. I couldn't live that life. So, I took a different path. But the life in the casinos failed me. And when that happened, there was nothing left for me. I had gambled away all our money, leaving nothing for Elaine and my daughter. I was ashamed and angry."

Henry finally looked up at Jack with tears in his eyes.

"Have you ever tasted the barrel of a gun before, Jack?"

Jack stared into Henry's eyes and shook his head no.

"I have, and it doesn't taste so good. When I knew I had fallen in too deep, the only thing I wanted to do was run away, and a bullet was going to free me from the mess I created. Then, as I stared into that barrel, a thought occurred to me. During the years I'd been practicing law, I learned something about the jury mentality. I learned that half the game is making the jury want to find in your favor. I figured out the price one has to pay to get the verdict. The jury in a tort case isn't worried about sending an innocent person to prison. Morality and conscience aren't part of their thoughts. They decide based on their emotion. I learned that about the jury, and then I thought, why not use that to fix my problem. I came up with a plan. My brother Peter Cantor was a useless plaintiff's lawyer and Ulysses Ullman was a quack doctor who wanted easy money. They were both game for a quick million. All we needed was to give the jury what it needs—reason to rule in my favor. Creating public anger against Pearl-Line was easy. Take its best product that the public had embraced and turn it into a monster. It wasn't difficult to anticipate the public's reaction once Ulysses went on TV. That was the price of the verdict."

Jack leaned back and stared at Henry. "Why did you tell me all this?"

Henry shook his head as he stared into the distance. "Peter Cantor is not your typical lawyer. He grew up in the streets, and he survived by lying, stealing and even killing. I never had to live that life, because I was adopted at a younger age. Even though he left the streets, the instinct to survive at all costs is still embedded in him. This scam against Pearl-Line was supposed to take him all the way to the promised land. But, now he knows that he's fallen into your trap. There's nothing he wants more than to get free, and he will find a way, like he always has. You are the one person standing in his way. Killing you will solve all his problems, in his mind. He's a simple guy. He shoots first and asks questions later. I don't know what your strategy is, but I know that Peter Cantor will kill to keep this thing from unraveling. You know too much, and there is nothing you can offer him to convince him that you won't come after him again. He will make sure you are not alive to talk about it. But you already knew Peter wants you dead. I'm telling you all this, because I know the game's over for me."

Jack nodded.

"I thought you had a right to know the truth before he kills you. So, Jack, now it's your turn. You are a smart guy. Why would you walk into that trap?"

Jack thought for a long time. "Have you ever thought about what life is?"

Henry stared at Jack with a blank look.

"I have for a long time, and I think it's something that I've always known, but never took the time to truly understand. There is no final goal that'll deliver you to your dreams. Making a lot of money is something we all strive for, but once you get there, we need something else. Life is nothing more than understanding where you are and deciding what is important at that moment. That's all it is. At the end of the day, money doesn't decide who wins or loses. The only winner is the man who can lie in his bed in his final days and find comfort in the life he lived—a life where he understood what was important and a life that was spent going after it. We are all going to be lying in that bed one day. When that day comes for me, I want to find peace and comfort with what I've done with the time given to me.

"You ask me why I'm walking into Peter's trap. It's because saving Tessa is what's important to me. And, I'm going to walk into that trap and find Tessa. I will find a way to get us out. Everyone talks about living a life, but not enough people ask how you lived your life. After this day, I want to be able to answer that question."

Henry didn't pull away from Jack's eyes. He understood, and wished he could talk some more. Jack stood and waved at someone. "Please take the handcuffs off."

Jack turned to Henry. "We need to go and change."

"Change for what?" asked Henry.

Two men approached them. "Stand still," said one of the men as he wiped camouflage face paint onto Henry's face.

"What are you doing?" asked Henry.

"We need to dress for the trap I'm setting for Peter," said Jack.

73.

Snake stared at the men after he laid out the plan. Will Jack's plan work? Jack was risking his own life based on the steps he believed Peter would take. If he was wrong, both Jack and Tessa likely would die, and Snake would have played a role in their deaths. He looked at his men, all retired deputies from the Sherriff's Office. "It's a long beach, gentlemen. We have to be ready to make our move the first chance we get. We will split into twos and spread out along the edge of the beach and follow Jack's movement. As soon as we see Peter Cantor or Ulysses Ullman, we have to grab them. Don't wait for orders. This entire plan is intended to smoke them out into the open."

Snake looked over at Jack and Henry, speaking in the corner of the conference room. He walked over to them. "We are ready. My guys will be in position within the hour. I've spoken with my buddy at the Sherriff's Office. They are not happy, but I didn't give them any options. They'll be hovering around the streets near Half Moon Beach and will come in as soon as we tell them where to go. You need to let me know as soon as you locate Tessa."

Jack smiled at Snake, but didn't respond. Snake still didn't like the plan, but he knew Jack had made up his mind. There was no turning back, and Snake had committed to go along with the strategy. It wasn't because he couldn't say no. It was because he believed in Jack, even if some would call it blind faith.

He thought back to the time he first met Jack. Jack had come down to Naples to conduct an internal investigation into a securities trading arm of a major bank. Jack's investigation broke open a massive Ponzi scheme run by the two most senior guys at the securities firm. Snake was the Sherriff back then and led the team working with the Financial Crimes Bureau. He worked with Jack to uncover a massive drug ring that was tied to the Ponzi scheme. The money from the Ponzi scheme was used to purchase narcotics, which would be delivered by ship to Naples, and then transported by vans to Miami for sale to distributors. He remembered getting the team ready to make the arrest at the Naples dock. They waited, split into twos all around the dock, waiting for the shipment to arrive. Paul Coon was with him. He had looked nervous all day, but Snake didn't think much of it. Then, Coon pulled his gun on Snake. Coon put the barrel against his forehead. At that moment, Snake thought it was over. Out of nowhere, they heard shouts. "Freeze! Drop the weapon!" Coon froze and raised his hands in surrender. As the deputies took a hold of Coon and handcuffed him, Snake saw Jack, standing behind them, staring at him. Through his investigation of the securities firm, Jack had figured out that Coon was part of the conspiracy and was on the take. He reported it to the Sheriff's Office, knowing that Coon was part of the stake out. Snake knew he would have died that night, if it hadn't been for Jack. Since that day, he believed he could trust Jack and rely on his instincts. A part of him believed Jack's plan was too risky, but the fact that Jack was running the show gave him confidence. That was good enough for him.

After a long few minutes, Jack turned to Snake. "You are going to have to pull the trigger. Make sure the first bullet hits Peter Cantor. He'll hold Tessa very close to him to use her as a shield. The moment you get any space between them, you pull the trigger."

Snake nodded.

"Thank you," said Jack.

Snake shook his head. "Don't thank me. Just come back alive."

Jack patted Snake's arm. "We are going to do a lot more than that tonight."

74.

The car came to a stop. A hand grabbed her arm and pulled her out of the car. "Just do as I say," she heard one of the men say. Tessa nodded. Tears were streaming down her cheeks. He pulled her by her arm, still tied behind her back. She didn't resist. She tried to focus on what she would do to stop them. They walked in silence until she could feel the sand beneath the sole of her sandals. "Stay here and don't move," said the man and then pulled off the bag covering her head before running off. Tessa stood on the middle of the beach. Even though it was late, the crescent moon provided some light through the thin clouds. A few moments later, two figures appeared. She knew they had to be Jack and Henry. They were barely visible as they walked toward her. She turned toward the brush on the edge of the beach trying to see where the two men were hiding, but she couldn't see. A part of her wanted to run to Jack to warn him, but she was afraid of what they might do. She knew the only thing preventing them from shooting Jack was that they didn't want to kill Henry. She had to think.

"Can you make out who's who?" asked Manny.

"No. They are both wearing a hood," said Peter, looking through his night vision binoculars.

"Which one do you want me to shoot?" asked Manny, staring into the scope of his rifle.

"I don't know yet. Just wait until they get a little closer."

"Are you going to tell me what the plan is?" asked Henry.

"No," said Jack.

They walked in silence for a while until Jack saw a figure in the distance. "See her?" asked Jack.

Henry didn't answer.

Jack took out his phone and sent the text message to Snake, "I see Tessa."

They continued their walk toward Tessa. They were within thirty feet. Jack could see Tessa's face. She was shaking her head, trying to say something. "Walk next to me," said Jack as they approached her. Once they were within three feet of her, Jack pulled Henry down with him as he brought Tessa down to the sand.

"Shit! I don't know which one is Jack," said Manny. "They both have face paint on their face. I don't know who's who."

"Fuck this," said Peter. He pulled out his pistol and ran out toward them on the beach.

Tessa heard Jack say to stay down. "The police will be here soon. Just stay still."

She looked up and saw Peter standing over them with his gun pointed at Jack. She remembered his face from her internet searches. Suddenly, she saw the resemblance. The same blond hair as Henry, the strong jaw line. "Get up," he said, staring at Jack.

Jack stood slowly. Henry slowly got up and stood next to Jack. Tessa remained on her knees, with her hands still tied behind her.

"That was good, you almost had us," said Peter.

"It's over, Peter," said Henry. "They know everything."

Peter looked over at Henry. "It's not over. Once I pull this trigger, we are home free."

"You are wrong, Peter," said Henry. "Everyone knows. This was a failure. Don't make it worse. Just…It's time to give up."

Jack stared into Peter's eyes, without speaking.

"Shut up, Henry," said Peter, staring at Jack. "See Jack, as smart as you are, you failed. You thought I'd go along with your plan and then just disappear, and you can go back to your life as if nothing happened. That's where you were wrong. I didn't go through all this trouble just to go back to where I was. I have too much to give up now."

"It's just money," said Jack.

"Yeah, just money," said Peter as he swung his fist and hit Jack's face. Jack fell to the sand.

Peter laughed. "That's for almost fucking up my plan. I needed to get that in before I killed you. Just money." Peter laughed, shaking his head. "That's funny, Jack. Say good bye."

Jack looked up at Peter as he sat up on one knee. "The problem you have Peter is you can't think beyond the obvious. You figured that I would just show up here with Henry and expect you to just hand Tessa over to me. I never thought you would do that, and you should have anticipated it. Yes, you can pull that trigger to try and kill me, but it never occurred to you that there could be a gun aimed at your head right now."

The grin on Peter's face vanished.

———————————

Snake and Bob found a position near the edge of the wide beach where they could make out figures on the sand. Snake could see three people standing near a large bush and one kneeling in the sand. He couldn't tell which one was Peter as they stood too close to each other. If one of them was holding a weapon, he couldn't see it.

"Shoot him, already," said Bob, looking through his night vision binoculars.

"I can't tell who's who. We have to wait."

———————————

"It's over Peter. There are cops all over this beach. Even if you pull the trigger, you'll never escape."

Peter cocked the pistol. "We searched the beach, Jack. There are no police hiding here. It'll take them a long time to get here. Good bye."

Tessa knew that he was going to pull the trigger right that second. With all her might, she leaped up at Peter and propelled her head into his face.

"I see him," said Snake as he saw one of the men holding a weapon as the dim moonlight reflected off it. He saw a figure leap up and collide with the man holding the gun. This was his chance. The one with the gun had to be Peter. He pulled the trigger. He and Bob jumped out of the bushes and began running toward the figures on the beach.

Tessa heard the gun discharge and saw Jack fall back. She heard another gunshot. The impact of her head against Peter's face stunned her and she felt dizzy. She fell to the sand as she stared at Jack lying on his back. The rush of emotions overwhelmed her. She no longer felt fear. She felt empty, fearing that she had lost him. Tessa stared up at Peter, who stood frozen. He slowly dropped his gun before crumbling to the sand. There were people running toward her. A man untied her and removed her gag. She crawled over to Jack and wrapped her arms around him. Other men came and hovered around Peter. At that moment, Tessa felt all her strength leave her body. Lying on top of Jack, she closed her eyes and let the consciousness leave her.

75.

"Everything's secure," said Snake as he shut off his phone. Bob knelt behind the medics surrounding Jack and Tessa. "No!" he screamed out as he covered his face with his hands.

A deputy walked up to Bob. "He's OK. The vest stopped the bullet."

Snake patted Bob's back. "I'm sure he's in a lot of pain, but he'll be alright."

The medics pulled back as Jack regained consciousness. Bob stood and ran to Jack trying to sit up and hugged him. "You stubborn fuck!" he shouted.

Snake let out a sigh of relief as he heard Jack say, "Get off."

"How're you feeling?" Snake asked.

"I feel like a truck crashed into my chest. How's Tessa?"

"She'll be fine," said a deputy standing near them. "She may have a concussion, but she seems OK." Jack sat up and tried to stand. Bob put Jack's arm around his neck and helped him up. Jack started toward Tessa. One of the medics turned to him.

"Her vitals are fine. Looks like she broke Cantor's nose with her temple. We are taking her to the emergency room to make sure she's OK."

They put her on a gurney and picked her up. Jack turned to Snake and Bob. "I'm going to go with them to the hospital. Check on Henry."

Snake turned and saw the deputies hauling Henry away in handcuffs.

"I think he's fine, physically anyway," said Snake.

Shelly ran to them and hugged them. "Everything's OK," said Bob. She handed Jack a towel to wipe off the face paint. Her hands trembled and she began to cry. Bob put his arms around her, and she buried her face into his chest. Bob looked at Jack and nodded. "Go."

Jack smiled and then ran to the waiting ambulance.

76.

She was trapped in the darkness. She reached for something, hoping to find a wall that could guide her out. She heard faint noises, and she tried to move toward them. She thought she saw a glimmer of light. Tessa's heart relaxed a bit. Then, she started to see a figure hovering over her. She tried to look, but couldn't make out who it was. It was a man, that much she could tell. Something about him comforted her. She stared at him for a long while and she found herself smiling. He reached out and gently ran his fingers down the side of her face. He was speaking, but she couldn't hear him. She blinked, and then he came into focus. She reached up and pulled him into a hug. She felt him crying as his body trembled. "I'm sorry," she heard him whisper. She held his head and looked into his eyes.

"Thank God you're OK," she said as she allowed the tears to drip down her face. "I though you died."

Jack nodded and stared into her eyes. The emotions she felt became unbearable. All of the moments she spent thinking about him came rushing out of her. She pulled his face toward her and kissed him. She felt Jack's arms come around her to pull her into an embrace. She didn't want the moment to end, but then he pulled away. He held her hand and just smiled. The ambulance pulled up to the hospital. They pulled her out and pushed the gurney into the emergency room. Tessa saw Jack speaking with the deputies. She waved at him and he smiled.

"How's Henry?" asked Jack.

"He's in shock, but he's fine. He's meeting with the detectives now. We'll see if he spills his guts," said Snake.

"What about Peter Cantor?"

"He died on the beach. Whoever was with him, got away. We have men searching the beach. There is an APB out for Ulysses Ullman and Sara Cantor. We'll find them."

Jack shook his head. "All this, just for money."

"It's a powerful thing Jack, especially if you don't have much of it."

Jack didn't answer.

"Now what, Jack?"

"I've got to go back to Madison and tell my story and end this litigation against Pearl-Line," said Jack.

Snake looked up and Jack followed his gaze. Media vans were approaching in droves. Jack turned to Snake. "Good luck."

"Aren't you going to stay to tell your story?"

Jack shook his head. "I want to save it for Madison where all this started. Let the Sherriff give his statement to the press. He doesn't know enough to say too much that'll impact what I want to say in court."

Snake nodded. "I'm sure he'll just say they're still investigating."

"Yep. Truth will have to wait."

Jack smiled and patted Snake's arm. "I'm going to go check in on Tessa."

77.

Tessa lied in bed, thinking through what she just experienced. Her hands trembled. She was in disbelief that she had come so close to dying. She relived the final moments when she saw Peter fall, and seeing Jack lying on the sand. She wondered how she wound up here. Just a week before, she was auditioning for the Philharmonic, and tonight, she was in the midst of a shootout on a beach in Naples. She sat up when she saw Jack step into the room.

"How are you feeling?" he asked.

"I think I'm OK. They want to keep me overnight to make sure."

"They'll take good care of you."

Tessa nodded.

"I need to go back to Madison first thing in the morning."

"Why?"

"I need to finish the job for Pearl-Line."

Tessa stared into Jack's eyes. "How did you know?"

"I didn't. It was the only shot we had and we got lucky."

Tessa nodded. "Have you told the client?"

"Not yet. I'm heading over there now to fill them in."

"They will be happy they hired you."

Jack smiled. He stared at her for a while and then bent down to kiss her forehead.

"When will I see you again?"

Jack sat in silence for a long while. "There are things I have to take care of."

Tessa looked at Jack and saw that he wasn't looking back at her. She nodded, recognizing that he wasn't coming back to her. She felt a sudden emptiness. It saddened her, but she accepted it. She tried to force a smile. Jack sat quietly without saying anything.

"Get some rest," he finally said, and then walked out.

Tessa stared at the closed door for a moment and then closed her eyes as a tear dripped down the side of her face.

78.

Jack and Snake met with Helen, Susan and Mike at Pearl-Line's offices.
They sat in silence as Jack told them about the scam concocted by Henry
and the fictional research by Ulysses Ullman. He told them about Tessa's
kidnapping, the planned exchange of Henry for Tessa, and the shooting at
the Half Moon Beach that led to Peter Cantor's death. Helen and Susan sat
in disbelief as Jack wrapped up the story.

"Is everyone OK?" Helen finally asked.

"Tessa's resting at the hospital. Henry is being held at the Sheriff's Office.
The police are looking for Ulysses and Peter's wife, Sara," said Jack.

"How about Isabella?" asked Susan.

"She is fine. We knew they were going to try to kill her, so we had Snake's
men keep an eye on her."

"What's next?" asked Helen.

"I'm heading to Madison in the morning." Jack turned to Mike. "You
need to get us in front of the judge tomorrow afternoon. It shouldn't be too
hard, especially with Peter Cantor dying. The media will be all over this by
the morning."

"I'll take care of that," said Mike.

Jack nodded and then stood. "I need to go and prepare."

"We'll take Pearl-Line's private jet," said Helen. "We'll have it ready
first thing."

"OK," said Jack as he and Snake stood.

Helen walked to Jack and hugged him. "Jack, I don't know how to thank
you for all of this."

Jack smiled and walked out with Snake.

"Need a ride to the hotel?" Snake asked.

"No thanks. I'm going to walk. Do me a favor, Snake."

"Anything."

"Make sure Tessa's OK, and see that she gets to the airport safely."

"I'll go with her and make sure she'll have a police escort," said Snake.

Jack made his way back to the hotel. He opened the door to his room. His body was exhausted, but he had work to do. He called room service for a pot of coffee, and he stepped into the shower. The cool water cleared his head. Jack turned on the television and saw the breaking news—the shootout at the Half Moon Beach. One dead, one arrested. Details still coming in. He poured a cup of coffee. Knowing that Tessa was safe at the hospital gave him comfort. He now shifted his mind to the next day, when he would have to tell a story in the Third Judicial Circuit Court in Madison County that will kill the Pearl-Line litigation. It had to be a story that people would react to—a story that will shift the public sentiment and force it to find a new villain. Jack leaned back on his chair, closed his eyes, and plotted out the story that was going to help him finish the job—to save the company.

79.

Tessa woke from a dream she could not remember. The nurse brought her a tray of food. She nibbled at it and then put down her fork. Thoughts of Jack filled her head, and memories of the way he left the night before made her feel empty. The nurse brought her a change of clothes. She quietly dressed after the doctors cleared her to leave. A man pushed her out in a wheelchair. She saw several deputies and Snake. Snake stepped up to her.

"Hi Tessa, how're you feeling?"

"I'm OK," she said looking down.

"We're going to take you to the hotel so you can pack up your things and then we'll take you to the airport."

Tessa nodded. Snake helped her off the wheelchair and walked her to an unmarked car. Two sheriff's cars were parked in front of it. Tessa and Snake got in the back seat.

"Where are Jack and the others?" Tessa asked.

"Henry's in custody. Jack and the rest of the team are on their way to Madison, Illinois for a court hearing."

"Jack said you and he knew each other for a long time."

Snake nodded. "Yeah. He worked on a case down here some years ago. To make a long story short, he wound up saving my life. We've been friends ever since."

"He gets around, huh?"

Snake smiled. "Yeah. He's the kind of guy people won't forget. Good man."

Tessa turned away from Snake and stared out of the window, thinking about Jack.

"I hope I'm not stepping out of bounds, but…" Snake didn't finish.

Tessa turned to him. "What?"

Snake smiled. "He cares about you."

"I don't think so," said Tessa.

"He risked his own life for you."

Tessa looked away. "No." Tessa paused for a long while as she thought through the fact that he was on his way to Madison. "He risked his life for Pearl-Line. I was part of his strategy. Because of what happened on the beach, he now has everything he needs to save Pearl-Line."

Snake shook his head. "It's not that simple."

Tessa turned back to Snake. "I think it is."

80.

The cars dropped them off at 155 North Main Street in Edwardsville. The media filled the stairway up to the courthouse. The Pearl-Line PR people had done a good job, thought Jack. He and his team fought their way into the courthouse and into Judge Wood's courtroom. The gallery was filled with reporters. Jack walked to the podium and stared at the empty bench. Bob and Shelly sat at counsel table. Helen, Susan and Mike found seats along the row of chairs just behind them. They waited a good twenty minutes until they heard the bailiff.

"All rise!"

Judge Wood came out and took her seat. She stared at the bruise on Jack's face for a long while.

"Good afternoon, Mr. Hatchet."

"Good afternoon, your honor."

"Are you alright?"

"Yes, your honor."

"You requested this emergency conference, and based on what I've seen in the news, I gather this is an important hearing."

Jack nodded. "Yes, your honor."

"Please proceed."

"Your honor, a lot has happened in the past two days." Jack paused for a long few seconds. "Lives have changed. A person has died and others will spend a long time longing for the freedom of life that they squandered away. And all of that relates to the Pearl-Line litigation. I'm grateful to be able to tell my story here, where we proclaim to search for justice and truth. In a big way, the people who have stood here have failed the system."

Jack pointed to the empty jury box. "And, the ultimate finders of the truth have failed the system. The Pearl-Line litigation was never about justice. It was never about unwrapping the layers of lies to get to the truth. Everything that has transpired evolved for a singular goal—money. The few individuals who knocked down the first domino to put this conspiracy in motion had one objective—to make money fast by fooling the world and making a company open its coffers. It all started in an office at my law firm. Henry Lane, an associate at my firm, made the decision that he wasn't going to live and play by the rules. So, he came up with a simple plan—convince the population that Pearl-Line needed to be punished. He did that by going after the single product that was adored by the masses. A cream that allows people to live their youth forever, even as our insides couldn't defy the path that nature has paved for us. He found a hungry news anchor to interview Ulysses Ullman, who told a fictional story about the YF Cream causing horrible diseases. He found Peter Cantor who was willing to kill to make another dollar. And he found Isabella White to serve as a vehicle for the disease, and a doctor, David Chen, who appears to have fabricated her medical records. With that network of people willing to lie, they set in motion a series of events that would take away the hopes and desires of an aging world, and to take down a company that profited from those same hopes and desires.

"Today, as I stand here, my adversary Peter Cantor lies dead in Naples, Florida. My associate and the inventor of this criminal conspiracy, Henry Lane, is sitting in prison. Ulysses Ullman and Sara Cantor are fugitives on the run. I don't know what will come of Isabella White or Doctor Chen. The authorities will do their job and reach their own conclusions on what role these individuals had in this conspiracy. What I do know is that truth prevailed today.

"I don't find contentment in Peter Cantor's death or the time the others will spend in prison. We are all driven by something. In their case, they were driven by money, like so many others. There is nothing wrong with wanting to make money, and we are all willing to get close to the line to get our share. They chose to cross it, and now they have to accept the price that comes with blurring the line between right and wrong. And this question of who else may have crossed the line will need to be answered with respect to all other plaintiffs and lawyers who have sued Pearl-Line."

A woman stepped into the courtroom and handed a note to the bailiff. He quietly walked to the bench and handed it to Judge Wood.

"One moment, Mr. Hatchet," she said as she put on her reading glasses and read the note.

"I am advised that a full-blown investigation has been launched by the prosecutor's office and local police in Madison regarding the Pearl-Line cases, with the cooperation of the Collier County Sheriff's Office. Looks like your prediction was correct, Mr. Hatchet. Now, turning back to why you are here, what is it that you would like for me to do? You requested this conference for the White case. The only other action in which the Cantor firm sued Pearl-Line is on behalf of Emma Pierce. I don't believe you have filed a motion to dismiss that case, although I would certainly entertain an oral motion," said Judge Wood.

"We did not file a motion to dismiss the Pierce action. This hearing was intended to be nothing more than a status conference where we have an opportunity to inform the court of recent developments that the court should be apprised of, including the fact that Ms. Pierce's counsel has died. We will be reviewing the files of every complaint that's ever been filed against Pearl-Line, including Ms. Pierce's complaint, and once we have digested that information, we will either seek appropriate relief before the courts or make necessary referrals to criminal prosecutors for them to do their job."

Judge Wood smiled. "Very well Mr. Hatchet. Now that Ulysses Ullman's research has been shown to be a part of this criminal conspiracy, I suspect there will be a lot of voluntary dismissals by the plaintiffs. Your prediction about criminal investigations should provide added incentive."

Jack nodded. "I suspect that as well, your honor. Unless, of course, people enjoy being the subject of a criminal investigation for fraud and conspiracy."

Judge Wood laughed. "You have a peculiar way of putting things, but I believe everyone will get the message loud and clear. Anything else, Mr. Hatchet?"

"That's all I have, your honor. Thank you for taking the time to hear us today on such short notice. We do appreciate it."

"Would anyone else like to be heard on this matter?" asked the Judge, looking out toward the gallery. No one stood and the courtroom fell silent.

"Very well. Thank you, Mr. Hatchet. Court is adjourned."

81.

The reporters rushed Jack, but their questions were devoid of any substance. Whatever they wanted to ask had already been answered during Jack's presentation. The questions revolved around how Jack got his bruise, how he uncovered the scam, and other questions that did nothing to advance the ball on solving the Pearl-Line litigation. Jack thanked the reporters and joined the team waiting outside the courtroom. Susan walked up to him and hugged him.

"Thank you, Jack. That was brilliant."

Helen grabbed Jack's arm once Susan stepped back. "I can't believe I was a witness to what you just accomplished."

Jack smiled. "We'll have to wait to see if it worked, but I have a good feeling about it."

"We have to go celebrate," said Helen.

Jack smiled. "Actually, I need to get back to New York and take care of some things."

Helen smiled. "Say hello to Tessa for us."

Jack looked at her with a curious look.

"It's a woman thing. We have an eye for these things. Take the Pearl-Line plane. We'll take a commercial flight back."

"Helen, I couldn't. There are no direct flights to Ft. Myers from here."

"Nonsense, Jack. This is the least I could do for what you have done for us."

"Thank you."

Helen smiled. "Hurry. Go."

"On my way," said Jack as he picked up his brief case. Bob and Shelly followed.

82.

Jack sank into the leather seat. Bob sat on the other side of the small table across from Jack with a blank look. Shelly was seated next to Bob.

"What's wrong?" asked Jack.

"That was unbelievable what you did in there."

Jack smiled. "Thanks, so why the sad face?"

Bob looked down. "I don't know. I wish I could've contributed."

"You did. We're a team," said Jack. "What I did in there didn't solve the problem. It's all the things we did this past week that got us here." Jack closed his eyes, hoping that sleep would come fast.

"Come on, Jack. There's nothing we did that in any way contributed to what happened in there."

"You are wrong, Bob."

Bob didn't respond. Jack opened his eyes and saw Bob staring out the window. He leaned in closer to Bob.

"Listen, this was not an ordinary project. We were winging it and we wound up in the right place. But Bob, listen."

Bob turned to Jack.

"There is no way we would've accomplished this without you, Shelly or Tessa. If you guys didn't go to the White Tequila, Ulysses Ullman never would've met Tessa or Shelly. He never would've given them his business card, and we never would've been able to send Tessa to meet him. If all I had was the typo in the complaint, at best, we would've had a plausible story that people likely would have ignored. It was Tessa's kidnapping, it was you occupying Henry while Snake and I snuck into his room, and it was Peter's failed plan to kill everyone who knew anything about our witch hunt that did him in and gave us a credible story to tell. We found a way to deal with each and every crazy situation, and every one of us contributed to the final story. You are as much a part of this story as I am. All I did was to piece everything together and tell the story to the judge."

Bob nodded and some color returned to his pale face.

Jack smiled. "Stop beating yourself up. Our entire team was integral to what we accomplished."

Bob nodded and then took a hold of Shelly's hand. She turned to him and smiled. Bob turned back to Jack. "Thank you."

Jack closed his eyes. "I would like to get some sleep now."

"Not me," said Bob. He waved at the flight attendant.

"Could you bring the young lady a cosmopolitan and me a vodka martini? And bring one for my friend too."

Jack opened his eyes. "What are you doing? I said I needed to get some sleep."

Bob laughed. "We are going to celebrate, and we aren't gonna be able to celebrate with you sleeping. You don't have a choice."

Jack shook his head in disbelief. The flight attendant returned with the drinks a few minutes later. Bob picked up his glass and offered it for a toast. Shelly laughed and met it with hers. They both stared at Jack until he finally picked up his glass and held it up.

Jack took a sip out of his glass and then turned to look out of the window.

"I know what you're thinking about," said Bob.

Jack turned to him. "What?"

"You're thinking about Tessa, aren't you?"

Jack smiled and took another sip. "No."

Bob turned serious. "Angela?"

Jack nodded. It was the first time he thought about her in a long while. He was so engulfed in the chaos of trying to save Tessa and solve the Pearl-Line litigation that he had not spent a second thinking about what he was going to face back home.

"Sorry," said Bob.

"I have to deal with it."

"What about Tessa?"

"What about her? She doesn't need this—to be wrapped up in my mess. Especially after what I did to her…" said Jack as his voice trailed off.

"What do you mean? You didn't do anything to her. She made her choices."

Jack shook his head and closed his eyes.

"You mean you knew?" asked Bob.

Jack nodded.

"You knew they were going to take her?"

"I wasn't sure, but I thought they might."

"How could you have let her go?"

"It was wrong, but I had to. It was the only way to blow open the conspiracy."

"You risked her life to save Pearl-Line?"

Jack opened his eyes. "I'll have to live with that."

"That's why you risked your own life to save her," said Bob, looking into Jack's eyes.

Jack looked away. "It was wrong, and I knew it. That's why she doesn't need me. It's unforgivable what I did to her."

"I agree it's unforgivable, but don't you think it's for her to decide?"

Jack shook his head and closed his eyes.

"Do you think she knows?" asked Bob.

"Yeah."

83.

A man waited at the terminal holding a white sign with her name on it.
Tessa walked toward him and the young man took her luggage. She followed
him through the sliding glass doors.

"I was told to take you to Astoria," he said.

"Yes. Thank you."

Rain poured out of the sky when they stepped outside. The driver asked
her to wait. He ran to the parking lot and came back with his black limousine.
They drove through the congested Queens streets. Tessa stared out of the
window into the pouring rain, thinking about the craziness she just lived
through. Her thoughts drifted toward Jack, and sadness filled her heart. She
wanted to relive the moment when they made love. But the warmth always
vanished as soon as she thought about the way he said goodbye. She was just
part of his strategy, and once he achieved his goal, he left her at the hospital.
She didn't like reliving the pain. She shook her head and told herself that she
wouldn't think about him anymore. The car stopped in front of her small
white house with green shingles. She opened the door to her house to a pile
of mail that had been deposited through the mail slot in her door. Tessa put
her luggage down and picked up the mail. She set them down on the kitchen
counter and made a pot of coffee. The smell of the brewing coffee made her
feel like she was home. It warmed her against the pouring rain outside. She
leaned against the counter and started sorting through the pile of mail when
she saw it. The white envelope was sent by the New York City Philharmonic.
She held it up and stared at it, afraid of what the letter might say. She brought
it with her to the coffee maker and held it against her chest while she poured
the coffee into the mug. After a few moments, she slowly opened the envelope.

Dear Ms. Malino, we are delighted to inform you that your live preliminary performance was exceptional, and we would like to invite you to a semi-final audition on May 23 at 6 p.m. Please confirm that you are able to perform that day.

Tessa stared at the letter for a long while. She brought it to her chest as tears filled her eyes. She looked up at the ceiling. "Thank you, father," she said, and she felt him smiling.

84.

Jack checked back into the Essex House where he spent the night before traveling to Naples. Exhaustion began to set in. He hadn't slept for days. He collapsed onto the bed and closed his eyes. Thoughts of Angela began to fill his mind, but he didn't have the strength to dwell on them. He rolled over on his side and all thoughts began to fade as sleep set in.

The sound of his cell phone ringing woke him. Jack turned to the alarm clock, which read 8:30. The room was dark from the drawn curtains, and he didn't know if it was evening or morning. He answered the phone.

"How're you feeling, buddy?"

"Hey, Bob."

"Looks like your handy work is paying off."

"What's going on?"

"Pearl-Line's all over the news. Dismissals are being filed in courts all over the country. Helen Tsang was interviewed and she said she owes everything to Jack Hatchet and his team."

"Good."

"You coming into the office today?"

Jack held the phone against his ear as he walked to the window and opened the curtain. He saw that it was morning.

"No. I need to go see Angela."

"Alright. Let me know if you need anything."

"Thanks, Bob."

Jack stood in the shower, thinking through the day ahead. He wondered how the conversation with Angela would go. He threw on a pair of jeans and a T-shirt and went down to the reception desk. He handed the woman his valet ticket. She printed up his bill and was almost embarrassed to hand it to him. Jack looked at the $600 bill and shook his head. He asked her to put it on his credit card. The valet brought his car around. Jack headed to the West Side Highway. He dialed the number and Angela answered right away.

"Hi, Angela."

"Hi. I saw you on the news."

"It's been a long week."

"Are you alright?"

"Yeah."

"Where are you?"

"On my way up to see you."

Angela was silent for a while.

"I guess we have a lot to talk about," she finally said.

"Yes."

Jack pulled up to the house and rang the bell even though he had a key. She opened the door and stood in the doorway without speaking. She took a step back and Jack walked in.

"Do you need coffee?"

"Yes, that would be great."

"Let's sit outside on the deck. I'll bring it out to you."

Jack nodded and walked out through the kitchen to the deck. He sat down on the wicker chair that at one time was his favorite. Angela came out and handed him a mug of coffee. He took it and sipped it. Angela sat across from him and stared out toward the pool.

"I think this day was coming for a long while," she finally said.

Jack put his coffee down. "Yes. We just chose to hide from it."

Angela turned to him and smiled. "Why do you think so?"

"We didn't want to acknowledge that we had failed."

Angela nodded. "I've retained a lawyer and...I thought we should just get it over with," she said.

"OK. We'll work it out. I'm not going to fight you," said Jack.

Jack stood. Angela walked over to him and hugged him.

"I need to get some things," said Jack. Angela pulled away and nodded.

Jack packed some clothes and walked downstairs. Angela waited for him in the foyer.

"I guess this is good bye," she said.

"Yes. Take care of yourself. Just because we are going our separate ways doesn't change who you are and what you mean to me. Call me if you need me for whatever reason. I will come for you. I wasn't much of a husband to you, but I will be a better friend."

Angela began to cry as she opened the door. Jack kissed her forehead. "Goodbye," he said and stepped out of the house.

He started the car and looked back toward the door, and he saw that it was closed. At that moment, he accepted that it was the final goodbye.

85.

Tessa played the last note and then bowed to the judges. Some smiled, while others just stared at her. She walked backstage and looked around. As she placed her violin in its case, she remembered the first audition when she was surprised to hear Jack's voice behind her. She didn't hear his voice tonight, but she turned to look anyway. She stopped in front of Pepe's and stared at the door for a while. A young couple holding hands walked in. She smiled at them, and then made her way to the subway station.

Her cell phone started ringing as she unlocked the door to her home. She saw it was Shelly.

"Hi Tessa."

"Shelly, how are you?"

"I'm good. Still trying to calm down after all that excitement. How are you?"

"I'm well."

"So, what have you been doing with your time lately?"

"I just had an audition for the Philharmonic."

"That's wonderful, Tessa."

"Thank you."

"Have you heard from Jack?"

Tessa paused. "No, why?"

"I would've thought he would've called you. In any case, we got the bonus check from Pearl-Line."

"That's great."

"Jack got the firm to agree to let you, me and Bob share half of the five million dollars among us as a bonus. The firm will keep the other half."

"Excuse me?"

"I have a check with your name on it for eight hundred thirty-three thousand dollars, and I would like to hand deliver it to you."

"My God, Shelly. That's so much money. I don't think I can accept it."

"Don't' be silly, Tessa. You earned it more than anyone. It's yours, and I'm going to hand deliver it to you tomorrow. Will you be home?"

"Yes, I'll be home."

"I'll see you tomorrow."

"Shelly, how is Jack?"

"I haven't seen him. He took a leave of absence from the office."

"Is he OK?"

"He's had a lot going on in his personal life. He'll have to tell you himself, if he wants to."

"OK. I was just curious."

"I know. I'll see you tomorrow."

Tessa hung up and stared at the phone for a while. Shelly's call brought her back to that night on Half Moon Beach. It was the first time she had confronted her own mortality, and the only person she wanted to be with was Jack. Her chest tightened and she felt her eyes welling up with tears. She turned her head hoping to forget.

86.

SIX MONTHS LATER

Jack found a two-bedroom apartment on 14th Street and Fifth Avenue. He liked the working fireplace, the small terrace off the living room that looked out into a courtyard. It reminded him of the years he lived alone in the city, before he had met Angela. The exhaustion from the Pearl-Line litigation and the separation from Angela made him want to detach from his life. He informed Thurman that he'd be taking a sabbatical. Clients new and old called looking for him to represent them, and those calls were referred to Bob. Bob was enjoying the recognition that he always deserved but never before experienced. He was no longer under Jack's shadow.

Jack's routine was to wake early each morning and run up to Central Park and back down to Union Square. After a shower, he would sit out on the balcony and sip his coffee. He enjoyed the simple life, and he chose not to debate in his mind when he should go back to the office.

The separation became a final divorce in September. They found a reasonable mediator who divided up their assets that enabled Angela to stay in the Westchester home, and gave her a percentage of his income from the law firm. Jack still felt the pain of knowing he had failed in making life work with Angela, but he appreciated the freedom of no longer having to ask who held her heart. Thoughts of Tessa often filled his mind, but he chased them away as quickly as they entered. Bob couldn't understand why he wouldn't call her, and he chose not to explain.

He heard his doorbell ring. He pressed the intercom.

"It's me Shelly."

Jack pressed the buzzer to let her in. A few minutes later, he heard a knock on his door.

"What brings you here?" Jack asked.

"I know you didn't want to be bothered, but I needed to give you something."

Shelly pulled out a package from her purse and handed it to Jack.

"What is it?"

"I don't know. Tessa mailed it to me with a note, asking me to give it to you."

"Tessa?"

Shelly nodded. Jack furrowed his eyebrows and unwrapped it. He saw three wooden paint brushes. He stared at them for a long while and then looked at Shelly.

"I don't know," Shelly said. "She called me to make sure I received it. She said she'd been carrying it around for a long time, and just wanted to give them to you."

Jack nodded.

"You should call her," said Shelly. "As smart as you are, you really can be dense at times." Shelly didn't wait for a response, and left quietly. Jack stood still, staring at the brushes. As he pulled them out of the package, he noticed a card inside. He opened it.

Jack, I bought these brushes for you after we were at Pepe's. I remember we were talking about what you may be passionate about. You mentioned painting and then you stopped talking. You didn't have to say anything else. I understood. People go through a lifetime, without ever knowing what's important. Not in terms of our needs in life, but something deeper and more honest. I bought these at a time when you making the decision to paint again meant something to me. I didn't want that memory to be left behind. I had been carrying them around for a long time, looking for the right moment to give them to you. That moment never came.

—*Tessa*

87.

Tessa received the letter from the audition committee that she had been invited to the final audition. She gave up her job as a floater at Thurman & Miller and concentrated on her violin. The bonus check from Pearl-Line allowed her to play music night and day without having to worry about money.

October brought cold winds. She found herself sitting next to the warm fireplace, staring at the ashes going up the chimney. Tonight was her final performance before they made the decision. She played the melody in her mind. The last log burned out and Tessa put on her black overcoat. She opened the door to see the leaves had turned yellow and red without her noticing. The dry smell of fall and burning fireplaces filled the streets of Astoria. The sun had already set. The sky was gray, with thin clouds covering the sky. Tessa picked up her violin case and headed to the subway.

She walked up the subway stairs and saw the bright lights of Broadway. It started to rain, and she feared it would get heavier. She tucked her violin case under her coat and quickened her pace. By the time she arrived at Lincoln Center, she was drenched. She found the ladies room and patted her face dry with paper towels, and brushed her hair back with her hands.

The backstage looked familiar. It was her third time there. She took off her coat and set it down on an empty chair. She opened her violin case and she smiled at her old friend.

"Time for you to go on," she heard the man say.

Tessa walked around the thick ropes and stepped out onto the stage. The familiar judges sat.

"Good evening, Ms. Malino, and congratulations for making it this far," said the man in the middle. She noticed he was wearing a green tie tonight and not the yellow bowtie that he wore during the prior two auditions.

"Thank you," said Tessa.

"Anytime you are ready," he said.

Tessa tucked the Stradivarius under her chin and played her favorite piece by Tchaikovsky. She closed her eyes and let the music play. It was effortless. The violin played by itself. The music flowed like water and it filled the large auditorium. At that moment, nothing else in her life mattered. Life was defined by that escape, where the single most important thing was the music that God had given her.

She opened her eyes as the last note flowed out of the violin. The six judges sat in silence. Some smiled while others nodded to show their appreciation.

"Thank you, Ms. Malino. That was beautifully done," said the man with the tie. "We will let you know shortly."

Tessa nodded. "Thank you." She tucked the violin under her arm and walked back behind the curtain. She placed the violin in its case as she felt a rush of sadness fill her heart. This was her last chance to show the gatekeepers that the world should hear her music. As much as she hoped that they would be fair, the sadness and fear of failure consumed her. She closed the case and remained kneeling on the wooden floor for a long while.

"Hi," said the voice behind her. Tessa looked up and saw Jack. She stood slowly and stared into his eyes.

"That was beautiful, Tessa."

"Why did you come?"

Jack looked into Tessa's eyes for a few seconds and then looked down. "I don't know. I wanted to see you."

"That's it?"

"Yes."

Tessa looked down, lost for words.

"Can I walk you out?" he asked.

Tessa nodded and picked up her violin case. Jack helped her put on her coat and they stepped toward the glass doors. The rain had gotten much heavier. Jack opened the door.

"It's pouring," said Tessa.

"Yes, but a little water won't harm us. I think we should just get wet."

"I can't get this wet," said Tessa lifting her violin case. "It's not waterproof."

Jack took off his raincoat. "Here, give it to me. I'll cover it with this."

"You'll get wet."

Jack smiled. "I won't warp. Let's go."

They walked out into the pouring rain.

"Where are we going?" asked Tessa.

"I was going to ask you the same thing."

Tessa stopped and looked at Jack. "I don't understand you. You leave me at the hospital, and then I don't hear from you for months, then you show up at my audition and act like nothing's happened."

Jack looked down at the ground without responding.

"Say something."

"I missed you."

Tessa stared at Jack, wanting more—wanting to understand.

"I didn't call you because…because I didn't think I deserved you. You are the most beautiful person I have ever met. You have a gift that can move a person to tears. Your warmth. Your passion. You deserve to be with someone as special as you, and I didn't believe I was that person. I'm the person who put you at risk, all in the name of doing my job. I go around and fix things. Sometimes I succeed, sometimes I fail. Sometimes I cross the line when I shouldn't, and I do it because I feel it's necessary. And everything translates into making another dollar. The one passion I thought I found was you. But after seeing what kind of person I am, I didn't want to become a part of your life and taint your beautiful existence. I wish I could have told you that I fell in love with you the first time I watched you walk down the subway stairs. But, I couldn't because knowing that I'm no good for you was enough for me to bury those feelings."

Jack looked up at her. Tessa couldn't contain the tears flowing down her cheeks.

"I came tonight because I wanted to watch you live your passion, and in my small way, let you know how special you are. I came to see you tonight to tell you I'm sorry."

Tessa wiped her tears with the back of her hand. "We are getting wet, you know."

Jack smiled. "Yes, we are."

"Can we walk to Pepe's and get warm by the fire?"

Jack nodded. They started walking toward the café. Tessa leaned into Jack's shoulder, and he put his arm around her. They walked in silence for a while, and then Tessa stopped.

"You don't get to decide what I need," she said as she smacked his chest.

Jack smiled and put his arms around her. She buried her face in his chest and began to cry. They stood in the rain, in the darkness, knowing that at that moment, nothing else mattered, other than their embrace.

Whatever we are, whatever we make of ourselves, is all we will ever have—and that, in its profound simplicity, is the meaning of life.

—PHILIP APPLEMAN

ACKNOWLEDGMENTS

This book would not have been possible without the help and support of all the amazing people in my life. I would like to thank my editor Kevin Smith for helping to bring this book to life. Thank you to my friend Sue LaColla for her insights and for agreeing to become a character in the book. Special thanks to Cameron Fuhr for his research on the boring medical stuff. I'm forever grateful to my friend Richard Doetsch for his guidance when I first started out on this journey more than a decade ago.

Thank you to my many friends and family for your support and encouragement. Many parts of your personalities are ingrained in the characters that come alive in this book.

Most importantly, thank you to my sons Alex and Will, and my wife Anita, for putting up with me all these years, and giving me a reason to wake every morning and strive to become a better person.